MEET ME AT THE LOCH

LOVE ON LOCATION

NC BARTON

To Aggie, my greatest adventure. You can read this when you're older.

SKYE

I'll be the first to admit this castle can be a lonely place. Growing up as an only child, I often imagined people filling the halls, but they were never quite so nosy. In the fantasy, they just hung on my every word, enjoyed my company, more interested in me than these old stone walls.

A tug on my sweater stops me, and the group stops too.

"So, are you a princess?" The little girl with blonde ringlets asks me for about the fifth time before wiping her nose on her shirtsleeve. "Like Merida in *Brave?* Are you Merida?"

Her cherub face is so earnest I swallow my laugh. "No, I'm Skye Ainslie."

The girl squints her eyes. "Are you sure? You look a lot like her. Why do you live here?"

I keep leading the group through the hall as I answer. I don't want this tour to take any longer than it needs to. "Well, when I was about your age, my grandma needed some help. So, we moved from LA here."

Her mother, with matching blonde hair, hands her a tissue. "Is your family Scottish royalty?"

I shake my head, wrapping my sweater closer around my torso.

1

It's only early September, but a chill is seeping in through the cracks in the ceiling.

"Why do you live in a castle then?"

"Well…" God, what a long story. "The answer varies depending on who you ask," I tick these off on my fingers to get the number right, "great-great-great-great grandfather Maxwell Ainslie won the castle from the Mortimers in a card game. The Mortimers claimed the game was rigged. They said the transfer wasn't legally binding, even got local officials involved, but it was legal, and Loch Ness Castle has been in the Ainslie family ever since."

I walk past the library I use as my writing room, wanting to keep my private spaces for myself.

"The joke was on Great-great-great-great grandad, though. The castle was in such disrepair it was hardly livable and stayed that way for generations. My grandmother did a ton of renovations and moved her family in. Then, my mother continued the work after we moved here." I run my hand along the wall, the stone rough under my fingertips. "This hallway used to be covered in cement. She spent an entire summer chipping away at it to reveal the original stone."

We head to the staircase and one of the guests points to the right. "What's down that hall?"

"It's our private bedrooms. We still live here."

The man with greasy hair and sensible sneakers thrusts his shoulders back. "We paid good money for this tour. We should get to see."

Forcing a smile on my face, I stop myself from questioning what exactly *good money* means to him. Instead, I say, "There's plenty more to see, don't worry."

My phone vibrates in my pocket, but I ignore it to continue the tour. We head down the stairs to the kitchen, then through the main dining room, always an impressive stop with the carved wooden fireplace, hunting trophies on the wall and an enormous chandelier made from elk antlers. Next stop is the library on the main floor, which was my mom's favorite room.

I open the heavy wooden door to the warm smell of fires in the hearth, slightly dusty books, and the whisky-ginger candle I light before every tour.

My group walks around checking out the carved plaster ceiling, the shelves of heavy leather-bound books, and that's when I notice the group is smaller than it was a moment ago. The man who asked me about the rooms upstairs is missing.

My pulse pounds like a war drum on the side of my throat, my cheeks hot. "If you'll excuse me, I'll be right back."

Running up the stairs, I head straight for the hall to the right. I peek through every open doorway with no luck. As I get closer, I see my bedroom door at the end of the hall is open. I know I closed it.

I take a deep breath.

I will not yell at the paying guest. I will not yell at the paying guest. Think of the online reviews. We need this income. I will simply ask him to rejoin the group.

Inside my room, standing next to my dresser, is the greasy-haired man, his grubby hands holding my green satin bra. A scoff comes out of my mouth. It is unbelievable.

The man drops the bra. "It was on the floor; I was just putting it away."

"Out!" All my well-intentioned plans soar out the window. "Get out!"

I stand aside as the man storms past me. "We deserve the whole tour."

"The *whole tour* does not include my pants drawer, sir!" I yell after him as he walks down the stairs and thankfully out the front entrance.

I run my hands over my face, my fingers cool against my flushed cheeks. I'll show the rest of the group the grounds and then send them on their way. We'll skip the ballroom; I haven't fixed the broken tiles in the corner, anyway.

The first thing I notice as I enter the library is that one of the older guests has helped himself to a whiskey. I sigh. It could be worse. Then I see that is in fact much worse. The blonde woman is thumbing through an ancient edition of *Dr Jekyll and Mr Hyde*, licking her finger each time she turns a page.

I'm about to take it from her hands when a crack stops me in my tracks. A man is holding a record sleeve; the record itself is shattered into hundreds of pieces at his feet. My face feels numb as I take the sleeve from his hands. Turning it around to see which album it is.

Please don't let it be hers, please.

It's the Rolling Stones "Sticky Fingers." Relief washes over me. One of my favorites, but mercifully not one of Mom's.

"The tour is over.."

There are a few groans, and no movement to leave.

"Thank you so much for coming." Again, not one person moves. The older gentleman is still sipping on our whiskey.

"Everyone needs to leave. Now!"

The group shuffles out the door with mutters of "money back" and we should've gone to Urquhart Castle. Once I am alone again it hits me what I've done. I can practically read the Yelp reviews now.

Dad's at a "business meeting" whatever that means. I'll tell him tomorrow. Today I'm done. I take a long bubble bath in our claw foot tub with a glass of wine and head for bed.

* * *

THE BELLS JINGLE on the bookshop door, and it sounds like home. Better than home, because there isn't any work to be done. No leaks to be patched. No chickens to feed. No tours to give. I still haven't told Dad about the disaster tour yesterday, but I'm not going to worry about it now that I'm in my happy place. I can pick a book at random and live any life, not the one where I'm a grown woman still living with my father.

Endless shelves of stories to escape into.

Okay, not really endless, as the bookstore in Foyers is actually quite small, possibly one of the smallest in all of Scotland. The stock is crammed into what used to be a living and dining room of a white stone cottage. I browse the shelves filled to bursting with books, walking past the small sitting area in the middle of the room with a red shaggy papasan chair. The shop is empty—completely empty. *Where is Gabby?*

"Gabby?"

"Is that you, Skye?"

"Yes. Is everything okay?" I suddenly feel like I walked into one of the mysteries I write. Is there a killer lurking around the shelf?

"Just making tea, dear! Want any?" she calls from the back.

"No, thanks."

I show myself to the crime fiction section and run my finger along the dusty spines, trying to decide which one to lose myself in. I reach to the top shelf, where the A's are, and touch the spot where my novel will go someday, if I ever get to publish one. Of course, in order to publish one, I'll have to get over this writer's block that has descended upon me like the fog on the loch in the morning—thick and impossible to see my way through. It's been months since I've written anything. Well, except for the instruction booklets I write for my job, but the ins and outs of a toaster oven won't snag me a book deal.

The bell on the door jingles. My friend Kate runs in, her black hair billowing behind her along with some stray leaves and a cool fall wind.

"Sorry I'm late."

"That's okay." We hug, and she gives me a kiss on the cheek, leaving a gooey smudge. I'm sure I have a fat red mark from her lipstick, her signature look since we were sixteen.

"Don't you want to get a bite to eat before your shift?"

She shakes her head. "Books are more important."

I laugh, but she's absolutely right. As we browse, Gabby comes out of the back holding a steaming cup and fills the small space with a floral scent.

After a while, Kate finds me in the reference section and hands me a pink book. Two people lean together, about to kiss, flowers surrounding them. It's cheerful and not something I would ever read. "What's this?"

"I finished it last week. It's delightful. You have to try it."

I hand it back to her. "I'll stick to murder."

Kate smiles as she places the book on top of my stack. "You need to broaden your horizons. If you don't love it…" She looks around, her green eyes searching for inspiration. "I'll give your next tour."

"I wouldn't inflict that on my worst enemy."

"Well, you won't have to deal with it once the Americans come, right?" She takes her books to the register. Before I can ask what she's talking about, over her shoulder, she says, "If you don't like it, you're a monster, and I'll buy you a pint."

"Deal," I say.

We take our books to the register, and I hand over my card. Gabby runs it, then tries the number. My cheeks burn as my stomach twists. I should've just asked her to hold them, but I thought I had enough to cover it. Kate swoops in, her red nails flashing as she hands over her card. "It's on me."

"Kate, you don't have to."

"It's not a problem."

Gabby swipes Kate's card. "See you hens next week at the meeting. Skye, I read your latest pages, and I have thoughts. Oh, and if you can stay a little after, my nephew is in town from Edinburgh. He's very handsome and has a good job in finance."

"Is he 6' 5"?" Kate asks, and I kick her behind the counter.

I'm not sure why everyone in town is so set on fixing me up, but not Kate. We're both twenty-four and single, which in this town is practically unheard of, apparently.

I smile but avoid the question. After the way my last relationship ended, I'm not really interested in meeting anyone, especially not someone who lives nearly four hours away.

As we walk out the door, the cool September air feels amazing on my still-flushed cheeks.

"I get paid Friday. I can get you back then."

Kate waves me away. "No worries. Once the Americans pay up, you'll be swimming in it, right?"

The Americans, again? My brain understands all the words coming out of her mouth, but not one of them makes any sense. "What are you talking about?"

Kate's already pale skin goes an unnatural shade of white. "Um, maybe you should talk to your dad. Oh, look at that…" She glances at her wrist, which has absolutely no watch on it. "I'm going to be late. Gotta run! Call me later."

Pulling out my phone, I text Dad.

Me: Are you home? We need to talk.

He replies with a link to a *You Heard First* article.

What the hell is going on?

I didn't know Dad read *YHF*—he's not really interested in celebrity gossip, that I know of.

Miles Casey's career isn't over yet. *Hollywood heartthrob and the star of the box office flop Clean Up Hitter (featuring him as a washed-up pitcher and Travolta as a talking baseball) was recently spotted at Paris International Airport waiting on a flight to Scotland.*

Sources close to Casey tell YHF he's been preparing for the leading role in the latest Natalie Rodriguez film at his LA bungalow. The role as a Scottish recluse is a departure from his recent family-friendly and arguably terrible films to a film with what our source called "substance." He's been hitting the gym to—

I stop reading. When I was younger, I had a massive crush on Miles Casey. I must've seen *Undercover Quarterback* a billion times. He has dark eyes that made my heart race. They twinkle when he laughs and simmer when he looks at the love interest in the movie. I went down the full rabbit hole and read every magazine article about him I could get my hands on. Not only was he smoking hot, but he also volunteered at beach clean-ups and visited children's hospitals. My crush was so overpowering that I even sent him fan mail. I close my eyes, cringing at the thought of it.

7

Dad used to tease me about it a fair amount, but that was over ten years ago.

Me: What's with the article?

Three dots appear, disappear, then reappear.

Dad: Be home soon. Explain l8tr. Love you. Dad

Not only is that not an answer, but he insists on signing his texts. Putting my earbuds in, I press play on my favorite album at the moment. Mick Jagger fills my ears with a guttural *yeah*, and sparklers ignite along my spine; all thoughts of Miles Casey fade to the background as I ride down the road toward home.

The pearly sky, flecked with dark-gray clouds, makes the hills look even greener, and in the distance, the loch sparkles. The crisp morning air rushes against my cheeks as a light drizzle mists everything with a glossy shine. Taking off my hat, I let the rain and wind run through my hair. I pedal harder and picture myself waving to Bessie and Nessie, our highland cows that like to hang out by the road, but when I round the corner, I throw on the brakes instead.

Standing there, whispering quietly and petting Bessie over the fence is Miles Casey —*the Miles Casey.*

In a kilt, no less.

Not just a kilt, but also a tuxedo top, the bow tie undone and hanging loosely, a small black leather backpack slung on one shoulder. His square jaw has a light dusting of stubble, and he looks rumpled, despite the fancy dress. Rumpled, but *so* sexy.

His dark hair is mussed, like at one point in the recent past it was tamed with product but has since escaped its shackles, a rogue curl brushing his forehead. He's even more handsome in person than in that silly teen sports movie.

What is he doing here? Dressed like that? He must be lost.

Miles's face is the picture of joy as he rubs behind Bessie's ear. Boy, does that kilt and knee socks combo ever show off his strong, muscular calves.

Propping my bike against the rickety fence, I listen to his deep voice as he whispers to Bessie. "Look at you. Aren't you just the prettiest cow? Yes, you are."

"Wonderful. Now that'll surely go to her head. Bessie's already the vain one."

At the sound of my voice, he whips around so fast his shiny dress shoes slip in the mud. Everything happens in exaggerated slow motion. His feet completely fly out from under him, and his entire body hovers before landing flat on his arse in the mud, his kilt flipped to his chest, revealing tight black boxers covering strong thighs and a substantial...

I tear my eyes away, landing on his face. His dark eyes are the size of saucers, his mouth is wide open in a perfect O—his expression looks so much like the one he has in the movie when the nerdy girl gets a makeover, I laugh. It starts small, then erupts from me like a bubbled-over glass of champagne.

Miles laughs too, our giggles mingling together in the misty air. He tries to prop himself up on his elbow but slips again, causing another bout of laughter from both of us.

I don't know what he's doing here, but I can't leave him in the mud. Stepping carefully on the slick patch of glaur Miles somehow found himself in, I reach my hand out to him.

MILES

*E*nding up flat on my ass in the mud about sums up how my journey to Scotland has gone so far. I reach for the hand of the woman with a halo of soft red curls framing her face. Her eyes are so blue they look like the sky, but not the gray clouds behind her. They look like the sky on the bluest day on a white sand beach on a tropical island somewhere. She's stronger than I expect, and I'm on my feet in one swift move.

"Thanks. I'm Miles."

She brushes her hands off on her tight jeans, and I can't help but notice her legs. They're long, with sculpted thighs that curve up in a lovely swoop to her hips. My eyes linger for a bit too long, and I glance away.

Skye's cheeks turn an adorable shade of pink. "I know. Are you lost?"

"No, we're shooting a movie here—well, there." I point to the castle looming in the background. It looks about a million years old. Her face is different when I turn back to her. Her mouth is set in a tight line.

"I live there."

I thought it was abandoned. From this angle, it doesn't look up to code.

"You're shooting a movie?" she continues. "Is that why you're out here petting my cows dressed like... like a Scottish Ken doll?"

A powerful gust of wind blows, and for the millionth time on this journey, I wish I'd thrown a pair of sweats into my carry-on bag. Goosebumps cover my thighs, driving her point about Scottish Ken home.

I cross my arms, trying to keep some heat in. "I was at a film festival with my brother and wanted to drum up some buzz about this movie. The plan was to change when I landed, but that was shot to hell since somewhere along the way, the airline lost my luggage..."

As I ramble on, I can't help but notice her unimpressed expression. Why didn't I buy a pair of sweats at the airport? *Because they had such cozy blankets in the first-class lounge.* I hadn't thought of it—I also hadn't thought to charge my phone, which is why I took a bus from Edinburgh to the Highlands instead of getting picked up. I try again to explain.

"It was all arranged so I could come early, before the rest of the crew."

She shakes her head and starts walking.

I grab my black leather backpack from where it landed when I ate shit and fall into step next to her. "It's part of my process to immerse myself in the character. I was nearly to the castle when I saw the cows. They're so cool. Like rock star cows with their shaggy hair brushing in their eyes. They're just missing the leather pants, although that would be a bit cannibalistic for them. Maybe some high-quality vegan pleather."

A tiny smirk plays at the side of her mouth. I'm amusing her at the very least.

"I didn't catch your name."

"Skye."

I laugh. *Skye*, as in the tropical blue of her eyes. There's something oddly familiar about the name. I can't put my finger on it.

"What?"

I bite my lip to keep my thoughts in my head. "It's a beautiful name."

Silence falls over our walk. I shouldn't have laughed. I'm acting like an awkward teenager when normally I'm extremely charming. *Come on, Miles. Charm her!*

I clear my throat. "Thanks for helping me back there. Hell of a meet-cute, huh?"

She looks at me, her piercing blue eyes flashing a shade darker. I want to scoop the words I just spoke out of the air, shove them back in my mouth, and then chew them in the slow, sexy way cowboys gnaw on the end of a piece of straw.

"Not that we...not that you... I mean, you probably have a boyfriend or a partner. I just meant if it were a movie, we would fall madly in love after this. Actually, if it were a movie, I would've pulled you down with me in the mud when you helped me up." My mind runs that reel; her body against mine, her soft curls tickling my neck.

Skye's cheeks turn pink, matching her rosebud lips, like she can read my mind. I push the thoughts away. I'm not ready to have feelings like that for anyone. Not after what happened in Barbados. Besides, I just met this woman. It's jet lag.

I sigh. "Let's start over. I'm Miles. Callum told me I could stay here before production for research."

Skye stops walking. The gravel crunches behind us, too loud for any more conversation. A dark-green Jeep that's more rust than car stops. Out steps a large man with an even larger smile and a gray beard.

"Ahhh, you *are* here." The man's eyes spark with amusement as he takes me in. I'd almost forgotten about the mud. "And it looks like you're in need of a shower. I'm Callum."

I take his outstretched hand. "Callum, it is so nice to meet you. Thank you again for letting me come before the other key creatives."

"Of course. We're happy to have you."

A small scoff escapes Skye, which tells me the "we" in his state-ment isn't true.

Callum looks past me on the path. "Where is your luggage?"

I let out a long breath. "Your guess is as good as mine."

"Well, come on. I'll give you the grand tour after you've had a chance to clean up."

"Dad," Skye interjects. "We need to talk."

"Aye. But later."

The frown deepens as she hops on her bike, her strong legs carrying her away.

"Hop in." Callum motions to the Jeep.

"But your seats…" I motion to the mass of mud on my kilt.

"Trust me, they've seen worse."

As the Jeep drives slowly up the gravel path, the castle comes into better view. It's much bigger than I expected. In fact, it's massive. It has to take up an entire city block. The stone is a worn-in rosy tan that pops against the gray sky. A large spire towers above the rest, crumbling with age.

How old is this castle, anyway?

I half expect a dragon to fly overhead and Daenerys to jump out from behind one of the hedges lining the grounds.

Skye's already off her bike, and I watch as she walks through a dark-wood arched door with a little iron window in it. Callum parks the car. We stroll up the couple of stairs and into the castle.

He leads me up the staircase lined with threadbare red carpet, through cavernous hallways, stones jutting out here and there. I shot a movie once where we spent a lot of time filming in caves, and this castle has a similar smell—wet rock. Not unpleasant, but unexpected. Not exactly what I'd call homey.

It's hard to imagine living here. How odd would it be to grow up in an honest-to-God castle? Maybe I can ask Skye later.

Callum opens the door to a room near the corner of the castle. It has a fluffy bed with a white comforter. A coat of arms hangs on the wall with what I assume are real swords. The window looks out over massive green fields, and off in the distance Loch Ness is twinkling in the sun that has broken through the clouds. It's picture-perfect. This film is going to look amazing.

"Bog's down the hall. It doesn't have an actual shower, but it has one of those showerhead sprayers. Very modern. I'll throw a jumper and some trousers in there for you. Skye can take you shopping a little later. Foyers won't have much in the way of clothes, but you can head into Inverness."

"Thank you. I really appreciate it."

Callum gives me a small salute before he shuts the door. Setting my backpack down on the desk near the window, I pull my phone out of the front pocket. Still dead. I search again through the main part of the backpack for my charger, which I know I tucked safely into the small pocket on the front of my luggage. My lost luggage. Still not there.

I set the phone down on the desk and head back into the hall to find the bathroom. Music thumps from behind the door directly across from mine. It's open just a crack, so I get closer. David Bowie spills out into the hall. The room inside is colorful with a bright-yellow shag rug covering the stone floor and a royal blue velvet chair sitting in the corner. A sweater sails from across the room to land on the bed, and I catch a glimpse of Skye stomping around her room, singing softly in just a black bra and jeans.

Oh shit.

She's getting dressed or undressed. Either way, I shouldn't be here. I back away from the door, but not before she catches my eye.

"What are you doing?" She quickly snatches the sweater and holds it to her chest.

I put my hand over my eyes as if that could help. "I was just looking for the bathroom."

"And you thought we always blast "Heroes" in the loo?"

"No, I…"

She shuts the door. That couldn't have gone any worse.

"It's over here." Callum comes down the hall chuckling, clothes in his arms.

"Thanks." I take the clothes from him gratefully. "Hey, I forgot to ask… Do you have internet?"

"Aye, most days we do. It's a bit spotty. The password is Brown Sugar." He lowers his voice. "The song, not the baking product. It's spelled the same, but the distinction matters to Skye."

I smile and immediately hear the Rolling Stones song in my head. "Got it."

The water in the clawfoot tub is hot, unraveling some of the knots in my shoulders. Not sure if there are more from the journey or from the unexpected welcome. It seems like maybe Skye didn't know we're filming here.

But that's not my problem.

I need to focus on my character. He breathed these stone walls like it was the only oxygen he needed. So I will too. Which will be a stretch.

I'm a city kid. Aside from some other locations for filming, I'm not used to this much silence and open space. But I'll have to get used to it quick if this film is going to be a hit. The premise of the film is already so out there; if I can't nail the authenticity of the character, it will all fall apart.

I sink a little lower in the tub, letting myself fully relax. This film will work. It has to. My career depends on it.

SKYE

As soon as I hear the water running, I leave my room to find Dad so he can explain what is going on and why Miles Casey is taking a bath in our home. Shoving my unruly curls through the neck of my jumper, I make my way down the hall when a loud crack startles me, and I run to find its source.

A chunk of ceiling fell in the hall outside my library, and rain is lashing in. My slippers smack against the stone floors as I hurry to the room where we keep supplies and haul the ladder out first, struggling with the heft of it. Next, I cut off a bit of tarp, grab the tools, and patch up the gaping hole as best I can, my stomach dropping with every teeter from the extremely tall ladder. It's just my father and me taking care of the place, and seeing his large frame up on this ladder makes me more nervous than the wobbles. So, I take a deep breath and ignore the height as I patch the leak.

What must it have been like to live in this castle in its heyday? When it felt like a luxury instead of a duty. Before it started to literally crumble into the ground? No one in my family would know.

Once the hole is fixed and the supplies put away, I make my way down to the kitchen, where my father is already bustling around humming "Ally Bally Bee."

Putting a hand on his shoulder, I move past him to make some coffee, rain lashing the green hills outside the window.

"A hunk of roof fell down in the hall off the library upstairs."

"Nah. Another one?"

I nod. "What's with the movie star in the tub?"

"Pet," my dad says apprehensively, which freezes me to my spot. Dad is never apprehensive about anything. He's more the jump in headfirst and figure it out when you land kind of guy. We have a lot in common in that way. "It's the solution to our financial troubles. Do you remember Mom's friend Anita, from the States?"

"Mom had a ton of friends from all over—"

"That she did." Dad's smile is warm and wide. "That she did. This was the actress, with the daughter some years older than you. They were over all the time."

We moved when I was seven. I have memories of LA but they're all hazy, like the sun is glaring in my eyes and I can't quite see them clearly. I remember it was warm.

"I don't know, Dad."

"Right, well, her daughter, Natalie, reached out to me. She's making a movie set here in the Highlands. Miles is the star. Very big movie. Nice people. She was looking for a castle… So, they're going to film here. At Dun Loch Ness. It starts in two weeks."

"What about the tourism board? Will they allow it?"

Dad's neck is red. "There was a meeting the other day. Vote was unanimous. They're all on board."

That's how Kate knows. I can't believe this. "You took it to a meeting before talking to me about it?"

Dad sighs. "Didn't want to get your hopes up if they turned it down."

"How long have you been working on this?"

He turns so I can't see his eyes while he mutters, "A couple months."

"Months?" I laugh, but it's brittle. "Why wouldn't you tell me?"

17

"You can get worked up, and you're not the biggest fan of strangers. I was worried how you'd take it."

Not the biggest fan is putting it mildly. I agreed to the tours after many, many discussions with Dad, and look how well those turned out.

How long will they be here filming? *Oh Lord.* "Where are they going to sleep?"

"Pet, it's a castle. We have more than enough room. That's part of the problem, as you well know. They're staying here, and they'll be paying a pretty penny for it. Don't worry."

I take a deep breath to ease the tightness in my chest. Miles Casey's going to stay here. Sipping my coffee. Eating my food. Bathing naked in my tub.

I tell myself to pull it together. It's been over a decade since I was that teenager with a crush. And despite my body's reaction to the thought of being in close proximity with Miles, I don't want to host a film production in our home. Who knows what hours they'll keep, with their lights and camera and action. How will I be able to write with them here? What if they want to shoot in my library?

"I wish you had discussed this with me before agreeing to it. They're going to turn our home into a circus. What would Mom have said?"

My father sighs, and guilt slicks my stomach. I shouldn't have gone there.

"She would've understood there's no other way to keep the lights on."

I don't meet Dad's gaze, knowing full well he's right. I would be lying if the fact that it was a Miles Casey film didn't make it so much worse. Why him? The only person I've ever sent fan mail to in my entire life. And after the letter he sent back...

There has to be another way.

"Maybe they'll bring more of their Hollywood people and shoot more movies here. It could be a significant source of income for the future, too."

I put down my coffee and stride toward the doorway, shrugging on my jacket. My father follows me.

"It might be fun even." Dad reaches out to brush a lock of hair out of my face.

I put on a woolly hat, trying to tame the mass of auburn curls and to show him I don't need his help.

"New faces, fresh perspectives. You'll see, pet."

I bite my tongue, slip out of my fuzzy velvet slippers and into my wellies, and then I'm out the door.

* * *

MY TRUSTY yellow bike is right where I threw it in the shed. The rain has died down, but the wind has picked up. It rushes against my cheeks, making what so far has been a truly terrible day a little bit brighter. Okay, not truly terrible—that's a bit dramatic—but not great either. On top of my father not discussing this movie plan with me, I didn't get to write. Not that it would've made any difference if I had.

Not one new idea has come to me since I submitted what I thought would be my best-selling book to my dream agent. Finally, I had written a book I felt was worthy of publishing. *It was the one.* The novel that would land a book deal, a best-seller, and a career writing something other than a detailed description of an air fryer.

Barely sixty minutes went by before the email appeared in my inbox. My heart caught in my throat as I'd opened the reply with shaking fingers then dropped into the pit of my stomach; you could almost hear the plop of it hitting acid like a bucket falling into a well.

It was a personal record for me, a rejection within an hour. I didn't leave my bed for a week. I watched *Clue* and *Death on the Nile* (the 1978 version, because Mia Farrow) on a loop, and ate cereal from the box. Since then, the words have dried up.

A large gust of wind brings me back to the present as I lean into it and pedal harder. I ride the same route every day unless the rain is too punishing. Down the hill into town, usually to say hi to Margie at

Thistle House and get a bit of lunch. But right now, I need to ride off this growing sense of unease that's settled in my chest. Or at least get a break from my father before my temper gets the best of me, and it turns into a proper fight. *Check me out.* I must be growing.

I can't believe he agreed to an entire movie production without even talking to me about it first. He took it to the board, which essentially means the whole town knew before I did.

This can't be the only solution. A bunch of Hollywood yahoos running amok all over Foyers. Hell, probably all over Scotland. That's not the kind of attention we want. Save all that fame and farce for the States. Plus, how will I get any work done? I need my book to be done in time for the manuscript contest, and I can't write with people shining lights about and taking over my house with director's chairs.

They'll have to find somewhere else to film.

As I turn a corner into town, the stone and stark white buildings are as familiar as slipping on an old sweater.

Margie is outside hanging up a bird feeder, her white hair neatly pinned back in a bun. She spots me and waves. "Skye!"

I'd rather skip my chat with Margie. I love her. She's like an aunt to me, or maybe more a great-aunt, but I know if I stop, she'll just want to talk about the movie. She won't understand why I don't want them there. I've never told anyone about the fan mail, and I'm not about to start now. Waving, I'm about to take a right when she yells.

"Skye, where are you going? It's Baltic out. Come in where the drinks are hot, dear!"

I sigh and arc my bike back onto the road toward Thistle House.

As I hop off, Margie says, "It looked for a second like you weren't going to stop here." She laughs like that's the funniest thing she's heard all week.

I follow her inside, inhaling deeply the smell of bangers, hash, and freshly brewed coffee. The small stone house is much lighter inside than you would expect. Arctic blue walls reflect slightly on the walnut floors. The tables are a lighter wood, each with a small bouquet of thistles and bluebells on them. Floor-to-ceiling windows at the back of the house overlook Loch Ness. On the far left side is a fireplace with comfy seats, each a different floral pattern, with cross-stitched throw pillows and hand-knitted blankets, all made by loyal customers. Family, really. The effect is cozy hodgepodge.

While I hang my coat on the coat rack by the door, Margie pours me a cup of tea, even though she knows I prefer coffee. She insists tea is better for my health. Fall has brought a cold mist that has settled over Foyers, especially in the mornings and the evenings, but the fire is roaring. I sit and hold my hands to it, my fingers warming up from the ride.

"Here, hold this." Margie hands me the mug. "Where are your gloves?"

"I forgot them."

Margie narrows her eyes and examines my face. "What's going on?"

Taking a sip, I hold in my cringe at the floral flavor. Not even black tea? This is going too far. Margie's still searching my face for answers. I mean to shrug, but just slump my shoulders instead. Everything comes tumbling out as it always does when I talk to Margie. "Dad pimped out the castle to a film crew."

Margie takes a seat, her face lighting up like I just told her I had a great date the night before. Margie's always trying to fix me up. Everyone's always trying to fix me up since Finn.

"I heard a little about that. Isn't that fun? A film. A proper Hollywood movie. Here! It's so exciting." Margie stands and runs to grab a handful of coasters, the Thistle House logo printed on each one. "At the meeting, Callum said they were staying at yours. But put these around the house, dear. You know we have lodging here, too."

"I wish they could all stay here, but Dad's already promised them beds in the castle."

Margie claps, rubbing her hands together like a cartoon villain hatching an evil plan. "Dear, this is wonderful. There might be a man your age, maybe even more than one. You'll have your pick."

I knew it. I knew when I told Margie, she would try to turn it into some kind of dating game, and to what end? This is not an episode of *Bachelor in the Highlands*. "And what, we fall madly in love and date long distance? I'm not doing that again, ever."

"Maybe he moves here, maybe you move there. You can figure that out later."

She knows I'll never leave again. The castle is too big a job for one person. Plus, the last time I tried to spread my wings, look what happened. I set my offensive herbal tea down.

"Nope. No fairy tale reality TV show ending here. It's just going to be a pain in my arse for a while. But I'll figure out a way for the castle to make money without the interlopers. I'll see you later, Margie. Thanks for the coffee."

The ride back is quick and blessedly dry. Once I walk in the door back at the castle, Dad hands me the car keys, whispering, "He's a nice bloke. They're all good people. You'll see."

"Dad—"

Miles walks down the stairs. I didn't think it was possible for him to look more ridiculous than when he was in his formal kilt attire covered in mud, until seeing him in my dad's clothes. He is swimming in them.

My dad says, "Ah, here ye are. Skye offered to take you into Inverness to get some things."

SKYE

*O*ffered. Apparently, I'd offered. I'm so *nice*.

But once Dad said it, I couldn't say no. We get in my car, and I crank up the stereo for two reasons. One, it's The Ramones, and The Ramones should always be played at full volume. And two, I want to discourage any kind of conversation. It's a forty-minute drive to Inverness on a clear day. In the rain that's now coming down in relentless sheets, it'll probably be closer to an hour. I'm still in shock that my father didn't tell me about this whole renting out our home to complete strangers. Well, not complete strangers, if a humiliating letter from nearly a decade ago counts.

"So, you're a music fan, huh?" Miles practically shouts over Joey Ramone.

I nod.

"What's your favorite band?"

Even though I don't want to talk, I answer automatically. "The Rolling Stones."

"Oh yeah. That's cool. I met Mick a couple times."

I turn down the music. "What?"

"Yeah. I met him on set. He and Keith. They were doing a song for the soundtrack of *That Night*, and they came to set to check it out. Get a feel for the film."

My heart is in my throat. I don't want to be impressed by his shameless name-dropping, but *Mick Fucking Jagger*. "What was he like?"

We talk about Mick and Keith—he calls them by their first names.

"When they showed up, I knew they were a big deal by how everyone else was acting, but I had no idea who they were."

I suck in a breath. "Shame on you."

"Hey! I was eleven. It was the nineties. If it had been NSYNC, I would've been hyped."

Despite myself, I laugh.

"Don't worry. My music taste has evolved since then." Miles gazes out the window, watching the countryside go by. "What got you into classic rock?"

"I listen to all sorts of music," I deflect, not wanting to share that my mother is the reason. Miles tells me about his record collection. We both love vinyl. I almost forget that I don't want to be in a car with him, that I want to find a way for the production not to come here.

"Everything just sounds rich—" Miles stops what he's saying and gasps.

"What?" I ask.

He looks at me and smiles, then points back out the window. "Rainbow."

The hills are green, wet and lush with the rainfall, stones jutting up here and there. In a stream, as if it's shooting directly from a cloud, is a hazy but vivid rainbow. My chest fills with pride, like I'm somehow responsible for the beauty of the land.

"It's gorgeous."

"Aye."

"Have you always lived here?"

I pause, considering my answer. "For the most part."

Miles smiles at me, his eyes twinkling. "There's a story there."

"For another time, maybe."

I get some coffee while Miles does his shopping. I have a draft due by Friday for work, but I can't exactly write it up on my phone. Anyway, I have a more immediate problem. I call my friend Logan, who works for the tourism board.

"Skye, long time. How's it going?"

"Great. How is the babe?"

"She's growing like a weed. She's three now, and the next one is due in December."

I already knew. It's all Logan posts on his feed. I just wasn't sure how to launch into it. "That's awesome."

Silence crackles over the phone.

"So…what's up?" Logan asks, sounding just the tiniest bit suspicious.

"Yeah, so…" I explain to Logan about the film production and my need for them not to use Castle Loch Ness.

"I don't know, Skye. I'll look into it, but two weeks is pretty short notice. If Dun Loch Ness needs the money—"

I appreciate his referring to the castle as "in need" rather than me.

"—why not let them shoot there? It sounds like it could be a lot of fun."

How can I explain my gut reaction that inviting this circus into the castle would be disastrous? My mother had been a star at one point. She was a singer-songwriter and made three albums, one of which got really big. She met my father after the release of her second album. When they married, she continued singing and released one last record before falling pregnant with me. She gave it all up and never said why. Once, when I was thirteen, I gathered all my courage and asked her plainly why she quit. She could've been a big star, like Adele or Lily Allen.

She said, "I changed. It wasn't who I was anymore."

I didn't understand. I still don't. Would she want the fame she left behind knocking on our door now?

Besides, how can I write with all the distractions? Once I sell my book, we can pay for repairs with my advance. If I write a bestseller, we can keep the castle afloat with just my income.

And then, of course, there's the stupid letter.

Remembering Logan is still waiting for an answer, I say, "It's hard to explain. In my gut, I just know it'll change everything."

There's a beat, and then Logan says, "Change might not be such a bad thing. But I'll see what I can do."

Swapping my phone for my book in my bag, I feel better already. Logan will find something, and then the whole production can move to Lewiston or Dores—anywhere but here.

I tuck into the book Kate made me buy. I've been inhaling it— gulping air like I'd just hopped off the bike after a steep hill. It's about a pop star and a baker falling in love. I usually only read mysteries or thrillers, sometimes the odd literary fiction, but I'm hooked on this romance despite myself. None of it is based in reality. Proper fiction, practically a fantasy novel, really. But it's the first romance I've read, and it's a revelation. Someone doesn't have to die in a book in order for it to be exciting. Who knew?

"Good book?"

I startle, spilling a little coffee on the page I'm on.

"Oh, I'm sorry." Miles frowns. "I thought you saw me coming toward the table."

I'd been so lost in the story, I hadn't. Somewhere along the way in his shopping, Miles had changed out of the enormous trousers and into a pair of dark-gray jeans and a black jumper that hugs his body in such a seductive way, I imagine my fingertips gliding along the soft knit.

"There's a bookstore back there," Miles says, jarring me out of my daydream. "I can buy you a new copy. What book is it?"

Heat floods my cheeks, and I suddenly don't want Miles to know I'm reading a romance. It's low spice, from what Kate says, but all the same, I shove the book into my bag.

"No, it's fine." Then I think about how little of the novel I actually have left. I'm itching for another romance to lose myself in, and I don't have any at home. "On second thought, I'd love to stop at the shop for a new book, if you don't mind."

"Not at all. My treat. I'm in the market for something new to read, too. I finished the one I was reading in the airport."

I smile, not sure I want to let him buy me a romance book, or anything for that matter. I've already warmed to him more than I expected on our drive over here. I don't need another reason to like him. Especially since once I figure out how to stop this production from happening at the castle, he probably won't speak to me again.

"We'll see. I know a better bookstore than this one, though. Come on."

* * *

We throw Miles's packages in my car and walk the short way.

"How far is it?"

I see Leakey's in the distance and point. "It's right over there."

Miles's face lights up, and I suddenly know why people use that phrase. It's like a literal light is shining from his cheeks. "In the church?"

I nod, not able to keep myself from smiling. "It was almost a nightclub. When the church decided to sell, there were two bids. They thought the bookstore was a better option."

Across the street, a woman yells, "Miles!"

A young girl in a tiny red skirt waves, and Miles graciously waves back. He puts a hand on the small of my back in a protective gesture that sends electric pulses through my sternum down to my toes. He leads us through the open forest green door as the young fan screams, "I love you," with her phone held in front of her face.

Miles looks embarrassed. "Comes with the job, I'm afraid."

I nod, dipping my toe into dangerous territory. "I bet you get a lot of fan mail, too?"

He shrugs. "I guess. My assistant Jake goes through it all. Sends them a nice reply."

Thank the heavens. He doesn't read them. Maybe he never even saw mine. Maybe the reply was from his assistant. "So, you never read any of them?"

"I used to when I first started out. But I haven't for years. It's better for my mental health."

Shit. Years. How many years? Like ten?

Miles walks through the small entryway of the two-story masterpiece that is Leakey's Bookshop before I can ask any more questions. I see it with new eyes, just as Miles must be seeing it now. The space is open and covered from floor to ceiling in books. A balcony that wraps around the entire building, making up the second floor and a rickety iron spiral staircase leading up to it. The walls are all mint green, purple, and light blue, softening the immense interior. It's like walking into a fairytale castle. Smack dab in the middle of the enormous space is a wood-burning stove filling the space with a cozy campfire smell.

Miles turns to me. "It's incredible."

A secret thrill rushes through me just like when we saw the rainbow. Like I'm responsible for how amazing this place is.

I head off to find another book and leave Miles to wander. The romance aisle is full to the brim with colorful spines. Orange, fuchsia, plum, sapphire, sea green. It's like walking into a rainbow. So different from walking through the crime fiction aisle. I look through the A's and find a mint green cover with a football player and a ballerina on it. I read the back, and it sounds fun. While holding on to it, I pick up a few others, reading the back. There are so many to choose from. All with a variety of scenarios, ranging from realistic to fantastic. Some, the couple are old friends turned lovers, some are enemies turned lovers, and some are strangers turned lovers.

Little pinpricks tingle the back of my neck as the idea forms. I could write one of these books. I could write a romance.

I don't believe in love at first sight like in the books, or a lasting love of any kind, really. Look at my parents—madly in love, my mother gave up her dreams for my father to live out a fairytale in a castle no less, and my dad still ended up alone. Exhibit B—my one foray into love ended with me alone, heart shattered, worse off than when I began. But just because I don't believe in it doesn't mean I can't write it. It's fiction, after all. I wrote a book where multiple people were murdered, and I don't actually want to kill anyone—well, most of the time. I can write about love without believing in it. Clearly, there's a market. Look at all these books.

I find my way to the craft-writing books. So many already grace my shelves, *Save the Cat Writes a Novel*, *Bird by Bird*, *On Writing*, but if I'm going to write in a completely new genre, I'm not pompous enough to think I won't need a little help, especially since I just started reading the genre myself.

Happily Ever After, Beat by Beat by Trudy Lamour looks amazing. It's a beat sheet for romance novels, exactly what I need. Another one catches my eye, and I'm pulling *Write Naked* by Jennifer Probst off the shelf to read the back cover, when Miles walks into the aisle.

"There you are. This place is incredible. Look at this cool copy of *Slaughterhouse-Five*." He holds up a black, white, and red cover with a large bomb in the center. In a wacky font under the title, it has the best line in the novel: "Everything was beautiful, and nothing hurt."

Miles steps forward, bringing with him the heady scent of cinnamon and clove. He takes the book out of my hand before I even realize what he's doing. "What did you find?"

Color rises in his cheeks as he reads the title. "Oh, are you a writer?"

My mind spins with how to answer. My imposter syndrome snarls loudly in my ear. I take the book back and add it to my stack. I always hate this question. "Sort of."

"Sort of?"

"I write, but it's not anything serious." Just my passion, my dream, the reason why I get out of bed some mornings. "Just for fun." And so I don't spiral into an existential black hole.

In an attempt to end the conversation, I start off toward the register.

"That's awesome. What do you write?"

My second most dreaded question. I wrote a cozy mystery about a woman who owns and operates a landscaping business and also stumbles into solving a murder. I wrote another, more serious mystery about a woman living in Cornwall who stumbles upon some remains while on a run and solves the murder. I wrote a time-traveling cozy mystery where the protagonist stumbles upon a time machine and goes into the future to find they were murdered, then has to travel to the past to solve it. It seems stumbling is a big theme in my work. All of the stories sound ridiculous when I try to explain them, so I say, "Crime fiction, mostly. Or I guess you say it's the mystery genre in America."

Miles steps up as I place my books on the counter. "My treat, I insist. I ruined your other book."

I think about protesting, but I can't deny how nice it feels to have someone, particularly an extremely handsome, nice-smelling someone, buy me a book. "Thank you."

MILES

The whole car ride home, I sneak glances at Skye. I meet a lot of beautiful women in my line of work, but she's gorgeous. And she's a writer. I've always admired writers. Putting their thoughts on the page, turning words into feelings, it's so cool. Not the most amazing adjective, I'm aware, but I'm not the writer.

"My friend Elsie is a writer. She wrote the screenplay we're going to shoot. I'll introduce you when she gets here."

Skye nods but keeps her eyes on the road. The rain is pounding the windshield, so it might not be the best time to talk. Instead, I gaze out the window as the dark-gray clouds swallow what's left of the day. By the time we make it back to the castle, it's dark.

"Thanks for the ride."

"Yep." She opens the car door but then turns to face me. "Thank you for the books."

Then she runs inside.

I gather my bags and make a run for it, too. Callum greets me as I enter the stone hallway.

"I hope you like roast," he says with a large smile. Everything about Callum is large, from his enormous beard to his booming voice. He takes up space with no apologies. It's comforting. "Dinner will be ready in an hour."

"Sounds wonderful." I'd had a slice of pizza at the mall, or shopping center as Skye informed me, but I'm still starving.

I make my way to my room. First order of business, I plug in my phone with my new charger. As I'm unpacking my other purchases, my phone buzzes to life. Six missed calls and thirteen texts.

My first call is to Jake, my assistant and personal trainer. I was already spending so much time with him, and then my previous assistant quit to go back to school, and Jake threw his hat in the ring. It just made sense. He wanted to come with me during this prep time, but I refused. My character is a loner. Just him and his old housekeeper, who's more like a grandmother to him than a servant, living in this castle. Every day is the same until the housekeeper dies, and after a period of mourning, he has to hire a new one. The new servant is a young, beautiful, headstrong woman who's obsessed with the Loch Ness monster, and my character falls madly in love with her despite himself.

How would my peppy, let's-work-out-at-five-in-the-morning assistant fit into my brooding loner character? He wouldn't. He'll join me when the rest of the crew gets here.

Actually, come to think of it, spending time with Skye isn't really going to help me get into character either. I just met her, and already I'm having a hard time putting her out of my mind. Her laugh—I haven't felt as good about myself in a long time as I do after making her laugh.

But I can't lose focus. I'm here for the film. I can channel all that energy toward the housekeeper character. Save it, use it.

Jake answers on the third ring. "Where have you been? I thought you died. Like, literally, I was calling hospitals. *Hospitals, Miles.* Until the *YHF* thing popped up an hour ago. Then I could see for myself you were just fine. Why didn't you call to say you made it?"

Shit. *YHF* loves reporting on my every move. It gives my films lots of free publicity, but I don't always love seeing my half-awake coffee runs all over the internet, and truth be told, it makes dating challenging. "It's a long story. What *YHF* thing?"

Putting Jake on speaker, I scroll to the internet on my phone. After a couple of attempts at connecting, disconnecting, and reconnecting, it comes up. I go to the open search tab, Miles Casey YHF today, and hit refresh. Before looking, I picture myself in a tuxedo top and kilt covered in mud plastered all over Google. But the only person who could've gotten a picture would've been Callum or Skye. My gut lurches at the thought. She wouldn't. Would she?

A picture of me, looking not half bad in my new sweater if I do say so myself, walking into the bookstore from this afternoon pops up. Skye is by my side—smoking hot—her leg outstretched, midstride, looking like it goes on for days. Her hair is billowing behind her like she just walked off the set of *Outlander*. Even from the far vantage point, her blue eyes pop.

"You're there less than twenty-four hours, and you already have a date? Who's the hottie?"

"It wasn't a date."

No. Although, going to that bookstore had been her idea. I wonder what she's doing right now. I click on the image and read. They have her name and her Instagram handle. How do they find these things so quickly? Will she be pissed? My heart sinks as I answer my own question. Of course, she'll be mad. It's a complete violation of her privacy. I have to find her and show her this before she sees it on her own.

"Hey, Jake, I gotta go."

"Okay. Have you been keeping up on your workouts?"

I haven't. The film festival had been so busy, and I virtually just got here. I wasn't going to do sit-ups in the middle of the airport. Now that would've been all over *YHF* for sure. So I just make a noncommittal noise.

"At least tell me you've been doing the planks and the mountain climbers."

There's no use lying to Jake. "I haven't. But I will."

"Do a two-minute plank right now while I'm on the phone."

There's also no use in arguing with Jake. "Fine."

I put my phone on the desk, stand, and drop to the floor Batman-style. It may be childish, but I get a kick out of it every time. While I'm holding plank, tightening my core, I say, "I want to start running again."

"Running? Why?"

"I miss it. Anyway, I think this character is more lithe and less bulky."

Jake sighs. "Okay, I'll come up with a plan and email it to you. One more minute. Then ten mountain climbers."

* * *

THIRTY MINUTES LATER, I hang up with Jake. He somehow turned "just one plank" into a whole circuit workout. I need another shower—well, bath. But I have to find Skye first.

There's no answer when I knock on her door. I make my way down the stairs and nearly run right into Callum. "Ah, there you are. Dinner's ready."

I'll have to tell her at dinner. In front of Callum. Will he be mad that, because of me, his daughter is all over the internet?

My gut twists, but I smile. "Great."

Callum leads us through a hall to the side of the staircase, then through a large, ragged stone arch into a grand dining room. The walls go up to a vaulted wood ceiling. Dark oil paintings hang from the walls that look just about as old as the castle: some are landscape paintings, some formal portraits of men in different stoic poses, all with a tartan hanging from a shoulder or in their kilt.

On the far wall is a fireplace with a roaring fire, and the head of an elk hangs above it. A long, almost black wooden table sits in the middle, large enough for forty people. Three place settings are waiting, along with a delicious-looking spread of food. But the room is empty. Skye isn't there.

"Go on. Pull up a chair," Callum says as he takes a seat.

I sit as instructed. Skye comes through the doorway, her usually fair cheeks pink, water droplets dripping from her hair. I stand as she enters and looks at me like I'm insane.

I sit back down immediately. What was I thinking, standing like she's the queen of England?

"I swear those chickens are possessed by the devil himself. They got out again. I can't even figure out how they're doing it."

Callum laughs.

"Ah, so funny. Laugh it up. I don't see you nearly getting your eyes pecked out by demon chickens."

This sets Callum off again, his large belly laugh so infectious I can't help but join in. After a few beats, Skye does too. We dissolve into laughter, and everything feels lighter. Wiping tears from her eyes, she says to Callum, "Pass the wine, old man."

The roast is tender, the wine rich, and the Yorkshire puddings are little pillows, smothered in gravy sent straight from heaven. How have I gone my whole life without ever having a Yorkshire pudding? In an attempt to make up for lost time, I reach for a third one. Skye gives me a mischievous look across the table that sparks something in my chest.

"I see you're a fan." She motions her head to the Yorkshires.

"To what I'm sure would be my trainer's utter disappointment, I am." Jake. That's when I remember the *YHF* photo. I set down my fork and pick up my wine, taking a fortifying gulp. I can do this. They might think it's funny. Both of them seem to have a sense of humor. "So, funny thing…"

In my most charming, most jovial way, I try to explain the picture online. Skye pulls out her phone and brings up the *YHF* article in question.

"Oh my God. I look terrible. Look at my hair. It's a rat's nest."

"You look stunning," I say, not understanding how she can't see what a goddess she is, striding down the street, wind rustling through her locks like she's commanding it to do so.

Callum takes the phone out of her hand. "Pet, what are you talking about? You look fetching. You look just like your mother."

Skye levels him with a stern stare.

Callum holds up a hand. "It's a good thing."

She puts her head in her hands, her fingers running through her curls. I'm lost, watching the motion.

She looks up and says, "How did this happen? Does it happen to you all the time?"

I assume the question is rhetorical. When both Callum and Skye continue to stare at me, waiting for my answer, I realize it's not.

Does it happen all the time? Yes. Do I want them to know that? No. I'm not sure why. I don't want them to think less of me or worry about the kind of attention the castle might get with me being here.

"Sort of." I attempt to soften it with a smile. "Really didn't think it would happen all the way out here, but I guess it did." My fake smile fades. "Yeah, if I'm honest, it happens pretty much all the time."

"I can't believe this." Skye gets up from the table, grabs her phone from her father, and strides out the door.

Callum sighs.

"I'm very sorry, sir."

Callum rises and pours some more wine into my glass. "You don't need to be. Honestly, it's not your fault. I knew when we invited the film to come here, we'd get outside attention. It'll be good for the town. Mark my words, Leakey's will have a banger week in sales. Skye's just upset. She'll cool down. She always does."

I nod and sip my wine. My next bite of Yorkshire is glue in my mouth. I hate that Skye is mad at me. I want to run to her and apologize, but Callum suggests space. Space is the last thing I want from Skye.

"Penny for your thoughts?"

I drop my fork. "Just thinking how amazing this place is." And your daughter. "I'm drawn to it in a powerful way." By it, I mean her. Why am I so fascinated with Skye? I take a sip of wine. We just met, after all. I haven't felt this strong a pull since Lana.

The wine sours in my mouth.

Look how well that turned out. I was in love with Lana from the moment she walked out onto the beach, her long brown hair flowing in waves bigger than the sea behind her. It wasn't just her looks, either. It was her laugh, her energy. I thought our souls were connected, but I couldn't have been more wrong. I was falling in love, and she was playing an altogether different game.

What am I doing entertaining romantic thoughts about Skye? She'll just stab the little pieces of my heart that are left rattling around in there. Besides, she's clearly not interested in me that way. And on top of everything else, it would be unprofessional. I need to take this role as seriously as I'd like the Academy to.

I will not pursue Skye in any way. I will not act on this odd pull. But I should still apologize.

"Thank you for dinner. If you'll excuse me, Callum."

SKYE

I clomp up the stairs, as if my anger can shoot from the soles of my feet and shatter everything in its wake. I cannot believe my face is all over the internet.

Miles's words pop into my head. Pop isn't the right word—more like ceaselessly run on a loop like a record snagged on a scratch. *You look stunning.* He said *stunning* with eyes so warm that I thought I might melt under their gaze.

I stomp harder, as if I can physically trample out any feelings I have for Miles Casey. *Feelings? I must be tired.* He's attractive and charming, but I don't need to go melting for any man. The last man I had feelings for left to pursue his music career in America. Finn McDougall. We'd known each other our whole lives, really. He asked me to marry him when I was nine and he was eleven. I stuck my tongue out at him and threw a handful of dirt right in his face. We didn't properly start dating until I was fifteen. We dated for years. Everyone thought we'd marry someday—even me—and then he left with a guitar in his hand and stars in his eyes.

Finn wanted me to join him in New York, and I did for a bit. I'd always wondered what my life might have been like if we'd stayed in America. Going back felt right. But when I got there it was like I'd landed on the moon. New York was so different from anything I knew. It was bright even at night. When you looked up at the sky there were no stars, just the reflection of all the neon. There was noise all the time. Garbage trucks, taxis, horns, music; even the odd alley cat was louder than any Scottish feline I had ever heard.

And the energy—there was so much energy. When I stopped at a crosswalk for a red light while walking around the city, I could feel the buzzing of the people around me, raring to go, barely contained balls of ambition and grit. It was… *exhausting.* I was already planning on coming home when my mom got sick. I left as soon as my dad called.

Finn and I tried long distance for a while. But how do you connect with someone living on the moon—someone who can't remember what gravity feels like anymore?

Enough Finn thoughts. I need a bath. I throw my phone on the bed—not wanting to look at it anymore—and get my things together. Favorite nightgown, check. Book, check. The only thing missing is a nice glass of wine, but I'd have to go downstairs for that, and I'm too mad to look at either of their faces.

It's no big deal, pet. Maybe not to him.

Dad is the one who wanted all of this attention in the first place. And then to bring up Mom on top of it. It's not the first time I've been told I took like my mother, but with her gone, it's like antiseptic on an open wound.

Submerging in bubbles, the smell of lavender and eucalyptus filling the room with a steamy mist, I lay my head back on the rim of the clawfoot tub and try to imagine the story I'm going to write. The love story. From what I've read so far in my craft books on romance, I need to introduce my characters and explain why they don't want to fall in love. I smile. That part should practically write itself. I know a million reasons why not to fall in love. One, it never lasts. Two, it's more trouble than it's worth. Three, you can lose yourself and be swallowed whole like my mother was. Dimming her light so we could shine. Four…

A knock startles me.

"Skye, are you in there?"

I'm hyperaware of my nakedness. I can feel every bubble on my skin. One pops near my clavicle, and I let out a small yelp at the sensation. Miles is outside the door, and the only thing separating us is a thin piece of wood. I imagine him wearing what he had on at dinner, that tight sweater and those jeans that look like they were tailored to accentuate his thick thighs, walking into the room, gently touching my face, tilting my chin up to him, and planting a soft kiss on my lips as his other hand sinks into the water.

"I just wanted to say how sorry I am."

My cheeks, already warm from the hot water I'm soaking in, burn as if he can see through the door. Or read my thoughts. Or both.

"I didn't think that kind of thing would happen out here. Honestly, I didn't. But even so, I should've warned you it was a possibility."

I want to say something, but no words come, a running theme for me these days.

"For what it's worth, you look amazing. In the photo, I mean." Miles sighs, and I picture his handsome brow furrowed and flustered. "I'll let you bathe in peace."

* * *

I'M up before the sun. Every morning, I rise in the wee hours, and in my nightgown and crushed velvet paisley-patterned robe that makes me look extremely bohemian, I go to the east wing, where I've made one of the small libraries into my writing studio. Beyond the shelves of books, there is a large green sofa and a red leather wingback chair next to an arched stone fireplace.

Over the past few months, I've dreaded my morning ritual. Most days, I have to drag myself here. I sit in front of an empty screen and feel just as vacuous as it is. Occasionally, I'll put myself out of my misery and practice my mother's old piano in the corner.

But today there's not a dull ache of dread behind my eyes. Today, there is a hum pulsating through my body. Something I haven't felt for a very long time. Desire. A desire to put words on the page.

I quickly make a fire in the hearth, then start on the second order of business: coffee. After filling the back pitcher of the Keurig with water, I wait impatiently for the sweet aroma of coffee to fill the room. Snatching the cup as soon as the last drop ripples into the brown liquid, I bring the fresh coffee to my lips, the earthy aroma only raising my excitement.

My writing desk sits in front of a window that overlooks the grounds. The field below is black, the tall blades of grass silhouetted against the midnight blue of the sky. The sun still won't rise for another hour or so. This is my favorite time to write. Just me and the faeries.

For the last step in my ritual, I light my candle and shove the negative thoughts out of my brain. With coffee steaming next to me, I sit in my blue tweed chair and open my laptop. My fingers fly over the keys. It's like someone turned on the water, and what had been a leaky faucet is now gushing. Or the Fall of Foyers after days of heavy rain. The words don't just pour out… They are torrential. My fingers can hardly keep up.

An hour and seventeen minutes later, the sun is rising above the hills, and I have written almost an entire chapter. I've never written that much that fast, even on a good day before. It must be the genre switch. Maybe I was always meant to write romance. A tiny voice deep inside tells me it's something else. It echoes in my chest. *It's the muse. It's him.*

I stand and stretch. That's ridiculous. I'm attracted to Miles—of course I am. Who wouldn't be? He's indisputably handsome. He's a Hollywood heartthrob, for Pete's sake. But a muse? Come on.

* * *

41

BACK IN MY ROOM, I throw on clothes. The demon chickens won't feed themselves. The day is golden, sun shining through an opening in the clouds, sparkling on the dew like glitter on a nightclub floor. Or so I imagine. I've never been much of a club girl, but my heroine in the second cozy mystery I wrote was. It looks like nature partied all night, and this is the aftermath. Beautiful, silent, and still. Well, silent until I get to the *chickens*.

After the chickens are done and I escape with my eyes, I go to the barn where the horses are. We have five Shetland Ponies. I love them all, but my favorite is Pippi. She was born when I was eight and obsessed with *Pippi Longstocking*. I read my late grandma's copy over and over. In the novel, Pippi loved her red hair and it made me feel better about mine.

"Hey, Pippi." She nuzzles into my hand as I offer her a carrot. "We'll go for a ride later today, okay? In the afternoon."

Maybe Miles would want to go too? In the light of day, I can see that I overreacted about the photo. It's not like it was his fault, and his apology was so heartfelt. We could ride to the Loch, then maybe stop for a pint. My pulse quickens at the thought. If nothing else, it would be a great scene for my book.

Practically skipping back to the house, I picture Miles's strong hands gripping the reins.

My father is in the kitchen and hands me a cup of coffee. "Here ye are, pet." His face breaks into a smile. "Don't you look happy today. I see you're over the whole thing, you know, the internet."

I resist the urge to roll my eyes. "Yes, Dad, I'm over the entire internet." My face actually was plastered *all over* the internet, but by now, people are already on to the next thing, hopefully. I take a seat at the table in the corner of the kitchen, with a large lead-paned glass window on one side and the fireplace on the other, and pull my phone out of my sweater pocket. I scroll to my Instagram and drop my phone on the table.

"Alright there?" Dad sits at the table, adding two plates of eggs, toast, and bangers.

I pick my phone back up. "Yep, just slipped. Cold fingers."

My fingers are cold, but that had nothing to do with the slip. I have—I look again because I just can't believe it, but it's true—I have 13,000 new followers to my little IG writing account. My handle is @writteninthe_Skye. A little cheesy, but also clever, without being too clever. I started it when I queried my first book, four years ago now. It's never had much of a following. My posts are sporadic at best. Agents and publishers these days want to see you have an online presence, so I chuck a picture of myself with my laptop or a notebook up there every couple of weeks. My best picture by far—most liked as well—is a picnic blanket at the Fall of Foyers, laptop open, steaming thermos, and my legs, which I thought looked rather nice that day, in black stockings and my green wellies stretched out in front of me. I click on it now, and the twenty-seven likes it once had has skyrocketed to over eight hundred. People have shared it. *This is madness.*

I quickly go to my website and check out the backend metrics. Over a thousand people have visited my website since I checked last week. Over a thousand! People have signed up for my newsletter. Holy hell. This is huge. I'll have to actually write a newsletter to send out.

"Y'alright?"

A smile takes over my face, and that hum I had this morning has turned into a vibrant buzz. I feel like one of those New Yorkers at the crosswalk—a barely contained ball of energy.

I need to find Miles, accept his apology, and then maybe invite him on a horseback ride.

"Have you seen Miles?" I stand, grabbing my plate and cleaning it. I'm too excited for food this morning.

"He left."

All the blood that had been electrically coursing through me drains to my toes. "He left?" It's not possible. Maybe he just left to exercise or visit the cattle. He seemed quite enamored with Bessie. "When? Where did he go?"

"I gave him a ride while you were out doing your chores. He said he needed to do some more research, but if you ask me, I think he was just trying to give you some space after the whole *FHY* thing."

"*YHF. You Heard it First.*"

Dad shrugs. "Right."

"Did he say when he would be back?" This is not possible. Did I really drive him away? The first handsome man who had come to town in nearly an age, and I made him leave.

"Nah. He left his number." He pats his pockets, and I silently pray that my father, who can lose his reading glasses while they are sitting on top of his head, did not lose the number. Please.

"Ahh, here it is."

I take it from him, hoping that on the scrap of paper is some note for me. Something like:

My dearest Skye,

Please text me, and I will return post haste. I have only gone because I could not stand that I angered you, my red-haired beauty. I know we have only known each other for a matter of hours, but my feelings for you are as bright as a raging fire. Our connection was instant. Tell me you feel it too, and I will come running back.

Yours,

Miles

Not that I have any of those feelings for him. Not that he would suddenly turn into a Victorian nobleman either. Post haste? Who says that? Maybe I should be writing historical fiction. Or maybe I should lay off the *Bridgerton*.

The paper only says Miles next to a scrawled, almost illegible number.

"Did he leave this for me or for you?"

Dad chews his eggs. Suddenly he's worried about speaking with his mouth full. I've had entire conversations with the man through a rack of lamb. Where are these manners coming from?

"He just handed it to me and said here's my number."

I put the paper in my pocket and charge out of the kitchen.

MILES

When I woke up this morning after doing my two-minute plank, I looked up the bus schedule and made a plan. I tried apologizing, but she just ignored me, and I've found in situations like this, it's best to give it a little space. It couldn't hurt my character development to have some time on my own and explore Scotland a bit.

Callum graciously agreed to drive me to where the bus picks up. When he dropped me off, he said, "You don't have to leave. Skye gets like this. She'll tire of being angry and come around. Eventually."

"It's fine. She has every right to be upset. It's an invasion of her privacy." And it was all my fault. "Besides, it'll be good to see a little of the surrounding area. My character is supposed to live and breathe Scotland."

"Aye."

Before I left the car, I gave him my number. I thought about leaving a note for Skye, too, but if she didn't want to speak to me last night, she probably doesn't want to hear from me this morning. What would I say, anyway? I cringe, remembering how I called her stunning. It's true, but she must think of me as a lovesick puppy.

I've been walking around Foyers since. The streets are charming but small, and before I know it, I'm at the edge of the loch. The water is smooth this morning, like glass, not a ripple of movement in sight. But my eyes still scan, hoping I'll see something. I stare until my face is so cold my cheeks are numb.

I find a local pub that's already open for breakfast. An older woman greets me with a warm smile. "Ahh, you must be one of the film people?"

I return her smile. "Is it obvious I'm not from around here?"

"Aye. Too bonnie, for one. You must be the star."

I laugh. But can't deny it. "Apparently so."

"I'm Margie. It's nice to meet you. Have a seat, and I'll fix you up."

After a filling and delicious breakfast of eggs on top of the most scrumptious hash I've ever tasted, I sip my coffee and look out at Loch Ness again. It's massive, the water receding into the horizon like it has no end. In the cool morning, a heavy mist, almost as thick as clouds, hovers over the water and clings to the tops of the trees as if the atmosphere is too tired to rise into the sky. Ahh, Skye.

What is it about her? She's beautiful, sure, but it's more than that. There's something in her eyes. A challenge, but also a promise. Passion. That's it. She's filled to bursting with so much passion. I wish I had even half that much fire for anything in my life.

"Looking for the monster?" Margie stirs me out of my thoughts, topping up my coffee.

I smile. "Yeah." Better that than admit I'm indulging a schoolboy-style crush while simultaneously having an existential crisis. "Ever seen it?"

"Aye."

I freeze with my coffee midway to my mouth. She can't be serious.

"Just about a'body that lives around here has a story. I'm no different."

This is wonderful—exactly what I need. I'll immerse myself in the stories of the locals and get a feel for who my character is.

"Would you mind telling me about it?" I gesture to the other chair at the table.

Margie glances around the almost empty pub. There are a couple of older gentlemen sitting at the bar, and a younger woman by the fire, knitting. "Sure, for a minute." She sets down the kettle and sits with a sigh. "When I was a lassie, I went out fishing with my father. It was a morning like this one, where the fog mixes with the top of the water and you can't tell where one begins and the other ends."

I lean in, imagining myself in a boat slicing through the mist. Margie goes on to tell me about a creature rocking the boat as it glided by at a speed she'd never seen from an animal or ship before. They could only just make out a silhouette as it passed underneath them in the water, but the shadow stretched on and on. It had to be four times the size of their rowboat. They paddled as fast as their arms would allow to shore and never spoke of it to each other again.

"Wow."

"Aye."

"Did you ever see it again?"

Margie laughs, and it's so melodious I nearly join her, even though I don't understand the joke. "Child, I never went back on that loch again. The size of that beast…" Margie shakes her head and goes back to refilling cups.

* * *

THE SCOTTISH COUNTRYSIDE blurs by out the window in every hue of green you can imagine. I boarded the first bus that came. Pulling out my notebook, I make some notes about Margie's story. Imagine living next to this beautiful body of water your whole life and never going in it, not even dipping a toe in. Her fear must be immense.

The bus stops, and the driver calls out, "Last stop."

Shit. I'm back in Inverness. I was hoping to go somewhere new, maybe a bit more rural. I check my phone to see if there's another bus or a train I can catch. There's one in about an hour. I wander around, find some coffee, take five pictures with five different fans, then buy myself a purple baseball cap with a thistle stitched on it. It's not my best disguise, but I didn't see any fake mustaches, so it'll have to do. I can imagine what Skye would say about my hat, or more, the eye roll she'd give me.

The bus finally comes. It's warm, clean, and not too crowded. Perfect. Sipping my coffee, I gaze out the window at Loch Ness as we ride along. I start to replay the conversation I had with Skye in the car until I realize what I'm doing. I need to put her out of my mind. This is a research trip. I need to be present. Dark clouds have rolled in, and they are perfectly reflected in the glassy surface of the water. I watch closely for any hint of movement.

After almost an hour, we arrive at Urquhart Castle. The wind is bitter against my face as I make my way there. The man I buy a ticket from informs me I have the place to myself on account of the storm coming. "Best be quick, lad."

I nod and give my thanks. The wind blows harder, and fat rain-drops fall, one after another, picking up speed. I zip my rain jacket, shove my hands in the pockets, and stroll around the ruins. And I thought Castle Loch Ness was in bad shape. Compared to this place, it's brand-new. The stone here is a similar shade of pinky tan. One whole wall of the largest part of the castle is missing. I climb the stairs and look over the railing out at Loch, the stone rubble beneath my feet. The water is full of ripples now, with the wind in full force and the rain splattering onto the surface. I close my eyes and inhale deeply, the smell of the wet rock, moss, and something I don't have a word for—earth, maybe. If my character lived here, he would fix this wall stone by stone.

This film is going to be amazing. I open my eyes and take in the lush green hills dotted with trees, the leaves just starting to turn golden. It's a refreshing change from palm trees. I fish my phone out of my pocket to take a picture. My brother is always sending me pics from different locations. Always jetting off for his latest period drama or another Bond-like spy thriller, while I'm usually working out for my next sports movie or Marvel knock-off. It'll be fun to send him a location pic back. I can count on one hand how many times I've left the US for one of my movies.

This film is exactly what I need, my ticket out of second-rate superhero movies. The director is fresh. She's only done a few independent films so far, but all got rave reviews from the critics. This is her first film with a real budget, and there's already a buzz around it. I could be up for an Oscar if I can focus. I'm nearly thirty. It's the perfect time to pivot to more serious roles.

With the past few movies, I didn't give my best performance. But it was the uninspiring script, the low-budget costumes, the taxing shoot schedules. Sometimes I wonder if acting hadn't fallen into my lap as a kid, if it's something I would've chosen for myself. Maybe I would've been a carpenter, done something with my hands. It's silly to think about, really. How many people would kill to be in my shoes? I've just had a run of bad luck with the movies I've been in recently. *Love and the Loch Ness Monster* is going to be different.

As I snap the picture, a rumble of thunder vibrates my chest, and a few seconds later, a flash of lightning streaks across the sky—time to go. I try to text it to my brother, but my phone dies.

* * *

TRAMPING through the rain over half an hour later, I find a white stone inn nearby that thankfully has a room available and a bar attached to it. The room is simple, all I need really, and it has a standing shower. After I plug my phone in and shrug off all my wet clothes, I spend far too long under the water spray.

Once I'm dried off and dressed in the fresh clothes from my backpack, I grab my phone to head out the door, but I see I missed a text from Elsie.

Elsie: Did you get the new pages?

New pages of the script? I'd already memorized half the old pages.

I start punching in different replies, erasing each one. Finally, I just decide to call her.

It rings three times before I hear a very bleary-sounding Elsie on the other line. "Miles, why the hell are you calling me at eleven o'clock at night?"

Shit. The time difference. I didn't even think about it. What time must it have been when I called Jake yesterday? I mentally try to do the math when I realize it doesn't matter. I can't go back and un-call him, and he had clearly been awake enough to answer and force me to work out. "Sorry. I'm in Scotland. I just completely spaced the time difference."

"You're in Scotland already?" Elsie sounds more awake. "Where?"

"Um, around where we're going to be filming. What's with the new pages?"

"You haven't read them yet?"

"No, not yet. Is it just minor changes?"

There is a long silence. Did the call drop? "Elsie?"

The sound of a cup clanking on the other end lets me know she's there, just not talking to me. "I need some wine for this. Hang on."

Another few beats pass, then a loud slurp. "Ahh. Okay. I had to write in a brother."

"A brother? Are these fake pages?" Elsie is a notorious prankster.

"They're not fake."

"Her brother, or my brother?"

"You have a brother now."

Part of what I fell in love with in the script was the quietness of the two-character tableau. Just me, her, and the phantom of the Loch Ness monster. "Why?"

"The studio—"

"You mean Emily and Marissa."

"Yes, but I agree with them that it needed more tension. It's an out-there concept. Another name will help with the box office, too. Read the pages. You'll see they're better. The counterbalance of another male in the mix gives your character more depth."

I'm not completely sold, but I like the idea of more depth. It could open up the possibility for a larger range of emotions. Jealousy can be powerful. "Do you know if they've cast the brother?"

Silence, which means she knows.

"Elsie, you have to tell me."

"I don't have to do anything. Besides, how would I know? I'm just the lowly screenwriter."

I laugh at this. Elsie always knows everything. Everyone loves her. Whether she *should* know or not, she usually does.

"Elsie, come on. I won't say who I heard it from."

I hear a deep breath on the other end of the line. "Ty Marshall, okay? They cast Ty Marshall."

My fingers go numb, like I'd slept on my arm funny. "I have to go."

"Mil—"

I hang up before I drop the phone.

SKYE

*M*iles is gone. It's completely fine. That's what I wanted in the first place. I don't need him here to write my horseback riding scene.

It'll be business as usual. I get on my bike and ride into town. The Thistle House is hopping when I get there, and I wave to the men at the bar. They're here so often that their bahoochies are probably shaped like the stool, or vice versa.

Kate is knitting by the fire, so I go to join her. Without even looking up from her turquoise wool, she says, "You missed out this morning."

My shoulders tense because I know what she's going to say before she says it. "Oh really?" I watch Margie clean up a table by the window.

Kate looks up at me, her striking green eyes alight, and leans forward as if the bodach's at the bar care what we're saying. "Do you remember that movie you made me watch a million times when we were thirteen about the football star and the nerdy girl who became a cheerleader?"

"We were fourteen, and I don't remember having to force you."

"Were we? Oh, God… Remember the dance we made up to the song in the credits?"

I grin. The theme song to the movie was OutKast's "Hey Yeah" and Kate and I made up an epic dance and lip sync number that we even performed at the local pub, with all the town cheering us on, just about dying laughing into their pints.

"Well, the football player was here," Kate says, breaking me out of the memory.

"Here?"

"And he's a braw-looking man. A real snack."

I let out a breath. "You've been watching too much Kardashians."

Kate narrows her eyes. "You don't seem surprised. Oh, hold on a second… He's here for the movie at the castle, isn't he?"

"Yes. Miles came before the rest of the crew, for research."

"Ahh, Miles, is it? Miles looked good in that movie, but he looks even better at thirty-five."

"He's not thirty-five." I can see his Wikipedia page in my head, the one I'd read and reread about four times since Miles showed up on my doorstep. "He's twenty-nine."

"Is he now? What else do you know about Miles?"

Born in Brooklyn. Never been married, no kids, never a serious long-term relationship to speak of, but is always dating glamorous women. A little like young George Clooney before he met Amal. But I don't want to admit—even to Kate—how much I know about him, so instead I ignore the question completely and get up to grab some coffee from the pot.

Margie comes back out of the kitchen, "I could've got that for you."

I wave her away, knowing full well she would've brought me another foul, flowery tea.

"You missed your lad."

I sip my coffee so I don't huff in frustration. She's trying to get a rise out of me, and I won't give her the satisfaction. "He's not mine."

She winks at me. "Not yet, hen."

53

* * *

As PIPPI and I go for a ride in the afternoon, I take in the landscape with fresh eyes. The sky is a blanket of clouds in quiltwork patches of gray. The farther they recede into the horizon pops of robin's egg blue poke through. *The blue of her eyes*—the heroine in my book, Sorcha. I make a mental note to put that in the scene. The air smells fresh and just a little sweet, as if the rain is not yet done with us today. I entertain the idea of pulling out my phone and filming some content for my now sizable following, but I feel Pippi beneath me, raring to go. I give her a swift kick to let her know she can run to her heart's content. The wind blows my hair back, and I grip the reins tighter. It feels like I've traveled back to a simpler time, where there is no TikTok, Facebook, or Instagram. Where I would write my books at night by firelight with a quill and ink pot, my fingers stained in the morning just like Joe in *Little Women*.

The rest of the evening passes uneventfully. I want to ask my dad when Miles said he'd come back. I also don't want him to know that I care, so I don't.

* * *

THIS MORNING, there's no hum buzzing through me. There's no desire to put words on the page. There's only habit and routine. It's empty, but I do it anyway. Fire in the hearth, coffee in hand, candle lit, arse in chair, laptop open.

I try to write a heartfelt, sexy scene with Miles—yes, my male main character has his name, but I'm going to change it later—and Sorcha riding horses through the countryside. But all I get down is a paltry description of the hills and, of course, "Her robin's egg irises shone brighter than the sky peeking through the gray clouds."

It's awful. A right load of shite. The sun is already rising, and I get all of one hundred words done. At this rate, my novel will be published when I'm eighty.

The tiny voice echoes in my chest. *It's because he's not here—your muse.*

I try to drown it with more coffee. Twenty more minutes. I'll do a timed sprint, get a mess of words in, and then do my chores. I set a timer on my computer, wiggle my fingers as if I'm casting a spell on my keyboard, and I'm off.

Twenty minutes and fifty words later, I click my laptop closed. I want to slam it, but clearly, I won't be able to afford a new one anytime soon…or ever.

The next morning, it's the same, and the day after that, and the day after that. On the sixth day of Miles being gone, the writer's block has fully settled in, and I don't write a word. Not one new word down. The voice in my chest whispers to me.

Call him. Text him. Ask him to come back.

While I'm dressing, while feeding the demons with beaks, while cooking dinner, even at the dinner table.

"Pet, are you okay?"

"Fine, why?"

"I've been asking you to pass the salt for a good three minutes."

I hand him the salt.

"Do you have your writing group tonight?"

Is it already Tuesday? Wait… Didn't we meet last week? I rack my brain and realize Dad's right. "Aye. I should go."

I take my plate to the kitchen and hurry to the library. Rain lashes at the window, so I decide to take the car. Slipping into my wellies, I head to Thistle House. The windshield wipers working overtime, I can't help but wonder where Miles is in this weather. What kind of research on his character does he need to do, anyway? Is that the real reason he left, or was it my temper?

Thistle House is warm and blessedly dry when I enter, hanging up my wet coat. Kate, Gabs, and Bella are already seated in the cozy chairs by the fire, clacking away with their needles. I grab a whiskey from Margie and make my way over. A few years ago, when our writing group formed, it didn't technically start out that way. If it's not knitting, then there's not a group for it in Foyers. When I was a teenager, I tried to start a book club. We read *Gone Girl*. At the meeting, many of the members expressed concern for my mental state, that I would select such dark materials. They acted like I had us read the Necronomicon and suggested we try a few of the chants. It's not like I wrote *Gone Girl*.

God, I wish I had.

So, I joined the knitting group, and it turned out they were all avid readers. They read my pages and gave me feedback. Bella and Gabby started writing their own novels. Now we get to exchange pages, instead of them all reading just my stuff all the time.

"Skye!" Gabby smiles, her brown hair pulled back in a loose bun held together with knitting needles. Despite her sweet face, Gabby writes dark historical mysteries—emphasis on dark. Bella holds up the mitten she's working on to me in greeting, her long braids swishing with the motion, her dark skin glowing in the firelight. She's a nanny and is writing a cozy mystery about a bookstore owner who stumbles upon a dead body with her pet cat in tow. Our work used to have a lot in common.

Kate holds up her whiskey to me, and I clink it with mine. She's the only one of the group who hasn't tried her hand at writing yet, but she gives great feedback. I sent them some of my new pages the other day, thinking I was giving them enough time to read them. They would've, if I hadn't gotten the dates mixed up. In reality, 'not realized what date it was' is more accurate. I could've sworn we met last Tuesday, but no, that was the day Miles got here.

"We were just talking about Bella's pages. Then we'll do mine, then yours. Does that sound good?" asks Gabby, her cheeks a little extra rosy tonight, either from the fire or the nearly empty glass of wine next to her.

I nod, wishing I'd actually learned to knit so I'd have something to do with my hands. I hate going last. I'm nervous enough about how they'll react to the genre switch, which none of them have brought up. Now I have to wait until the end. We discuss Bella's latest chapters and get into a lively conversation on how many characters are too many. We move on to Gabby's latest chapters. Gabby's writing is clean, her research is thorough, and her plots are hole-free. She doesn't really need us, and any suggestions we have or feedback we provide, she usually doesn't do anything with. But she seems to enjoy our meetings, and she's a great facilitator. We spend her time questioning one of her character's motivations on whether it was believable for an uptight English woman in 1922 to stretch in the garden in plain sight of the neighbors. She convinces us it is.

Gabby sips her wine. "Okay, now on to Skye. New genre."

Kate smiles like a cat that's caught a canary. "Romance. How'd you get into that?"

I make eyes at her.

Bella chimes in. "Romance is my second favorite genre."

Gabby pushes the bridge of her glasses up. "So, the pages themself are, well, they're…"

I might throw up into my whiskey.

"They're marvelous."

Every muscle in my body relaxes at the same time, and a pleasant tingle moves through me. This must be what drugs feel like.

"I loved them," Kate says with a massive smile.

Bella is nodding so hard that the beads at the end of her braids are clacking together, almost like applause—an ovation for my pages.

"Sorcha is just a spitfire. I like her. I'm rooting for her. And Mickey…"

I've been calling the character Miles, but I did a quick find and replace, changing the name to Mickey before sending the pages.

"…oof, he's a dreamboat."

I giggle, not able to contain the pure elation this praise is giving me, but also because blouse-buttoned-to-the-top-button Gabby saying dreamboat is too much.

We talk for thirty minutes about my opening pages, and the response is overall very positive. They are excited to read more…but as of now, there isn't any.

I need to get my head back in the game. I need to text Miles.

* * *

I LAY in bed writing texts and deleting them.

Me: Do you know when you might come back?

Delete, delete, delete.

Me: Do you have an ETA for your return date?

Delete, delete, delete. Sounds too corporate.

Me: You up?

Delete! What is this, a booty call?

What do I want to say? I want him to know that I'm not upset anymore about the whole paparazzi thing. That it's safe for him to come back without enduring my wrath.

Me: Hope the research is going well. I just wanted to say, I know it's not your fault about the whole picture thing. I'm sorry.

I read it over and over, delete the last two words, then hit Send.

I'm about to plug my phone in when three dots appear. They disappear, then reappear.

Miles: Thank you for understanding. For what it's worth, you did really look incredible.

My stomach flips. His words at the dinner table play in my head for the millionth time. *Stunning.*

Me: You didn't look half bad yourself.

Delete! Who am I? The only things missing from that statement is a cigarette hanging out the side of my mouth, a martini in one hand, and an eyebrow waggle.

Me: What have you been up to?

I send it. What am I? Twelve now? Really sophisticated conversation.

Miles: Monster hunting :)

I can picture his face, lit up like when he was petting Bessie, and I smile.

Me: When are you headed back this way?

I'm about to hit Send when another text comes in.

Miles: I'll tell you all about it tomorrow, if you'd like?

Me: Can't wait.

I put away my phone before I can judge my last text, because while it may not be the most eloquent thing I've ever written, it is absolutely true.

* * *

THE NEXT MORNING, the words fly from my fingers. The desire is back. Maybe it was the feedback from the girls, but I know that's not true.

Miles will be back today.

I sail through my chores and take extra care getting dressed, even putting on proper makeup—not just my usual swipe of mascara and halfhearted comb through my hair.

Miles will be back today!

I'm just about to get on my bike for my morning ride when my watch buzzes. The tourism board is calling. It must be Logan.

"Hello."

"Skye, you owe me big-time," Logan says.

In the distance, I see a figure walking steadily toward me, in dark jeans and a cream fisherman's sweater. Tall, dark, and handsome— that saying was invented for Miles Casey.

"Skye, are you there?"

"Yes. I'm here. Lost connection for a moment." To earth. "What did you say?"

"I said I found an alternate castle on the other side of the loch where the Hollywood people can shoot. Your quiet little castle and quiet little town can stay that way."

Quiet. Dormant. Devoid of any inspiration. No muse.

"Um, actually, Logan, my dad convinced me it'll be good for everyone. Bring money in, help the economy, all that."

"You sure?"

The blood rushes to my ears, roaring loudly. What about my mom?

She would understand. I hope. "Yep."

"Okay, I'll call Dun Hares and tell them the whole thing's off. Are you sure?"

Miles is only feet away from me, his smile wide. Even if he did read my stupid letter, even if it really was him who replied, it was so long ago, there's no way he remembers. What's past is past.

"I'm sure."

MILES

*S*kye's out front on the phone, so I hang back, slow my pace. Her hair is catching the morning light, making it look like fire. I want to reach out and touch it, so I put my hands in my pockets instead.

Once she tucks her phone away, I approach and tell myself to be cool. I'm Miles Casey. I walk into far more intimidating situations than this on a weekly basis. What is it about this blue-eyed, long-legged woman that sends adrenaline coursing through my veins?

"Of all the roads in all of Scotland…" I say with a smile. That was cool.

She returns my smile with one of her own, and it shatters me. "I would argue *you* walked onto *mine.*"

I raise both my hands. "Fair point."

Skye looks down at her bike. "I was going to go for a ride, but…" She seems to be considering her next words, then looks up at me, her blue eyes so breathtaking I catch myself from staggering back. "Unless you might want to go for a horseback ride."

"With you?"

She laughs. "Aye."

My heart floats out of my chest. I expect to see it hovering between us like a party balloon. "Yes, please. I would like that very much."

So much for being cool.

She smiles. "Let me just put this away."

I can't help but watch her as she goes. Her jeans hug her curves in all the right places. When she heads back toward me, she motions for me to join her. I want to run, but I walk — fast.

"The horses are just back here."

"Is what I'm wearing okay?"

"Yep. It should be fine, but if you want to change, you can. I actually need to get a few things too."

We agree to meet at the stables in fifteen minutes. I shuffle around some things in my backpack and notice I have a couple of missed calls. Whoever it is will have to sweat it out, because there is no way I'm making Skye wait.

I walk behind the castle and into the field where there is a large barn. Skye introduces me to the horse I'll be riding. Foxy is a beautiful old Clydesdale with shaggy white feet and brown markings all over. Skye hands me an apple to feed her. Foxy munches it gratefully as I stroke her soft neck on the side.

"She likes you."

"I like her too." I look at Skye, her blue eyes piercing right into my thoughts. "She's gorgeous."

Her cheeks turn a light shade of pink, and I think she knows I wasn't just talking about the horse.

We get both horses saddled up and ride toward the loch. We take a trail that winds through the trees instead of the road we drove on before. It's so green. Green grass, green trees, green moss covering them. It smells sharp of pine and dirt and a subtle floral scent that I can't quite place. I wonder if it's Skye. I watch her up ahead, her soft curls flowing behind her, bouncing with each step, and I imagine myself burying my face in her hair. Would the smell get stronger?

Skye looks back, and I glance away quickly so she doesn't think I'm a creep for staring at her all the time.

"You're good on a horse," she says, a note of surprise in her voice.

"I've had training." I nod. "Rode them in quite a few movies over the years."

"Ahh, yes." She lifts up her pointer finger. "I saw that cowboy one. What was it called?" She snaps her fingers. "*Spurned.* You were on a horse in that whole thing. I just forgot."

I laugh. "My performance was that memorable, huh?"

She falters, and I quickly add, "I'm kidding. It was terrible. But that movie was a lot of fun to make. I loved the horse. His name was Wayne, named after John Wayne. He was a handful." I pat Foxy on the side. "Nothing like you. You are such a good girl."

Skye smirks, an adorable half-smile, and turns back to the trail. "Let's see what you got, then."

She gives her horse a kick, and they're off like a shot.

It's true that I've been trained, but it's also true that it's been years since I've been in the saddle. I give Foxy one more pat. "Okay, girl. Please, *please* make me look good."

A swift kick to her sides, and we're off. The wind is fresh on my face. My sweater blows snug against my torso. I feel alive. I feel free. Maybe I should get a horse. But where would I put it at my place in LA? Maybe I should move somewhere quieter.

During my travels around the Highlands, when I wasn't worried about Skye never forgiving me, I felt at peace. The silence is soothing. And I was only stopped by fans a handful of times. I'd be lying if I said I didn't miss a quick drive to get my favorite green smoothie, but the countryside suits me more than I thought it would. Maybe I'm just over-identifying with my character. Wouldn't be the first time.

I bring my focus back to the trail. We're headed down toward the loch now, and I catch up to Skye. She's slowed her mare down to a trot, and we ride side by side. We take a trail right on the banks of Loch Ness. The water stretches out, rippling in the wind this morning. Streaks of black mix with every shade of gray you can imagine, settling into a stark white on the horizon. I never knew so many subtleties of gray existed before coming here. My eyes scan the water automatically for movement.

"So...monster hunting?" She raises her eyebrows as she asks.

I smile. She must've caught me searching. "Aye."

She laughs. "Aye?"

"Trying it out. For my character."

I tell her about my adventures over the past week, staying in small towns, hearing about people's experiences with the loch and the monster.

"Everyone who lives near the loch has one, according to Margie."

Skye nods. "Believe me, I know."

I tear my eyes away from the water to look at Skye again, a far more breathtaking sight. The gray makes any color against it pop, and Skye is all color, from her red hair to her blue eyes, to her pink sweater that perfectly matches her cheeks on this ride, to her dark green boots.

"Do you have a story?"

She looks startled, so I clarify. "About the Loch Ness monster?"

"We all call her Nessie."

"I'm catching on to that." I laugh. "For some reason, it feels overly familiar for me. Like I haven't earned it yet or something. Have you seen it, though?"

Skye looks off in the distance. "Nessie stories are best told next to a fire, preferably with whiskey."

"It's a date, then."

Her eyes twinkle when she turns back to face me, and my heart drops into my shoes. I've been telling myself I shouldn't indulge my attraction toward her. But when she looks at me like that? It's undeniable, forceful. It feels like an earthquake. I'm powerless to stop it. I just have to hold on tight and pray I don't get clobbered.

Then she's off again at a gallop.

We ride for a couple of hours before Skye stops in a small field on top of a hill. She ties Pippi up to a tree and pulls an apple out of her bag for her.

Over the course of my career, I've ridden a ton of horses but never put away or tied one up. That was always the trainer's job. I fumble to knot the reins. Skye leans over me, her arm brushing mine. Her hair caresses my face, and the scent of lavender is overwhelming. As she moves back, her hip grazes my fingertips. My body is electrified everywhere we've made contact.

Skye tosses an apple my way, and it soars past me in my stunned state. She laughs as I grab it off the ground and feed it to Foxy.

"I'm usually a better catch." Foxy's greedy lips tickle my hand. "Whoa. Look who's hungry…"

Skye brushes off her hands and pulls out a buffalo plaid blanket. "I am."

"Me too. I could eat a horse." Skye barks out a surprised laugh, and I realize what I just said. I give Foxy an apologetic pat. "Sorry, girl. Not really. It's just a saying."

Skye shakes her head. "Foxy may never forgive you."

She lays the blanket on the grass and sits. Next out of the bag comes two sandwiches, two more apples, a small bag of chips, and two bottles of water.

I clap. "You brought a picnic."

"Aye. Figured we'd get hungry."

I sit, and she holds up one of the sandwiches. "Fancy a piece?"

"A piece? There're two. Can I have the whole thing?"

She stares at me for a frozen moment, then bursts out laughing.

"What? If you want to save some, that's fine, I guess. I'll take a piece."

"A piece is a *sandwich*," she says that last part in her most American accent.

"Oh." I take the *piece* and unwrap it. "I thought y'all spoke English here."

"Well, ye heard wrong." She smiles. "We speak Scottish. It's like English, only when we blather on, it's more interesting."

We eat and enjoy the view. The loch is shimmering in the sunlight that has pushed through the clouds as the day has worn on. In the far distance, a hazy mist covers the hills, some of the greenest I've ever seen, even through the fog, with just the occasional pop of yellow. But the real beauty is Skye. I can't take my eyes off of her. At the same time, I'm trying really hard not to stare. The light is catching the side of her cheek. Her skin is so fair, it looks drawn on. It's such a contrast to the red of her hair. And her figure. I can't say I wasn't plenty distracted by her on the ride. Her strong legs gripping the horse, her shoulders squared and her—

"So, what's this movie called anyway?" Skye asks, interrupting my thoughts. For the best, really. If I'd kept going, I might not be able to get off this blanket without considerable embarrassment.

"The movie? It's tentatively being called *Love and the Loch Ness Monster.*"

Skye smiles. "What's it about?"

"It's about…well… It's about love and the Loch Ness monster." I laugh.

I tell her the basic story, the one from the new pages. Two brothers living with their old housekeeper until she dies, and they hire a new one, a young, beautiful woman. Both brothers fall madly in love with her, but she doesn't even really notice because of her obsession with the Loch Ness Monster. Even explaining the new story with my brother sours my mood. Ty Marshall. I can't believe they cast him for the part. I should walk, except I can't. Not after the last few flops I've made.

This film has bones to it. My character has depth. It could mean awards, for all of us. I sit up and brush off my hands.

I can't think like that. To make good art, you can't think of the reception, not during creation. Not for me, anyway, but maybe that's been part of my problem. Maybe I should give a little more thought to how my films will fit in the market.

"Hmm," Skye says. "Sounds interesting. Are there any other characters in the film?"

I shake my head. "Not really. A few minor ones. They were hoping to cast some local extras. Want to be in a movie?" I waggle my eyebrows.

"No. Absolutely not."

She says it so harshly, it takes me by surprise. She must notice my reaction, because she quickly says, "Not that being in the movies isn't great. It's fine, that's your job. It's just, all that…" She motions with her hand, and I have no idea what she means by all that. "It's not for me."

There's a beat of silence before Skye goes on. "My mom was famous." She looks away and swallows hard. "She chose a simple life, and I respect that. Not that I wouldn't love a different job. Just not yours."

I smile. "What do you want to do? Or, I mean, that sounds silly, like *what do you want to be when you grow up?* You're already a grown-up."

She looks off in the distance, her eyes focused on the water. "I want to write. I get paid to write instruction booklets, mostly for appliances. But one day I'd like to get paid to write my novels."

"I'm sure you will. Are you working on anything right now?"

She pauses, her apple halfway to her mouth. "I've been tinkering with something new."

"I'd love to read it sometime, whenever it's ready for outsiders."

She turns her blue eyes on me, and there is a softness to them that I want to pause and look at for hours.

We finish our lunch and ride back to the castle. Skye hurries away once we get there, not even turning to look at me when I try to thank her for the ride. She just throws a hand up over her shoulder. Disappointment is bitter in my mouth. I had hoped, imagined, that after the ride, while we were tying up the horses, she might lean over to help me with my knot like she did on the picnic. But this time, I would tilt her face to mine and kiss her soft rosebud lips. Not this time.

I check my phone and see I have more missed calls and a couple of texts. I click on the first one.

Natalie: Call me! NOW!

Oh no. This can't be good.

I dial her number while moving around the field, trying to get the best service.

"Miles! I've been trying to reach you for days! Where have you been?"

"Sorry. Service is spotty out here to begin with, and I was way out there. I have some great ideas for my character, though." Natalie is an old friend and the director of the movie we're about to film.

"That's great. Really, it is. We can hash all that out later. I'm calling about the *YHF* post. The redhead in the photo, that's the owner's daughter, isn't it? Of the castle where we're going to shoot for eleven weeks. You're not dating her, are you?"

I think back on our trip to the bookstore, our conversations in the car, our horseback ride, and our picnic. Are we dating?

"Miles. It's a yes or no question."

"No...not really." We hadn't technically called any of them dates, and it seems like the answer Natalie wants to hear. A relieved sigh on the other end of the line tells me I'm right.

"Good. You can't."

"What do you mean?" Not that I want a serious relationship or anything. But a nice dinner with a woman I enjoy spending time with doesn't sound half bad. I can have dinner and still focus on the film.

Natalie speaks clearly through the phone, shattering my imagined candlelit table, my fingers brushing Skye's as I pass the wine. "Under no circumstance can you date Skye Ainslie."

SKYE

$\mathcal{I}$ practically run to my laptop. It's very unlike me to write in the afternoon. But I'm feeling inspired. So inspired, I don't even light my candle before opening my computer. My fingers soar over the keys. The words come out as if they are already written.

After I finish up a scene, I write another, then another after that. I introduce some side characters. Then I finally get to the scene that's been trying to burst onto the page since I sat down.

A picturesque horse ride under a Technicolor blue sky. It's fiction. Not everything has to be gray. Sorcha and Mickey stop on a hillside for a picnic with a breathtaking view of the glittering loch below. They have crackers, cheese, grapes, and wine. A small drop of wine lingers on Sorcha's lips. Miles takes a gentle finger and wipes it off, his skin hot and firm on her lip. His hand moves to the back of her neck, finding the sensitive flesh under her hair. He leans in...

"Skye, dinner is ready."

No. Who needs food when they are about to kiss?

He leans in, his eyes smoldering in the sunlight, and...

"Skye, we're waiting on you, pet."

I let out a long, low breath and close my laptop. It's best to stop in the middle of the scene, right? Didn't Murakami say that? Because then you can come back and jump right into the world.

I head downstairs to the dining room, and the table is set with a beautiful roast chicken. My mouth waters as I sit down. I must be hungrier than I realized. Miles is sitting across from me, looking just as scrumptious as the chicken. Scrumptious? Oh Lord... Romance writer brain. But he does look good, in a fitted dark-green sweater that seems to barely contain his biceps as he passes me the potatoes.

I reach for them. "Thank you."

He smiles, and it's like someone turned on the sun. "Thank you for the ride this morning."

My cheeks warm at his phrasing.

"Ride?" my father says, making my cheeks burn. "Take the horses out?"

I nod.

Miles pours a little gravy on his potatoes. "Yeah. We rode all over and then had a picnic. It was great."

"Had a picnic, did ye?" My father has mischief in his eyes as he says it. Cheeky bastard. "That's wonderful. And a great way to spend the day before you have to buckle down for the film. I heard from your people. They should start arriving tomorrow in the early afternoon or evening."

I move my food around on my plate, suddenly not as hungry. What if all these people being here changes things, and I can't write like I have been? What if I won't get to spend time with Miles anymore because he'll be too busy?

"Are they? Guess I should check my phone once in a while." Miles's smile falters, too. He says to my father, though it feels for my benefit, "I shouldn't be busy with the film the whole time. I'm not in all of the scenes." Then, almost to his plate, he says, "Not anymore, anyway."

Dad and Miles make small talk about some crime show from America called *The Wire*. I've never seen it, so I tune them out and let the back of my mind knit words and ideas together. When the knitting is louder than the conversation at the table, I excuse myself and head back to my writing room.

* * *

I WRITE at a more measured pace this time, and this time I do light the candle and make some hot chocolate. It feels good to be inspired. It's been so long, I wasn't sure I would ever feel that way again, like this whole writing thing was a cold that I finally shook. I'm delighted it's not.

Once my mug is cold and the candle is a pool of wax, I tune back into my surroundings and hear music. Not just any music, but music so familiar, it's etched into my bones.

Closing my laptop, I head downstairs to find the source. The ground-floor library is dark, even with the lamp on and the fire roaring in the hearth. This library is larger than the one I write in. There's a large leather couch and loveseat, with two soft red damask chairs positioned around the fire. On the shelf nearest to the sitting area, instead of books, it's records, hundreds of them. Most of them were my mother's, but some are my dad's, and over the years I've also added to the collection. The record player sits on a long wooden table behind the couch, spinning away, my mother's voice booming out. She had such a melodic voice, deep but feminine. Like a Scottish version of Nico or Fiona Apple.

I used to love listening to her records. When I was growing up, I'd put them on, and she'd come in and casually change the album. She'd say, "Have you heard this one?" or "I have this song stuck in my head; I have to listen to it now." She never said she didn't want me to listen to the albums she made, but I got the hint. After she passed, I couldn't bear to put them on. Not just hearing her voice again, which is its own exquisite kind of fresh pain every single time, but also the waiting. Expecting her to come into the room and change the record. Only now, she never does.

The notes of the song playing reach right into my heart and

squeeze until I can't stand the pressure anymore. I shut off the record player. Miles sits up from where he was lying on the couch, his script that was on his face falling to the floor.

"Was I being too loud?"

"Where did you find this?" I hold up the record sleeve.

Miles motions to the record wall. "Just on the shelf."

I shake my head. "You just picked this at random?"

There's no way. What are the odds?

Miles stands and comes over to where I'm standing. He looks pensively at the sleeve. "It wasn't entirely random. It's going to sound"—he sighs—"silly, I guess."

I carefully put the record in its case and put it back on the shelf, choosing a Simon and Garfunkel record instead. "The Boxer" rings out through the room like sage smoke.

Miles continues, "But I was looking through the records, and I thought the woman on this cover looked a little like you. So, I put it on."

I go to the bar cart, pour a whiskey, and raise my eyebrows at Miles. He nods, so I pour him one too. After I hand it to him, I sit in the chair closest to the fire.

"I'm sorry. I should've asked about the records before I put one on."

I shake my head. "It's fine. You can put on any you like. Just not that one."

He sits back on the couch. "Got it."

"Or any by that artist."

He smiles. "Not a fan?"

"She was my mother."

"Oh, that explains the resemblance."

I nod and take a deep inhale, smelling the whiskey, the fire, and something spicy, sexy.

Miles.

"Want to talk about it?"

"Nope." I hum with Paul Simon's hums in the song, unable not to.

Miles smiles and scoots forward on the couch. "Are you a singer too?"

I laugh. "Only on karaoke nights at the Thistle, and lately not even at those."

"They have karaoke nights there?"

"They do. Once a month, then randomly if it's one of the old blotters' birthdays or something."

"Who would have thought? What's your song?" He holds up a hand and stands. "Wait, don't tell me. I can guess." Miles sips his whiskey, his eyes searching the ceiling for my song. "'Satisfaction.'"

"It's actually called "(I Can't Get No) Satisfaction," and no."

"'Paint it Black.'"

I shake my head.

He paces for a couple of minutes. Then he pauses to ask, "Is it a Stones song?"

"No." I smile. He's turned this into a game of twenty questions. I take another sip of whiskey, the amber liquid warming my belly, the fire warming my face, and Miles warming my heart. Whoa—this is fun, but that's a bit far. Save it for the pages!

Miles snaps his fingers. "'Blitzkrieg Bop.'"

"I'm not a masochist."

"What? That's a good song." Miles looks adorably confused, and I bite my lip, wanting to feel some pressure on them.

"A great song. But too fast for karaoke, too hard. Actually, come to think of it, the song I usually choose—well, when I used to sing—is kind of hard too, but for different reasons. Maybe I *am* a masochist. But really, I haven't sung in years."

"Years? Why?"

I shrug, and he quickly shifts back to his guessing game.

"'Welcome to the Jungle.'"

"No."

"'Me and Julio Down by the Schoolyard.'"

I shake my head and sip more whiskey. A small smirk tickles my lips. These are great guesses, but he'll never get it.

"Oh!" Miles puts a hand to his forehead. "What is that Pogues song? 'The Sick Bed of'...ahh, somebody. You know the one I'm talking about?"

"Ahh, I see. Since I'm *Scottish,* I sing The Pogues, who were Irish and Londoners."

"I didn't mean…"

My straight face breaks, and I laugh.

"I'm joking. Although it is offensive. But my mom knew Shane. He sang at the Thistle House once, completely blotto. Sometimes around Christmas, I'll sing "Fairytale of New York" but it's not my go-to song."

Miles throws himself back on the couch and sighs. "I need a hint."

Sounds from down the hall, make me pace a bit to get a peek. "Nope."

Mischief lights up his eyes. "I'll just have to see at the next karaoke night. When is it?"

"It's always the last Friday of the month, so in a couple of weeks. Next one will be extra fun because of Halloween, but like I said, I don't sing anymore."

"We'll see." He smiles, and heat spreads all the way from the tips of my ears to my toes.

He walks over to me, grabbing my empty whiskey glass, his fingertips lingering on mine. My head is swimming, my lips feel electric. "Refill?"

I look up into his warm eyes and then down at his full lips. He leans in. My face instinctively moves closer like a force beyond my control. It's like he's a magnet and I'm metal. He smells like cinnamon, cloves, and whiskey, plus a little something sweet. The scent is enchanting. Our lips are so close now, I can feel his breath.

The commotion from down the hall gets louder and louder until the library door swings open.

"Miles!" A gorgeous woman with long black hair, pale skin, and a figure that defies all laws of gravity buzzes into the room.

We jump apart like teenagers caught making out on a couch.

The tiny ball of energy comes over and kisses Miles on each cheek. I thought people only did that in the movies.

"Oh, thank goodness." She grabs Miles's glass and downs the swig of whiskey he had left. "Can you get me another? My flight was atrocious, and the car ride over here took forever. This castle is really far out here, huh?"

Miles and I are both stunned. The woman half-waves to me as she unzips her coat, revealing an even smaller figure than I thought she had at first. Well, her waist is tiny. Her bosom is not. "I'm so rude. I'm Ava Garreth."

Of course she is. I've seen her in close to twenty movies, probably. My favorite is the one where she played a spunky model-turned-detective.

Miles fills another glass for Ava and brings it over.

"Thank you. I have lots of ideas about our relationship in the film."

He comes to grab my glass, but I pull away.

"I should turn in."

Miles's face falls, or am I just reading into his expression?

"One more."

Ava is kicking off her shoes and tucking her lithe legs under herself.

I shake my head. "Early morning."

Miles nods. "The demon chickens won't feed themselves."

Ava laughs. "Chickens? This place is wild."

I run up the stairs. I thought the "crew" wasn't coming until tomorrow.

As I brush my teeth and get ready for bed, I tell myself over and over it's better this way. I can't indulge real feelings for Miles. It's not like he's even interested in me anyway. He's charming for a living. It's probably just a habit to be all smooth. Although he does look at me like I'm a freshly poured pint with just the right amount of foam at the top. But it doesn't matter. He's going to leave at the end of the filming and go back to his glamorous life. He'll forget all about me—

well, he might think of me sometimes when he's having a whiskey. He'll say, "I had an Irish girl once."

And I'm not even Irish. Honestly, I'm only half Scottish.

But I'll be here with my heart shattered, pining for the handsome man who's in America. Nope. Not again.

Especially not for Miles Casey. He's much better suited to someone like Ava, anyway. Someone glossy and put together. Someone who doesn't eat carbs.

I'll save all the kissing for the page. The romance will stay in the romance novel.

But what damage would it really do? If we did kiss? Or possibly more? I'm a grown woman. I could have a harmless fling. As long as I keep my feelings out of it, and so does he, we could indulge a wee romance.

I pull the covers up to my chin, still going back and forth in my head on what I should do. To kiss the handsome American or not to kiss the handsome American, that is the question.

MILES

$\mathcal{A}$va is yammering away, but I'm lost in thoughts of Skye. Right before Ava arrived, I'm pretty sure we were going to kiss. Our faces were so close, I could feel her breath on my lips. But then, as soon as Ava came in, Skye took off like her hair was on fire.

If I go now, I might be able to catch her before she goes to bed.

"So what do you think?" Ava leans closer to me, her eyes shimmering in the firelight. I don't know what she's talking about because I didn't hear a word she was saying.

"I have to go." In my mind, I'm already catching up to Skye, maybe as she's coming out of the bathroom, her face freshly washed. A small trickle of water running down her cheek to her silky nightgown.

"But what about my idea?"

"Yeah, sounds great," I say as I bolt out the door, passing Callum on his way in.

"Ah, your friend found you?"

"Yep." I wave over my shoulder as I bound up the stairs.

I slow my stride once I get to the hall. The bathroom is empty when I pass it. Walking to the end of the hall, I hesitate in front of her door.

Natalie's voice echoes in my head. *"Miles, you can't date her. We're going to be filming there for weeks. We're not set to wrap until a little before Christmas. What if you two have a lovers' spat? We can't just switch castles mid-movie. We'd have to reshoot the whole thing for continuity."*

I back away slowly from the door. It's better this way. The past few years, I've started to feel like my heart is whole again instead of slapped together with duct tape. I don't need to go falling for a beautiful woman who lives halfway across the world and has expressed no interest in me romantically. Well, that last part isn't true. I'm pretty sure she wanted to kiss me as much as I wanted to kiss her.

A woman's voice echoes down the hall as a door opens.

"The room is beautiful. I'm just wondering if there is anything slightly larger for Ms. Gareth."

Callum's voice booms, "Not if she likes heat."

Before either of them can see me lingering outside Skye's door, I duck into my room.

As I get out my running clothes for the morning, I let out a long, low breath. Focus. I just need to focus on my part in the film. The rest of the crew will be here tomorrow, Jake will arrive next week, and I'll be too busy to worry about Skye.

I try to sleep, but I just keep thinking. Instead, I pull up Skye's Instagram on my phone, scrolling photo after photo. Her captions are clever. She is a good writer—from what I can tell from these snippets. Posts with her face in them are few and far between. I find one with her standing in front of the loch, a scraggly tree branch dipping into the frame. The sun behind her is lighting up her hair like a rich glass of red wine, a glint in her eyes. I go to sleep wondering who took it.

* * *

In the morning, I drag myself to the kitchen for a cup of coffee before my run. I hate to eat before exercising—I get nauseous easily. But just a quick nip of coffee usually helps wake me up enough to not hate the first mile, and boy do I need to wake up this morning. I tossed and turned all night thinking about Skye, replaying our almost kiss in my head on a loop.

There's already a pot of coffee on, so I pour myself half a cup. Callum and Skye both seem to be early risers. Must be tending to the animals. I sit for a moment at the kitchen table and gaze out the window. The sunrise is throwing pink splotches at the clouds, and the sky behind it is an almost unnatural shade of lavender. I feel an itch to be out there in it. To feel the ground under my feet and the cool morning air on my face. I take one more sip of coffee before heading out the door.

Not really sure where I should head, I run down the dirt road and decide to retrace the route of our horseback ride, but not go as far.

The cows are looking dapper this morning, shaggy hair in their eyes. The mist clinging to the grass at their feet makes them look even more like rock stars on stage with a smoke machine. "Rock on," I call to them as I pass.

Muscle memory kicks in, and my feet find a comfortable rhythm. I put in my earbuds and turn on the Scottish folk music mix I've been listening to since I agreed to take the role. My blood pumps, heating up the chilly morning. I lose myself in the landscape, the music, the strong beating of my heart.

By the time I head back, I'm covered in sweat. I meant to do an easy three miles, but got a little carried away and probably went four, some of the hills on the way back making it not so easy. But it was glorious.

I slow to a walk. Once I'm close enough to the castle, I can see vans parked out front. Disappointment tugs my shoulders down. This will be my thirty-seventh film. More films than years I've been alive. I'm exhausted, and we haven't even started shooting yet. These days, I enjoy the planning, the prepping, the lead-up of everything more than actually being on camera. How many times can you look longingly—or furiously, or pensively—off into the distance? That's not the only source of my disappointment, though. I was enjoying my time alone with Skye. She took off the moment Ava got there yesterday. Will I get to hang out with her with all these people here?

I shake it off. It doesn't matter. I'm not here to hang out with Skye. I'm here to yank my career back onto some kind of respectable track. I have a job to do.

* * *

ONCE I GET INSIDE, the castle is bustling. There is a low chatter of voices everywhere. The smell of bacon and coffee wafts through the air. I want to find it, but I also don't want to see anyone yet.

I walk softly up the stairs. After I shower and dress, I'll be able to face everyone.

"Milesicle!"

Only one person calls me that. I turn to see Elsie at the bottom of the stairs. Her light-pink pixie cut hair is sticking up at odd angles, and she has a massive cup of coffee in her hand, and suddenly, my desire to hide fades away.

"Elsephant!" Elsie has written the screenplays for three other films I've been in. She is a genius, by far the hardest-working person in the room and the funniest. We became good friends after a particularly grueling shoot in Alaska, where I had to do a lot of scenes with very little clothing in the snow. That's when she started calling me Milesicle. Some days she would send me fake pages of more and more ridiculous scenes in the snow or on a frozen lake just to mess with me. She's like my little sister—well, if my little sister was a pale, pink-haired smart aleck.

I dash back downstairs, my hamstrings screaming at me that I should have stretched after my run. Picking her up, I swing her around in a bear hug, making her coffee splash everywhere.

"Whoa there. Don't mess with the caffeine."

Skye comes in the door, muttering under her breath, just as I'm putting Elsie down.

"I'll clean this up." I motion to the coffee droplets on the stone floor. "Skye, this is my friend, Elsie MacDonald. She's a writer too."

Skye nods.

Elsie smiles. "It's so nice to meet you. Thank you so much for letting us film here. It means a lot to me."

Skye half smiles. "It was my father's decision, really. I should... I have to go."

"Oh, okay."

As Skye walks upstairs, I watch her go. Those jeans are made for her. Elsie swats me on the arm.

"What was that for?"

"Put your tongue back in your mouth, dude."

I run a hand over my face and sigh. "Is it that obvious?"

Elsie laughs. "Yes. Are you two..."

I shake my head. "We've just hung out a couple times."

Her eyebrows shoot up to her hairline.

"No, not like that. Just friends."

"Okay. Good. We don't need that kind of drama on this set. Remember Barbados?"

Another film I'd been on with Elsie. We were making a sexy heist movie called *Swipe*, kind of a take on *Mr. and Mrs. Smith*, if they weren't married but had just met on Tinder and were thieves instead of secret agents. I started dating my co-star the first week of filming. She was so hot, and we had all these trivial things in common, like we both loved that old movie *High Spirits*. We both took our coffee black. Little things, but I thought we were meant to be.

It turned out she wasn't really a one-man-at-a-time kind of woman.

We stopped dating the sixth week of filming on a ten-week shoot. It was the most awkward time of my life, and unfortunately, it wasn't just awkward for me. It was terrible for everyone. The director came to Elsie to try to write fewer scenes with us together. But *we* were the movie.

"Don't worry, I already got an earful from Natalie. I won't date anyone on the set."

Elsie gave me a pat on the shoulder. "I'm not trying to *mom* you. You're both grown-ups. Do what you like. Just don't get us kicked out of the castle."

"We're just friends."

I drag myself upstairs to finish my workout, the planks won't do themselves, and nearly run into Skye at the top.

"Skye."

She just gives me a curt nod as she heads the other way. Did she hear me talking to Elsie? Her full lips are pulled into a small frown.

"Hey." My mouth completely forgets about everything I just agreed to and says, "Do you want to go for a walk later this afternoon?"

Skye's lips twitch at the side, and I know I made the right choice. "Aren't you going to be busy filming?"

"No… There's a table read. I'm pretty sure that's not until tomorrow, though." Eighty percent sure. Truthfully, more like seventy-six, but one thing at a time.

She nods, mischief dancing in her eyes. "You know what, I have a better idea than a walk. If you're up for it?"

I smile. "I'm always up." Skye's eyes go wide as quarters, and it dawns on me what I just said. "I mean… I didn't mean…"

Skye laughs.

"I'm just going to stop talking now." I cover my mouth with my hand.

"Should we meet around three?"

I nod, my mouth still covered.

SKYE

*M*iles just told that super cute girl with short pink hair that he was absolutely not into me. Once I got past the surprisingly swift sting, I realized this is perfect. We can hang out, (for muse purposes) and I don't have to worry about leading him on.

I get to work writing comments for one of my critique partners' pages, make lunch, finish a few chores, and then get ready to hang out with Miles. After I pull on my turquoise jumper that makes my eyes pop, I take some time with my makeup, lace up my nice hiking boots, and head down to meet him.

Coming down the hall, dressed in a white-collared button-up shirt, is a tall man with full, dark hair. He smiles when he sees me, his teeth so white against his dark skin; he looks like he walked straight out of an ad for toothpaste. Actually, I think I have seen him in a toothpaste commercial.

"Oh, hello."

I instinctively look behind me, but no, he is talking to me.

"I'm Ty Marshall." He holds out a hand.

Ty Marshall. It wasn't a toothpaste commercial I'd seen him in, more like close to twenty films. It's so odd having all these famous people just roaming about. Like seeing peacocks in the wild and realizing they're just birds. I shake his proffered hand; his palms are smooth and warm.

"Skye Ainslie."

"Ahh, the Lady of the Manor."

Lady of the Manor? Ick. "I guess so."

"It's wonderful to meet you. I just got turned around looking for the bathroom."

"Aye, it's right over here." I motion to the closed door. Exactly how many people will be sharing this bathroom with me while they are filming?

"I tried that one. It's locked. Is there another?"

"There are quite a few downstairs. Some of them even work."

Ty's brow furrows. His face doesn't look too happy about this bathroom situation either. Just then, the door opens. Miles emerges smelling of that subtle mix of cinnamon and cloves and looking handsome in a cream fisherman's sweater that highlights his dark hair and lashes.

"Miles." Ty smiles and holds out a hand to Miles, which—to my surprise—he sidesteps, keeping his arms resolutely at his side.

He gives a curt nod. "Ty."

I've never seen Miles act so cold. Usually, when he greets someone, his eyes light up and he gets bouncy. Like an excited puppy. I thought he was incapable of not being friendly, but I was wrong.

Miles turns to me, and his full-watt smile is back. "You look incredible."

Heat rises in my cheeks. I thought I looked nice, but incredible?

"Are you ready to go?"

I nod.

Ty frowns again, his perfectly manicured eyebrows pulling down. "I think Natalie is looking for you."

Miles gives Ty a slap on the back that seems a little harder than necessary. "Thanks, buddy."

He grabs my hand, and we head to the door.

What was all that about?

"Where are we going?"

I smile, dropping his hand as I throw on my coat. "You'll see."

I lead Miles out to the Land Rover and turn the key. "This Will Be Our Year" by the Zombies fills the car.

Miles surprises me again by turning it up and singing along. I join in and am about to pull out when, out of the corner of my eye, the door to the castle flies open. A woman with thick curly chestnut hair, luminous brown skin, and bare feet is running toward us, waving her thin arms in the air like she's mad.

"What in the world?" I say.

Miles follows my gaze. He puts his hand on his face and mutters, "Shit."

As the woman gets closer, I see it's Natalie Rodriguez. *The* Natalie Rodriguez. I'm not so much of a movie buff that I would recognize every director I came across. But Natalie is one of the hottest up-and-coming directors working right now. And by hottest, I mean that quite literally. She is absolutely gorgeous, with flawless light-brown skin, thick black hair, and dark eyes that take up most of her face. She looks like a Disney Princess if they drew them with more curves. The paparazzi *love* her. She directed one of my favorite movies—*Me, Myself and I*—and she was just featured in *Time's* One Hundred Most Influential People. Dad swears she and her mom came over all the time when I was little and we lived in LA, but I don't remember.

As she approaches the car, I roll down the window.

Natalie's cheeks are rosy from her jog. She takes a second to catch her breath. "Oh my god. Skye! You're all grown up. Oh you might not remember me but I babysat you a few times. I'm Natalie."

She holds out a hand with perfectly manicured black nails, with small jewels on the tips. I shake it, feeling her warm, soft skin.

She gives me a half-smile and turns her full attention to Miles. "We are all setting up in the dining room for the table read. Remember the table read?"

Miles smiles, and it is so wide and charming, it practically has a cartoon sparkle that goes along with it.

"Is that today? I thought it was tomorrow."

She shakes her head, her gorgeous hair swishing with the motion. I wonder if I could get my hair to look like that. More soft and luxurious, less frizzy and untamed. "No. It's now. My feet are freezing. I'll see you inside in three minutes."

I roll up the window and turn off the engine.

Miles shakes his head. "Sorry. Can I take a rain check?"

"Aye."

"Tomorrow? After my run?" He reaches out his hand and puts it over mine. It's like his skin is electrified. A jolt goes straight to my heart.

"Sounds like a plan."

* * *

WE WALK INSIDE TOGETHER, close but not holding hands. Miles heads off to the dining room with his head down. I nearly run to my writing room, my skin still tingling from Miles's touch. I need to get it all down on paper. When I reach to open the door, it's already open, the fire burning in the hearth.

The woman I met earlier at the bottom of the stairs, Elsie, is lying on the couch by the fire, her laptop on her stomach, clacking away. She sits up when she hears me come into the room.

"I hope you don't mind. I needed a quiet place to work, somewhere far away from the dining room and Callum said..."

It feels like I should mind, but for some reason, I really don't. "It's fine. But do you need to be alone?"

She scoots back so she is more upright but still leaning against the arm of the couch. "No, not at all."

I always work at my desk, but Elsie looks so cozy by the fire, with her laptop perched on her knees, that I think, why not? I unplug my laptop and bring it over to the chair by the fire. I put the blanket over my lap and get situated, crossing my legs. Opening my novel, I dive in. That's what it feels like, too—like I'm so immersed in the words, they surround me like cool water on a sultry summer day.

After about twenty minutes of clacking away, I notice Elsie staring at me. The look on her face seems like she's trying to figure me out. She was doing her fair share of typing, too, so I'm not sure what she's trying to decipher. I close my laptop. "Would you like some tea or coffee?" Elise shakes her head, so I check the time. Four o'clock— that's not too early. "Or I think I have some whiskey."

"Whiskey, please!" Elsie says while she clicks her computer shut.

Placing my laptop on the floor, I bring over two glasses and the bottle to the small coffee table. I pour us each two fingers, and then, on second thought, just a splash more.

Elsie holds out her glass to me. "Cheers."

"Slàinte."

"Oh, I love that." Elsie tries out our Scottish Gaelic way of saying cheers, not doing too bad a job of pronouncing it.

I point at her laptop. "Are you working on the script they're going to start filming?"

She shakes her head. "No. Not tonight. I'm sure I'll have some rewrites after the table read, but I was working on something new."

"Why aren't you at the table read?"

Her eyes look haunted at the prospect. "I can't. It honestly gives me a panic attack just thinking about sitting there while they read the entire script. I get defensive. I correct them if they skip lines or change little words. And I hold a grudge, so Natalie tapes it for me and I make all my edits in the morning."

"Aye, that makes sense."

"I'm sure you get it. You're a writer."

"Not published or anything," I'm quick to add. I don't want her to think I'm pretending to be something I'm not.

"Being published doesn't make you a writer. Writing makes you a writer. What are you working on?"

I'm going to tell her the same lie I've been telling Miles, that I'm working on a new murder mystery, but instead I say, "A romance novel."

My cheeks feel a little warm at the admission, or possibly the whiskey.

"Oh, how fun. I love romance novels. Have you read any Natalia Jaster?"

I shake my head, and Elsie goes on. "She writes romantasy, and the chemistry sizzles off the page."

I nod and make a mental note to check it out. "I only recently got into romance—novels, I mean. Obviously, I'm a grown woman and have had my fair share of actual romance." My cheeks burn hotter than the roaring fire. What am I saying? "Not my fair share, but a handful of relationships—well, one meaningful one." I clear my throat and get back to the safe topic of books. "I've read mostly contemporary."

Elsie nods, a small smirk on her face, probably from my whiskey-muddled ramblings. "Have you read any Lynn Painter? She's one of my faves in that genre, so cinematic. I can never figure out how she puts so many song lyrics in her writing. Her publishers must have deep pockets."

I shrug. "I haven't read any of hers either. I've just dipped my toe in, really. Up until recently, I exclusively read mysteries and thrillers."

Her eyes light up. "How fun! A genre switch. What's your book about?"

I take a long sip of whiskey so that I don't say Miles Casey. "It's about two people from different worlds who fall in love."

"Sounds intriguing. I'd love to read it sometime."

If Elsie read my pages, she'd instantly see it was about Miles and me, or would she? It might be a good test to see how thinly veiled I'd made his character. I give her a half smile. "It's not ready yet, but I'd love that when it is. What is your new script about?"

She tells me all about it. This one takes place in the Pacific North-west. There's bigfoot and a love story, but she hasn't quite worked out the plot yet.

An hour and two whiskeys later, we're sitting on the floor by the fire, me reading from her laptop and her reading from mine.

Screenplays are a different beast, but her writing is wonderful. Her dialogue is heartfelt without being sappy, and there's an undercurrent of mystery. The more I read, the more nervous I get about what she thinks about mine. We both agreed we'd just read the first five pages. When I look up after finishing hers, she is still intently reading mine. My pulse is banging wildly at the side of my neck. She must hate it. She must be having to reread parts because it doesn't make any sense. My thoughts swirl until I feel dizzy. "It's just a very early draft—in fact, it's the first draft. I know it still needs a lot of work."

Elsie nods but still doesn't look up from the screen. *Cursed whiskey*. I would never have shared pages so early if I hadn't been drinking. Well, except to my writing group, but that is different.

She's smiling. "This is great. The voice is so fun. Really good stuff, especially for a first draft. Forgive me, I'm a slow reader. I'm only about halfway through."

She likes it. I let out a sigh of relief. "It's fine. Take your time."

Grabbing the bottle, I pour us each a little more whiskey. Stealing glances at her the whole time as she reads, I watch her face change from delight to what looks like confusion. Her brows knit together. Then they shoot up and she lets out a little, "Oh..."

Is it too spicy? Did I go too far with the metaphors?

When Elsie finally looks up from the pages, she lets out a heavy breath. "Wow. You've got it bad."

"It's bad?"

"Oh, no. It's a saying. The writing is wonderful. It's just... Is this based at all on somebody in real life? An actor staying here, maybe?"

I shake my head quickly, switching our laptops back. "No, of course not."

I reread the opening pages. Our meet cute where Miles fell in the mud, dressed in his ridiculous tuxedo top and kilt. In my version, when I help him up, I fall on top of him—just as he had suggested after it happened—our bodies pressing together, our breath mingling in the morning air, our lips almost touching.

Elsie is on her phone, tapping away. Is she texting Miles? Oh God... What if she talks to him about the pages?

She turns the phone to me and shows me a picture of Miles on a red carpet, a white and gold backdrop behind him, dressed in a tuxedo top and kilt. "I was at the festival too. I saw his outfit."

I close my laptop. "It didn't actually happen—well, some of it did. But not like that..." I think about our near kiss last night. We hadn't actually done anything. What exactly am I trying to deny here? I sigh. "Okay. It's Miles."

MILES

I head to the dining room. Before opening the door, I take a deep breath and square my shoulders. I can do this. I am a professional, and I'm not even that late.

I open the door. Snacks, cheese, crackers, coffee, and several bottles of wine, all of it untouched cover the table. Everyone has a full water cup in front of them. Ava is speaking. Sitting next to her is Thora Townsend, her silver hair pulled back in a tight French twist, an oversized cashmere cardigan wrapped around her thin torso. Quite a change from the last time I saw her in Dior accepting her second Oscar. Next to her is her assistant, a young man whose name I can't recall at the moment. We've only met a handful of times before.

The rest of the table is filled with various members of the crew, personal assistants, and, of course, Ty. I wish Jake were here so I didn't feel quite so on my own, and I probably wouldn't have forgotten about this table read if he was. I resist the urge to check my phone for any updates on his ETA. It's bad enough that I'm late... Late and scrolling mindlessly on my phone like some tone-deaf teenager is not a good look.

As I enter the room, Ava goes silent. Everyone looks up from their scripts and stares directly at me.

Natalie clears her throat. "So, what is it, Miles? You just hate table reads?"

"Sorry. I really thought this was scheduled for tomorrow. I hate to admit it, but I'm a little lost without my assistant." There is only one empty seat at the table, right next to Ty, a little placard with my name on it waiting for me to sit. I look a few times in vain for another chair, but there is none. Can I stand?

"Have a seat. Join us," Natalie says, clearly unimpressed with my excuse.

I'm kicking myself that I got the time of this table read mixed up in the first place. I'm usually really on top of all that—well, with Jake's help. Maybe I rely on him more than I thought. Natalie and I go way back, but she is a professional first, friend second. I can tell she's pissed.

I mouth, *Sorry*, at her, to which she just rolls her eyes and motions for me to sit.

Reluctantly, I take the seat next to Ty. Glancing over his shoulder, I see he's on page seventeen. I pick up the script from the table and turn to the same page.

Ava reads, and I'm spellbound by the subtle approach she is taking with her character. From what I've seen of her other films, I sort of expected an over-the-top performance, but her delivery is quiet, yet compelling. I'm pulled in, and it makes the table read fly by. Except when I have to read with Ty.

Even his voice is grating. Too deep, like he's trying to sound like Tom Waits or Ron Perlman or something. Ridiculous, since I know for a fact his regular voice is much more nasally. The tension at the table when we say our lines to each other is palpable. We're talking *at* each other, rather than having an actual conversation.

We've gotten through a good chunk of the script when Natalie stops me mid-sentence. "I think that's good for now. Let's call it a night, gang. I know it's been a long day,"—she looks pointedly at me—"for most of us. We'll pick this back up tomorrow at nine and discuss notes."

There are nods around the table. *Tomorrow.* If there were a rock nearby, I'd kick it. Skye has a surprise adventure planned. We said tomorrow after my run. I'll have to find her and see if we can do it in the afternoon.

Ava and Thora start chatting, their assistants following them out. I'm about to beeline for the door to find Skye when Natalie says, "Miles. Hang back a minute."

My stomach plummets into my shoes.

"Oooh, someone is in trouble," Ty sneers.

I grit my teeth so I don't punch him in the face. I'm not a violent person, but something about Ty brings out a white-hot rage in me.

Once everyone leaves, Natalie silently opens one of the bottles of wine and pours herself a large glass. The glug of the wine echoes off the stone floors, punctuating the silence between us. I want to say something just to break the tension, but I also don't want to speak first. She pours a second glass and hands it to me, still without a word. Then she takes a seat closer to the fire. She motions to the other chair. I sit and try to gauge exactly how screwed I am. Is this booking the next flight and looking for a job in construction screwed? Or just keep my head down the rest of my time here screwed?

Once we're both situated with our red wine, it feels slightly less like a summons to the principal's office—*slightly* being the operative word. Natalie finally breaks the silence.

"So, the table read just slipped your mind?"

"I thought it was the morning *after* you all arrived."

"You didn't get my email yesterday changing it?"

I hadn't checked my email. It feels odd that email even exists in these crumbling stone walls and wild landscape.

"It won't happen again."

She nods. "What's the story with you and Ty?"

I take a sip of wine and look away. "No story."

She puts her wine down on the small table next to her chair and crosses her arms. "Miles. Don't bullshit me. You're a good actor, but a terrible liar."

I sigh. "Ty and I worked together before. We had some personal issues."

Natalie shakes her head. "Look, if you don't want to tell me, fine. I'm not your therapist, I'm not your boarding school matron, and I'm definitely not your mother. Right now, the bristling alpha positioning you two are doing could work on screen. Just make it work for you, okay? Don't let it make you lose sight of your character's ultimate need."

I nod. "My character's ultimate need."

She stands, pours a little more wine into her glass, her nails clinking on the bottle, and says over her shoulder as she leaves the room, "Love."

* * *

NATALIE'S WORDS rattle around in my head.

Love.

I put my wine on the table and go in search of Skye. I check the library where we almost shared a kiss yesterday, but it's empty.

I head upstairs and turn in the direction I saw Skye go the other day. The halls are dark and cold, probably a good ten degrees cooler than the other parts of the castle I'd been in. I'm just about to turn back and try knocking on her bedroom door when a laugh echoes from somewhere down the hall, and then piano music plays. Around the corner, light spills out of a large open door and, with it, the sound of voices.

When I walk into the room, Skye is sitting at the piano, her fingers poised on the keys, and Elsie is rolling on a large rug by the fireplace, laughing hysterically. Soft tears are running down Elsie's face, and she's trying to catch her breath. Skye is nodding and saying, "I know. I know."

Their joy is infectious. I smile. "Looks like I found the party."

Skye jumps with a yelp and accidentally bangs the keys. Elsie startles as well, the whiskey in her glass splashing out.

"Miles!" Elsie says, her arms flinging out wide. "Have some drink." She whispers to Skye in a not quiet voice at all, "Don't worry. I won't tell him a thing. I won't breathe a word. I'll take it to my grave."

Skye starts to laugh again, and they both say, "Grave," in a fit of giggles.

"How much whiskey have you two had?" I ask, unable to hide my smile.

"We are grown women. We will not be shamed if we get a little—" Elsie stands, stumbles a moment, and then sits back down on the couch this time. "Okay, maybe a lot bit drunk."

"Come on. Let's get you two to bed."

Skye nods and helps Elsie to her feet. They whisper together, this time quiet enough that I can't hear.

"Okay," Elsie says. "Let's go."

We drop Elsie off at her room first—hers is the first one to the left down the long hall where Skye's and my rooms are. "You promise you'll come to watch the filming."

"Aye, and you'll come to karaoke?"

"I wouldn't miss it." The two women embrace like they are lifelong friends, saying goodbye.

Skye seems less drunk than Elsie, but every now and then she stumbles, so I stay close just in case. "Do you play the piano?"

"A bit."

Is there anything she can't do? I smile. "Maybe you can play for me sometime?"

A mischievous smile flirts at the corner of Skye's pink lips. "Maybe, if you're good."

I laugh, but the way she's looking at me is making the chilly hallway suddenly very warm. I try to bring the conversation to a more neutral place. "I thought you and Elsie would get along."

She nods. "She's wonderful. So talented and smart. She's going to give me notes on my project."

"Oh, that's great." I'm a little jealous because I offered to read it, but of course, she would want the writer's opinion. "About tomorrow, would it be okay if we rescheduled it for the afternoon? We have to finish the table read in the morning."

When we get to her room, she walks in, leaving the door open, and goes to sit on the blue chair in the corner.

I linger at the door as she kicks off her shoes. "Will the afternoon work?"

"You don't have to stand in the doorway. Come in." She makes an exaggerated waving motion with her arm.

I step inside, but don't want to make myself too comfortable. She's been drinking, and I don't want to cross any lines.

"Shut the door. You're letting in the draft."

Skye is taking off her sweater, revealing a threadbare white tank top, her black bra visible underneath. My heart is in my throat. I want to reach out and touch her. I want to run my hands along the soft fabric of that top. I want to pull it up over her head and bury myself in her neck, then work my way down.

"Miles, will you shut the door?"

I swallow hard. "I should go. Let you rest."

Skye walks over and stops just short of pressing her body against mine. She swings the door shut behind me. Her face is so close to mine. She smells like a fancy cocktail, notes of lavender and whiskey. She says in a whisper, her lips almost touching mine, "It lets in the cold."

Her blue eyes are searching my face, and I can't find my voice. She puts her arms around my neck, and my hands find her waist instinctively. I want to kiss her—God, do I want to kiss her. But it wouldn't be right. I don't want our first kiss to be a hazy memory for her because she was two sheets to the wind. I want her full consent, and I want us both to remember it for the rest of our lives—or at the very least, the next day. She leans in, and I ignore every fiber of my being telling me to pull her in closer. Instead, I push her away.

"Skye, we shouldn't. You've been drinking."

She waves a hand at me. "Pssh. Drinking schminking."

I laugh. "Drinking schminking, huh?"

She smiles and shrugs as she sits on the bed and starts taking off her socks. "When did you stop reading your fan mail?"

I shake my head. "You're really interested in fan mail, huh?"

"Research for my book. When did you stop reading them?"

Searching back, I try to remember. "I must've been twenty or so."

She nods and starts to unbutton her pants. "Do you remember any of them?"

Raising my eyes to the ceiling so I'm not outright staring at her, I think back. "I saved some. There were a couple I used to reread. Actually, one was from Scotland…" My heart beats fast. It couldn't be. "I could have Jake send them."

When she stands, her pants fall to the floor, revealing black underwear and long legs. "No. You don't need to do that."

"Okay." I try to focus, get back on topic, peel my eyes away from her thighs. "Tomorrow afternoon, then, for our adventure."

I say a quick goodnight, knowing the more she takes off, the harder it'll be for me to leave. Leaning against her shut door, I try to catch my breath.

Tomorrow.

I can kiss her tomorrow.

I did the right thing. Only, I'm not supposed to kiss her at all. I'm supposed to be just friends with her so I can keep my job. This role could really put me back on track: more awards, fewer memes.

And what about all the fan mail stuff? I need to call Jake.

The bathroom door opens, and Ava walks out, a small towel wrapped around her. What is with the half-naked women everywhere tonight? I move away from Skye's door like it's electrified and am about to duck into my room when Ava spots me.

"Miles."

I give a half wave. "Goodnight, Ava."

She pads over lightly, her satin slippers smacking against the stone floor. "Wait."

I freeze, my hand halfway to my doorknob. I don't want to wait. I want to try to call Jake. Then go to bed and dream about Skye's arms around my neck until I fall asleep. But I already started this whole production on the wrong foot, so I turn to her and put on a large smile. "What's up?"

"Where were you this morning? I thought we agreed to talk more about that thing."

Thing? I have no idea what she's talking about. "I've taken up running again. I'm trying to get out there every morning around six-ish. You know, stay in shape."

"Running?" She looks deep in thought before she smiles. "Okay. That'll work."

"Work?"

"Right. My process, you know? Getting close with each other so it translates on screen."

"We can be running buddies, then."

I'm on the phone dialing Jake before the door is completely shut.

"What's up?"

"You know that little box I have where I keep letters and trinkets and things?"

"You have a box of trinkets?"

I sigh. He doesn't know about the box. It's not like we go through it together while wearing face masks and drinking wine. "I think it's in the closet. Can you look for it?"

"Sure. I'm out at dinner right now."

"It's no hurry. Just let me know when you find it."

"Sure thing."

I lie on my bed, my mind a mess. Trying my hardest to run lines to put myself to sleep, but my mind keeps wandering to Skye. She wanted to kiss me. She wanted me to stay. I can still smell her lavender scent in the air.

SKYE

*T*he world is too bright. I must've slept in. Checking the time, I see it's already after six. No. No. No.

I fly out of bed, the head rush that comes with it making me instantly regret my swift movements. Putting on clothes at a more measured pace, I try to show my hangover that I respect it, I will nurture it, and then it can kindly leave. I don't have a lot of time to write before my chores and then meeting Miles.

How much did Elsie and I put away last night?

The end of the night comes back in small flashes. Miles walking me to my room. Oh Lord... Did I take my trousers off in front of him?

The rest of the night is pretty fuzzy, though.

I make my way to my writing library, going over the scene I want to get down this morning. Since I only have a short amount of time, I turn it into a pomodoro session. Twenty-five minutes later, I got a decent amount of the scene written. I stand to stretch, looking out the window at the horse barn, the roof catching the first rays of sun.

I'm about to leave to tend to the chickens when movement out the window catches my eye. Miles is out there in running shorts and a long-sleeved fitted shirt that hugs his muscles in a way that is almost indecent this early in the morning. But he's not alone. Next to him is Ava, her dark hair pulled back in a high ponytail. She's in sleek black leggings and a pink sports bra. Not one ounce of fat jiggles as she runs—well, except in the bra. I look away and try to ignore the sting of jealousy that hits me like a slap to the face. They're just running together. What is wrong with me? It must be hangover brain.

At the door, I slip into my wellies and throw on my coat. Off I tromp, around the castle toward the chicken coop. They're always my first stop. Get the worst out of the way. As I'm rounding the corner to the coop, Miles and Ava come running toward me. Ava is laughing at something, her pearly white teeth gleaming in the morning light like some villainess in a Disney flick, or maybe I'm projecting.

They slow down, and I tuck my hair behind my ears. I should've put on makeup or at least run a brush through my hair. Ava and Miles are sweaty from their run, but they glisten more than anything. Miles looks particularly attractive this morning, his eyes bright and focused directly on me. It feels like he can see into my soul. Heat floods my cheeks.

"Good morning, Skye." He smiles. The morning suddenly feels warmer.

"*Madainn mhath*," I say with a small smile.

Ava grabs both of my arms. I'm so surprised, I immediately jump back. "Will you say that again? Does that mean good morning?"

Her voice is so high with excitement that it pierces right to the core of my hangover. I resist the urge to grab my head. "Aye. *Madainn mhath*."

Ava repeats it a few times under her breath. "You know, Skye, I'd love to pick your brain about…well, about being Scottish. Are you busy right now?"

"I have to feed the chickens and tend to the cows. As well as some other odds and ends to take care of."

"Oh, okay. What about later? We have some stuff to do this morning, but I'm free this afternoon."

I look to Miles. We have plans, but maybe he doesn't want Ava to know about it. Examining his square jaw, it comes back to me in a flood of memories that bring a burning sensation to my cheeks. My arms around Miles's neck. I tried to seduce him in my room last night —Miles, with that twinkle of mischief in his eyes. I clearly remember now, he wouldn't kiss me because I'd been drinking. My heart warms at the thought. I've never hung out with anyone so...thoughtful in that way.

Guys I've been with in the past are more likely to offer to help yank off your pants than suggest you should slow down. Turns out respect is incredibly hot. Honestly, it makes me want to try again, stone cold sober, and see what Miles says. I'm replaying the feeling of his hands on my waist when Ava jars me out of my thoughts.

"Will this afternoon work?"

Miles shakes his head. "No. Skye and I have a research trip this afternoon."

"What kind of research? Maybe I can tag along."

Miles and I both say, "No," at the same time.

Miles puts a hand on Ava's shoulder, and I feel a swift kick to the gut. I'm usually not this jealous of a person, but Ava is so perfect. "It's really specific to my character. I'll explain. Let's go in and let Skye get to her duties."

Miles leads Ava inside and throws me a wink over his shoulder. I float back to the chickens.

* * *

THE REST of the day takes eons. I write some more, the words easily flying from my fingers. I could write an entire novel just on the warm feeling I get from Miles Casey winking at me in his tight, sweaty shirt and running shorts that hit him at the muscular part of his thigh. When the afternoon arrives, I pick out a cute black top with buttons up the front and a pair of tight gray jeans.

We meet out front by the Jeep, but I have a thought. "Let's ride bikes instead."

Miles gives me a hesitant smile. "Bikes? Okay."

I get out my yellow beauty and then pull out my dad's bike for Miles. They're around the same height, so it fits perfectly.

Miles winces a bit at the first few pedals.

"It's a bit of a ride, but nothing too strenuous," I assure him. "You okay with that?"

He nods. "Yep. I'm good. I'm getting into running again, so I'm just a little sore. Or a *wee* bit sore."

I laugh, but his accent is getting better.

"As soon as I warm up, I'll be fine. This is great."

We ride into the gray and golden afternoon, the wild wind in my hair and the most handsome man at my side. It's like a dream.

After a while, I pull onto the side of the road near Loch Ness and get off my bike. Miles follows suit.

"It's better to walk the bikes from here so we don't ride into a tree or run into a root."

Miles nods, and we start off on the trail.

"This is one of my favorite places."

The trees blow in the slight wind. And for a few moments, we are silent, listening to the lapping water of the loch, the rustle of the leaves, and our bike chains turning.

"How's the writing?" Miles asks.

The morning was extremely productive, even with my lack of time. I wrote over twelve-hundred words in the blink of an eye, fueled by coffee and our near kiss the night before. Then, when I went back to it, I got another thousand or so. I smile. "Good."

"What's your story about?"

I sigh. What is my story about? Love, loss, fear.

You.

But instead of saying any of that, I say, "Oh, just you know, murdery stuff."

Miles laughs, and it booms against the trees and disappears into the mist hanging over the water.

I swiftly change the subject, not wanting to lie to him anymore. "How's the character development going?"

"Good. I think. I thought I had a pretty solid handle on it, but now that more of the cast is here, I'm not as confident anymore."

I'm not quite sure what he means, and it must be written all over my face, because he goes on.

"It won't just be about what I think the character is. It's going to be affected by all of our relationships and how we play with or against each other in the scene." He sighs. "I don't know if I'm ready for that, but it's happening so… not a lot I can do. Got to jump in headfirst. Truth be told, the whole being in front of the camera thing is my least favorite part."

"Isn't that the main part of your job?"

Miles laughs again. "Yep."

I nod. "What's with you and that Ty guy?"

Miles looks surprised. "Is it that obvious we have beef?"

"You have beef?" I have no idea what he's talking about. Beef? "Like for supper?"

Miles laughs. "Sorry. It means we have history. Not a super pleasant one."

"Oh, what a funny saying."

Miles laughs. "You're one to talk. While I was traveling, someone said to me, *"A pretty face suits the dish-cloot."*" He says it in an honestly great Scottish accent—better than yesterday's, even. "I still don't know what that means."

I laugh. "That's a classic."

"What's it mean?"

I look up at the clouds, which are getting darker by the minute, searching for how to explain. "It basically means that if you're attractive, it doesn't matter what you're wearing."

"So they were kind of insulting my fashion choices." He laughs. "But I get it, I think. Like Marilyn Monroe in a potato sack."

"Exactly."

It was smooth, but Miles essentially changed the subject from Ty Marshall. It doesn't seem like he wants to talk about it, so I don't bring it up again. The sound of the water's gotten louder. I veer off the trail and to my favorite spot. A little clearing with a massive willow tree, its leaves a mixture of deep yellow and some green stragglers that can't quite let go of summer.

Miles smiles. "This is just like in your Instagram photo."

He's looked at my Instagram? I know exactly what photo he means. I usually don't post photos of myself, or at least of my face anyway, but even I could see I looked bonnie in that one. I'm shocked Miles has seen it.

There's a fallen log under the tree, and I take a seat. Miles joins me, and we look out at the water. "This is the best place on the loch. Well, my favorite, anyway."

He nods. "I can see why. It's gorgeous."

Mist clings to water. It's hauntingly beautiful. "This is where I saw Nessie."

Miles sucks in a breath next to me, and it's so cute I almost laugh. "Really?"

I take a long inhale. "When I was a kid and we first moved here, my dad, mom, and I used to walk this trail together. There's more of a proper park a little ways farther. My mother and father were fighting that day. Once they started yelling, I ran away. They didn't fight often —hardly ever, really—but when they did, it scared me. Anyway, when I ran, I found this spot. It was a day like today, with heavy mist. I was throwing rocks into the water and watching the ripples. One of the ripples kept getting larger and larger. A huge silhouette came out of the water and then crashed back in with a massive splash."

Miles let out a breath, like he had been holding it while I was talking. "Whoa. That's amazing."

I smile. Miles listens with his whole body, leaning in, eyes locking on mine. It's intoxicating.

"Did it surface again?"

"No. My mom found me after that, and we all went home."

"What were they fighting about?"

I've told this story to a handful of people over the years, and no one has ever asked me what my parents were fighting about that day. It makes me reach back through my memory for it. "I don't really remember."

Miles nods. "It must be hard to have a singing career and a young family."

"She'd given it up by then."

Would it have been that hard? I know my mom traveled a lot when she was a singer, but if it was her dream, it seems like my parents should've been able to work it out. She shouldn't have had to give up all of it to make peace. I shift on the log but don't say anything.

Miles clears his throat. "Sorry. I just assumed that's what you meant. Not that I would know. I mean, I have a demanding career, but I haven't had any serious relationships to try to juggle during it."

Miles is, well, he's drop-dead gorgeous, he's friendly, and he seems to crave company. I can't figure out why he hasn't had any serious relationships. It surprises me so much that I ask, "Why not?"

Miles rubs his hands on his pants. "Oh, um…"

"It's none of my business."

"No, it's fine. I met a girl on the set of a movie. She was gorgeous, and we just hit it off. But she wasn't a one-man kind of girl, it turned out, and I…" Miles pauses, his eyes scanning the water, which is getting darker as the clouds roll in. He sighs before continuing, "I didn't see it coming. It hit me harder than I expected. I pictured a whole life with her. I really thought we were meant to be together. For a while, a couple of years at least, I held hope that she would come back. I sent her gifts, emails, texts. But she wasn't in love with me."

Miles's face is turned toward the hills, his jaw clenched. I don't know what to say. "That's awful."

He half smiles. "You know what the worst part is? I wasted all that time on a fantasy."

I run my hand along the log we're sitting on, feeling the coarse bark under my fingertips as I consider his words. But I'm not sure how to take them. "What do you mean?"

"It's just, I met other women—nice, stable, accomplished women —during the years following Lana. And I still clung to this hope that she would come back. We weren't even together very long. I just had it so set in my head we were meant to be. I squandered real-life chances at love, while what I had with Lana…" He shakes his head. "None of it was real."

"But none of it's ever real."

"What?"

"Love." A gust of wind blows my hair off my face, and bright-yellow leaves rustle on the ground. I cross my arms over my chest to try to warm up and contain my thoughts, but they spill out anyway. "Even when feelings are reciprocated, someone always loves the other person more. Someone is either left pining with a broken heart or has to contort themselves to fit in the confines of the other person's expectations."

Miles lets out a chuckle as he picks up a leaf by his foot. "Gee, tell me what you really think."

I scrunch my nose. "Obviously, I have a lot of opinions on the subject."

"But weren't you reading a romance novel the other day?"

I shrug. "I used to read *Peter Pan* as a child. That doesn't mean I believe in faeries."

Miles looks at me with warm eyes, twirling the leaf between his pointer finger and thumb idly. "What a shame. But you believe in Nessie?"

"I'm a believe-it-when-I-see-it type of person. I saw Nessie. I don't necessarily believe she's a sea monster, but something is out there."

"So I'm assuming, after that speech, you aren't in a relationship?"

I shake my head.

"Were you the one left pining or the one contorting?"

I laugh. "I'm that transparent, huh?"

Miles shrugs and lets his little leaf fall to the ground. "Shot in the dark."

"I was both, turns out."

"Ah, a classic overachiever."

I'm about to retort when a ripple breaks the surface of the water. Miles jumps up and runs to the edge of the loch. I follow, adrenaline pumping through me. Could it be Nessie? I've come here almost weekly since that day when I first saw her and never spotted a hint of her again.

As I get closer, I see it clearly.

Miles is still watching intensely as the creature dips below the surface. We both stand silent for a minute, and I'm just about to explain, when Miles lets out a massive whoop of pure joy. He turns to me like we're at a football game about to high-five after a hat trick, but instead of holding up his hand, he picks me square up off the ground and spins me around.

The world whirls by in streaks of blue, gray, and golden yellow. The only thing that is steady is the massive smile on Miles's face.

He puts me down and leans in close. I mirror him, and before I fully register the implications of any of this, I put my mouth on his.

His lips are pillows, and I sink into them like a sleep-deprived maniac. I can't get enough. He tastes of coffee and something a little sweet, almost like he had cinnamon toast for lunch. I open my mouth, needing to decipher the taste, needing more. He opens his mouth to let me in, and a moan erupts from somewhere deep in my belly. It's an animal noise, and it startles me so much I pull away.

I put my hand to my mouth as if I could shield the kiss there forever, as if the mist is threatening to snatch it back into the ether.

Miles turns toward the loch, and says, "I can't believe it. We saw Nessie."

"Miles…" I almost don't want to burst his bubble, but my mouth keeps going. Apparently, it has a mind of its own today. "It was a seal."

"A seal? No. It's a lake. It can't be a seal."

"They hang out in the loch a fair bit. They come in from the river."

As if on cue, the seal pops his little head up, closer this time, and swims around. We watch for a while as it glides effortlessly through the water, then dips down and disappears below the surface.

MILES

"A seal." My shoulders sag, and while I'm disappointed, my heart refuses to sink.

We kissed. Skye kissed me. Her lips are incredible. It was like the whole world fell away. Nessie could've been staring right at us from the water, and I wouldn't have cared. And that noise she made. I wanted to lay her down right there on the bed of fallen leaves, but then she pulled away.

I want to reach for her again, but I've made promises that I won't date Skye. Although, I never said anything about kissing.

The little seal swims around the loch. Drops start to appear on the water, and I can feel a few on my face—small at first and then larger and faster until we are in a full-on downpour. Skye squeals and runs under the tree, putting her sweater above her head. I join her, my clothes absorbing the drops. Why hadn't I brought a jacket?

"We should go. We'll be soaked," she yells over the lashing rain.

Her face looks so beautiful. A small water droplet runs down her cheek to her lips. I reach out and trace its path with my finger, then pull her toward me. She places her hands on my chest.

"Miles, we were just caught up in the moment."

I inhale deeply, smelling the lavender scent of her hair. "I don't want the moment to end."

All my promises forgotten, I lean down. Stars explode in my veins as our lips meet. I'm lost in her touch until a flash brings me back to the bank of the loch, followed by a crack of thunder so loud, my chest rattles with the vibrations.

Skye's eyes are wide. "Now we really have to go."

She runs to the trail, wheeling her bike with her, and I follow. We make it back to the road completely soaked, rain pounding the asphalt.

"Let's ride to the pub. It's closer," she yells over the downpour.

"I'll follow you," I call back, and it's the truth. At this moment, I will follow her straight into the loch if that's where she rides.

We ride to the Thistle House as the light begins to wane, silent the whole way.

She pulls her bike over and leans it against the side of the building around the corner from the front door. I do the same. The rain drips off the awning, but we are relatively sheltered. Before she opens the door to go inside, she turns to me. Now that I know just how soft her skin is, I want to touch her all the time. Could I reach for her hand? She points at the Thistle House. "There will be no kissing in there, got it?"

I frown. It's not like I was going to take her on one of the tables while we wait for dinner or anything. But now that the image is in my head, I lose my train of thought.

She waves a hand in front of my face. "Hello. You with me?"

I nod. "What about a little hand holding?" I don't know why I'm pushing this. I shouldn't be doing any PDA either. I just crave contact with her.

She shakes her head. "I've known these people forever. If we go in there all lovey-dovey, they will ask me about you for centuries after you're long gone. They don't know the meaning of the word fling. Well, to them it's a dance. But casual dating is not in their vocabulary."

"Is that what we're doing? Is this a fling?" I don't know why the word stings so much. Of course, we've only known each other for a couple of weeks. I live in another country. How could this be anything more than a casual affair? But her kiss didn't feel casual. Her touch didn't feel breezy.

Skye's cheeks turn bright pink, and she covers her face with her hand. "Ah, I'm... Of course, you were just caught up. You thought you saw a sea monster. Forget I said anything."

"No, no. I *do* want to kiss you again. A lot. All over."

She takes her hand away, and a tiny smile tickles her perfect lips. "Oh. Good. But we can't in there, okay?"

I nod. She's about to open the door when I put a hand on her arm. "There's something you should know."

Her face falls into the puddle beneath her feet with an almost audible plop. "You have a girlfriend." She takes a deep breath and talks so fast it's hard to keep up. "I can't believe it. I'm no cheater—"

I cut her off mid-tirade. "No, it's not that." I explain about the director's concerns and my promise not to date her.

"Aye. I overheard a bit of that. This is perfect. In there,"—she points to the building again—"we are just friends. But when we're alone, we can—"

I lean in and kiss her, running my hand through her hair. She pulls away, looking as dazed as I feel.

"Exactly," she says.

"Okay," I say.

I go to open the door, but this time she stops me. "One more thing. We are not going to fall in love with each other, right? No meant to be, no soulmate talk. It's just two mature adults expressing their attraction to each other."

Her blue eyes bore into me, and it's like she can see my soul, which is not supposed to be getting involved in this. I take a deep breath, gearing up for one of my best performances. "I will not fall in love with you."

* * *

I FOLLOW SKYE INSIDE. Thistle House is bustling. Nearly every table is full, each with a small candle flickering on it. Scottish folk music plays over the speakers, and the hardwood floors creak under my feet. We find a spot in the corner, but not before just about every person says hello to Skye and asks about "her fella."

She introduces me to each person with the assurance I'm not her fella, explaining about the movie. By the time we finally sit, I'm dizzy. Five people have auditioned for me, I've had three slaps on the back, one offer of a date, and half a beer spilled on my sleeve.

I let out a quick breath.

"See what I mean? Everybody is in everybody's business."

I nod. "I'm starting to see that."

Margie comes to our table with two pints of Guinness, not bothering to ask if it's what we wanted. The candlelight doesn't even penetrate the thick liquid as she sets them down and runs a hand over Skye's wet hair. "Yer soaked. How'd you get here? Swim?"

"We rode bikes. It was a lovely afternoon when we left."

Margie makes a farting sound and waves her arm. "Well, it's a right downpour now." She lowers her voice. "The room is available if you need it. You know where the key is."

I raise my eyebrows. Room? Margie turns her attention to me. "Ahh, my bonnie American. How is Scotland treating you?"

I can't contain my smile. "Better than I thought possible. It's reignited my soul, sparked my passion, and exceeded all my expectations."

Skye blushes an adorable pink, but it's all true.

Margie laughs. "Oh my. That is grand."

She takes our order—two fish dinners—and leaves, still shaking her head.

"Room?"

Skye's blush deepens. She takes a long drink from her beer.

"Aye, Margie has a couple of rooms upstairs, like an inn. One of them, she never rents out on a case it's haunted. But she says she keeps it open for me. When I was a teen, I needed a place to crash sometimes."

I run through all the scenarios of Skye and me heading up to that room after this, me helping her pull her black shirt up and over her head.

"No," Skye says abruptly.

My face must've given me away. "Why not?"

She's shaking her head and about to speak when a petite woman with straight black hair and green eyes weaves between the crowd of people in line at the bar, past the women waving to her by the fire, and sneaks up behind Skye, putting a finger to her lips when she catches my eye.

She puts her hands over Skye's eyes as Skye lets out a yelp. "Surprise." The woman drops her hands and grabs a wooden chair from a nearby table. The older couple sitting at it waves to her as she does.

Skye has her hand clutched to her heart. "You devil."

The woman reaches her hand toward me. "I'm Kate, Skye's oldest and dearest friend."

I take her hand and shake it. "I'm Miles."

She smirks like she can read my mind. "Oh, I know who you are. Did Skye tell you we were obsessed with that football movie when we were kids?"

I smile, thrilled by this confession. "*Undercover Quarterback?* Really?"

Skye is pinker than shrimp and fiddling with her beer. "We weren't kids, exactly. We were teens."

"Ah, well, that makes me feel a little less old."

Kate laughs and says, "We even had a dance."

Skye looks like she is going to murder Kate and hits her arm. "Haud yer wheesht."

This makes Kate laugh louder. Margie comes over with our food. "Stop being a bully. Let them eat."

Kate stands. "Okay, okay. I'll talk to you later." She gives Skye a kiss on the cheek and goes back to sit in a tufted chair by the fire with a group of women who are knitting.

After a few heavenly bites of my fish, I say, "So, this dance…"

She rolls her eyes and finishes chewing her bite. "We were fourteen. Give me a break."

"Fourteen…" I nod, doing some mental math. "I was nineteen when we shot the film, twenty when it came out."

Skye looks at me in surprise. "Oh, that's younger than I thought you were."

"Did I look older?"

She shrugged. "All the muscles."

I smile and hold up a bicep. Her eyes follow the line of my arm, the bulge when I flex. I smile and drop my arm. "About this room."

She shakes her head. "How would we explain when we pedal home in the morning?"

She has a point. I can't lose this job. "You're right."

* * *

AFTER A MASSIVE DINNER, the rain lightens up, and we head on our bikes back to the castle. It's dark, but the bikes have little lights on the handlebars that help. There is a true break in the clouds, and the moon shines down, helping to light the way. The sky is absolutely filled with stars. I've been in remote locations before and seen my fair share of starry nights, but this is on another level. It's like Scotland has more stars than the rest of the world.

The ride is quiet. I'm hoping to sneak Skye into my room, or sneak into hers, but before we even wheel the bikes into the shed, Minnie runs up to us, her red hair tucked into a neat bun. Minnie is one of the PAs. She's young but amazing at her job. This is the third film I've worked on with her. Once she gets closer, I can see the urgency in her face.

"Miles," she yells.

"Uh-oh," Skye says as she opens the door to the shed and wheels her bike in.

"Minnie! What's up? I didn't know you were working on this project. I want you to meet Skye."

She's out of breath and pauses for a moment with her hands on her knees, then takes my bike from me.

"They're in the middle of a design presentation." Minnie catches her breath and adds, "Nice to meet you, Skye." She turns back to me. "You need to go now. They've been looking all over for you. Didn't you get any of their texts?"

I shake my head. "No service." I may have had service at the pub. But the truth was, I hadn't checked my phone since we left. "Why didn't anyone mention it?"

We all start walking to the castle. I wish I could grab Skye's hand. I'm a naturally affectionate person. This *keeping things secret and not having any public displays of affection* thing goes against every fiber in my being.

Minnie grabs my arm and pulls me inside. I catch Skye's eye as she heads upstairs and give her a little air kiss behind Minnie's back. The smile Skye gives me in return lights up my chest.

"Can't I change first?" My sweater is still damp from getting caught in the rain.

"No. It's almost over," Minnie says. She leads me to the dining room where we had the table read, and it feels like déjà vu. Again, the only open spot is next to Ty. Thora is speaking, and a fair amount of the cast have glasses of wine in front of them. Everyone looks beat. The designer is nodding, listening attentively to Thora's question.

I silently sit down.

"That's an excellent point, Thora. I'm going to have to give it some thought, bring it to the team, and get back to you."

Natalie says, "I think that's all for now. We'll start filming in the morning. You should all have the schedule in your inbox, but if you don't,"—she looks pointedly at me when she says this—"please let me know now. Thank you, everyone."

Minnie comes to my side, and we're just about to leave together when Natalie says in a bone-chilling tone, "Miles, a word."

Minnie whispers, "I'll see you later."

I nod.

Once everyone has filed out, Natalie looks at me with her fiery, deep-brown eyes.

I start by apologizing. "I didn't realize the design presentation was so soon."

"Everyone was emailed."

I hadn't checked my phone. "I must have missed it. It won't happen again."

Natalie cuts right to the point. "Miles, are you sleeping with our host?"

"Callum? No. He's a nice guy. I just don't think of him that way." I smile, but it is not returned.

"Skye. Are you sleeping with Skye? You are a grown man, and under any other circumstances, I would say do your thing. But we can't lose this location. My mom was close with Callum's late wife. She pulled some strings to get us here. I will say it again to be super clear... *You* would be more easily replaced than this castle. Got it?"

I nod. "Understood."

SKYE

*T*head straight for my computer. We kissed, and *oh* what a kiss. It was the kind of kiss Shakespeare writes sonnets about, the kind of kiss Nora Ephron puts at the end of the movie. And I want more. When Margie offered me the room tonight, I really thought about taking her up on it. I could have peeled that sweater off Miles and run my hands down his muscular stomach...

Words fly from my fingertips with light tippity taps. By the time I head to bed, I've made a good amount of progress on my project. Most of them are words like provocative, titillating, sultry, and—my absolute new favorite—velvety.

I go to bed feeling like a kid before the first day of school, equal parts excited and nervous about what the next day will bring.

In the morning, I write until the sun is just starting to peak above the hills, and I know if I wait any longer, the chickens will morph into even scarier demons, like gremlins that have gotten wet. I'm just slipping on my wellies when Ava comes running down the stairs in tight jeans, high tan leather boots, and a shiny red bomber jacket.

"Skye." She stops once she gets down the stairs, not a hint out of breath, not a hair out of place. "I was hoping to tag along this morning."

"You want to come with me to tend to the animals?"

She smiles, and it's so bright you'd think I'd asked if she wants to get champagne cocktails. "Yes. I'd love to. I've never really been around a farm—well, I've hung out with horses, but not anything else."

I slip into my other boot, then put on my coat. We go out into the cold morning, so cold I can see my own breath. The pale-yellow light of the sun is just starting to slice through the gray clouds. I inhale deeply, smelling the grass wet with dew, the dirt, and moss. The air is at once floral and earthy, with a slight briny scent underneath. It smells like home.

Ava is watching me, smiling to herself. She looks away when we lock eyes. "You really love this place, don't you?"

Not wanting to speak, I nod, suddenly feeling silly for a lump in my throat and the tear in the corner of my eye. It's true I do love it here, but I can't deny that part of me really wants to spread my wings and see what else is out there. Just because New York was overwhelming doesn't mean that I want to stay in the place where I've lived most of my life. But I can't leave Dad alone in this big castle. What if something happened? Once I'm a bit more composed, I say, "Most of the time."

As we head toward the coup, Ava shakes her head. "I'm jealous. I've never felt that way about a place before. Well, maybe my grand-parents' house, but I didn't spend much time there. I moved a lot as a kid. Then I ended up in LA at eighteen, stars in my eyes and not a dime in my pocket."

"You moved there by yourself?" I don't know why, but I assumed Ava came from a Hollywood family, and acting was something of an over-glorified hobby for her while she had her family's money to fall back on. A completely unfair and unfounded assumption I'm seeing now.

"Yeah. As soon as I graduated, I got on a bus from Montana. No friends there, just this feeling." She motions at her chest. "I knew it would all turn out okay."

I smile, having a new outlook on Ava. "And it did."

Ava only half smiles as she mirrors my movements, scooping the chicken feed and sprinkling it over the ground. "After a few really terrible years, it did."

I'm about to ask more, but Ava tries to pet one of the chickens, and it screeches at her so loud that Ava screams, and I erupt into giggles. That sends Ava into a fit of laughter as well.

We go through the rest of the chores fairly quickly, with Ava asking me about the details of some of the tasks and about Scottish words for things. I'm surprised she is so at ease with chores. She doesn't flinch about mucking out into the mud to tend to the cattle, she doesn't balk at the landmines when we look after the horses... Aside from her scream at the demon chickens, you would never know she hadn't worked on a farm her whole life.

Even when it starts to drizzle on us, she doesn't suggest heading in or calling it a day. It's not at all how I thought she would be.

After all the chores are done, we head into the castle. I'm slipping off my boots when Ava surprises me once again by throwing her tiny, but extremely strong arms around me in a hug. "Thank you. Can I shadow you again sometime?"

"Of course."

Ava runs upstairs.

I head to the kitchen in need of another cup of coffee before my bike ride.

I stop in the doorway when I hear tinkling laughter, like a fork tapping fine China. My father is talking, and Thora Townsend, *the* Thora Townsend, is holding a cup of coffee and giggling—actually giggling.

They are sitting at our kitchen table, carrying on like old friends. In fact, they seem to be flirting. I can't wrap my head around it. Thora Townsend is a proper movie star. She's won a pile of Oscars over her career, which is long and varied. My favorite film of hers when I was a kid was a fantasy series in which she played the White Queen. But she's most well-known for her period dramas. And here my father is, chatting her up like they're at the pub.

I'm not angry on behalf of my mother. Mom's been gone a good six years now. My dad deserves company if he wants some, but a movie star of all people? Guilt coats my throat as I remember my current fling with a movie star. But that's different.

I enter the room and head straight for the coffee.

"Ah, pet. Have you met Thora?"

Thora gives me a half wave. "Good morning."

I smile. "It's nice to meet you."

My dad mumbles something to Thora, then grabs both of their coffee cups. He joins me at the counter and refills them. "See? Isn't it fun having all these people here?"

Ty walks in as if on cue. "That coffee smells heavenly."

The place is littered with movie stars, and not one is the one I want to see this morning.

I nod at my father and slink out the door.

* * *

MY RIDE IS swift and drizzly this morning. I pull up to the Thistle House and head straight to the fire, where Kate is knitting. I'm surprised she's here today. She works at a yarn shop called Knit Picking, which doesn't open till ten, so she's here most mornings before her shift. But on Fridays, they get deliveries, so she's usually not here by the time I arrive. I check my watch. I'm not early.

"Skye," Margie calls out, and Kate looks up and smiles at me. "Tea?"

My hands are practically shaking from the cups of coffee I've had at home. "Mmm, maybe just a little hot chocolate."

I sit next to Kate by the fire. "No work today?"

Kate shakes her head. "I stayed late last night doing inventory. Boss gave me the day off."

I thank Margie when she brings me my drink. Kate clacks away with her knitting needles. I never quite got the hang of the whole knitting thing. I do okay with one row, but then completely lose the plot when it comes to purl.

We've sat here in comfortable silence a million times before, but this morning feels different. Because this morning, I have a secret. I kissed Miles Casey. I'm going to have a proper grown-up fling with the most handsome man I have ever met.

The memory of his hands on my waist, his lips on mine, the rain falling all around us has me smiling into my mug.

"What?" Kate says.

I shake my head. "What?"

"What's with the smirk?"

I raise my eyebrows, the picture of innocence. "I'm not smirking. I just enjoy your company, and this hot chocolate is lovely."

Kate narrows her eyes. "Oh my God. You got laid. Is it that braw American?"

How does she see right through me? "I did not get *laid,* and you watch far too much American tele."

Kate is still looking at me suspiciously. "Well, something happened." She puts down her knitting, picks up her tea, and leans forward in her chair. "Dish."

I sigh, but if I'm honest, I'm dying to tell someone. I lean forward too. "You can't tell anyone. Like anyone at all. Swear it."

"I swear."

"Swear it on Christie." When we were fifteen, we got very into the BBC version of *Hercule Poirot.* We watched the episodes nonstop and *Death on the Nile* with Mia Farrow on a virtual loop. We read every single book Agatha Christie ever wrote. We read *And Then There Were None* five times in one summer. Since then, if we're really serious about something, we swear on Christie like it is our version of the Holy Bible.

Kate laughs. "Well, it's been a minute." She places a solemn hand over her heart. "I swear it on Christie."

I tell Kate all about our epic kiss by the loch, every single swoony detail. Then I tell her about our agreement to have a mature, no-holds-barred, no emotions fling.

Kate shakes her head and picks up her knitting. "*You* are going to have a fling?"

"Yes."

"*You?*"

"Yes! Why is that so hard to believe? Why do you keep saying *you* like that?"

"Because every single person you've ever dated, you end up engaged to." I'm opening my mouth to protest when she holds up a finger. "Even Seamus Flanagan in primary school when you first moved here. Remember, he gave you one of those silly candy rings and he told you not to eat it so it would stay nice."

I laugh. "He actually shellacked it so I couldn't eat it."

"He did?" She shakes her head and goes back to clacking away with her needles. "You see my point."

"We were kids."

"What about Finn?"

I sit back in my chair like she slapped me. We don't talk about Finn, ever. I set down my cup. "I should get going."

"Skye, wait. I'm sorry. I just don't want you to get hurt."

"That's why it's a fling. No one has to get hurt."

* * *

I RIDE HOME HARD, trying to pedal off some of my annoyance. How dare she imply that I will get attached to Miles? That I fall in love with every bloke I ever date. I run through the very short list in my head and pump my legs faster, as I see that she is infuriatingly right. There was Seamus in primary school, then Charlie in secondary school, and then, of course, Finn.

Just because I was serious with all of them doesn't mean I will be with Miles. I'm older and wiser now. I can see love for what it is—a big, fat farce. Miles and I can just make out a bit while he's here and say a fond farewell when he goes.

Riding down the road, wind in my hair, excitement bubbles in my throat. This is all going to work out. When Miles leaves, I will have a best-selling romance novel and a secret.

Coming around a sharp corner, I see a figure approaching me on foot. Miles is out for a run—sweat making his tight shirt cling to his torso. His body-hugging running tights leave little to the imagination, his powerful thighs flexing with every foot strike. Slowing down my bike, I hop off.

"Skye." He waves, speeding up as he runs toward me. It feels like the scene in the airport at the end of the movie. The handsome man running toward the attractive woman with sleek hair, or in this case, me with my curls wild around my face, to tell her he loves her and can't live without her. I shake those last thoughts out. No, this is just about attraction.

As he gets closer, I throw my bike down, run to meet him, and fling my arms around his neck. In one fell swoop, he hoists me up, his large hands on my ass. I wrap my legs around him. Our mouths meet like they are magnets, unable to resist the force of each other. It feels like years since our last kiss, even though it was only yesterday. I memorize the feel of his lips with mine. Soft, yet firm.

I pull back as I hear footfalls getting closer, and Miles puts me down. Ava runs around the corner, sweat glittering on her forehead. She literally doesn't sweat; she sparkles. Miles and I move apart quickly like teenagers caught knacking in a car park. But I'm pretty sure Ava didn't see anything.

"Skye." She stops when she meets us, her eyes go wide, and she points to my bike abandoned on the side of the road, the back tire still spinning. "Did you get in a wreck?"

"Ah, no," Miles says right as I say, "A wee one."

Ava looks between us both. Miles wipes the sweat off his brow with the sleeve of his forearm, then says in a horrible impression of someone surprised, "You did? I didn't realize."

I resist the urge to shake my head. How can someone who is a brilliant actor be such a terrible liar?

"Just hit a bump." I pick up my bike. "It's fine. The bike's fine. Everything's grand."

Ava smiles. "Ahh, well, we're only about halfway into a five-miler, right, Miles?"

He nods, but his eyes are drinking me in. Goosebumps ripple the back of my neck. "Do you want to join us?"

I shake my head and put out my leg, pointing to the toe of my boot. His eyes follow the line of my leg all the way up my body to meet my gaze, his brown eyes smoldering. He bites the side of his lip. "Not properly attired."

Ava waves. "Ahh, maybe next time." She runs away.

Miles mouths, *You're killing me.* I smile. He gives my butt a covert pat before he runs after Ava.

I pedal back to the castle as if my bike has wings.

MILES

*I*llicit kisses and brief touches fill the next few days. We are always interrupted, and I'm always left wanting more. Skye is a breath of fresh air. She is passionate, not just when we're kissing but when she talks about things. Even when she's lamenting feeding those stupid chickens, there is a spark in her eyes. I've gotten so used to glossy people who try to act like magazine cutouts of themselves. Like an interview is being conducted all the time. But Skye is real.

Finding time to be alone is tricky. Ava insists on coming on my morning runs. That must've been her grand idea that I agreed to in the library when she first arrived. I don't ever remember her asking if she could join me. It's okay, really. I don't mind her company, but if she weren't with me, I might be able to run somewhere and meet Skye.

The evenings are tough, too. Every time we decide to try to sneak into one of our rooms, we are interrupted by one of the many people crawling all over this castle. Hollywood has thoroughly infested it, except for my assistant Jake who as it turns out isn't coming. He called two days ago. On his way to the airport, he was in a car accident. He broke his leg and will need surgery, but he is lucky to be alive. I told him I'd hop a plane right back and help take care of him for once, but he wasn't having any of it. His sister took some time off to stay with him.

It would be harder to hide my relationship with Skye if Jake were here. In fact, I know I couldn't. I'd have to tell him, and that's not possible. Skye and I agreed to keep it secret. I wasn't in love with the idea at first. I'm more the wear my heart on my sleeve kind of guy. But I gotta admit, it's kind of hot. Either way, it's a necessity if I want to keep my role in this production, which, honestly, I'm not even sure about anymore. Thora is amazing, but I only have a handful of scenes with her. The bulk of my scenes are with Ty, who's a constant pain in my ass. Natalie's great, but she demands a lot, always asking me to dig deeper, give a little more. What if I don't have more to give? What if the performance I'm giving is truly all I have, and it's not good enough?

We're in the middle of a scene in the library, and I'm lost in my endless spiral of self-doubt.

"Miles," Natalie calls out. "It's your line."

I shake my head and adjust my kilt. "Right." I look at Ava. "Aye, sure. I've seen Nessie a dozen times. I can show ye, if ye like."

Ava's tiny hands fly to my chest. That stage direction is not in the script, and I'm so surprised by it that I stumble back. "Show me. Show me now."

"Cut," Natalie yells. "Let's take a five-minute break. When we come back, we'll shoot that one again."

Everyone nods, and I'm wondering if I can find Skye and sneak a kiss before we have to reset the shot.

"Miles." Natalie beckons me with the crook of her finger, and I have the sinking feeling of being summoned by the queen.

I try to act casual heading over. "What's up?"

Natalie lowers her voice to a whisper. "On the next take, can you try not to look so repulsed when Ava touches you? You're supposed to be *in love* with her."

"I was just surprised." Oh man, did I look repulsed? I wasn't. Ava is very beautiful, objectively. I'm just not attracted to her.

"You looked disgusted and a little terrified."

I sigh. "On the next take, I'll look enamored, I swear. I was just caught off guard."

She nods. "Is everything all right? You seem a little off."

"Have my performances been okay?"

"Yes, for the most part. You just seem...I don't know. Distracted." She lowers her voice even more. "Have I been working everyone too hard?"

I shake my head. "I don't think so."

She nods, but she's chewing on the end of her pen, her tell whenever she's nervous or unsure of something. "I'm giving everyone the weekend off. It's Halloween."

I'd kind of forgotten about holidays or days of the week, even. "Right."

"We should all go blow off some steam. Where can we go?"

Karaoke. But I don't want to say it out loud. I want it to be just a Skye and me thing.

Elsie comes up behind me with two fresh coffees and hands one to Natalie, then takes a seat in the chair next to her. "Go where?"

Natalie blows on her cup, steam wafting off it in the cold castle. "Somewhere everyone can have a good time."

"Thistle House has karaoke tonight. Skye told me about it."

Natalie smiles like a cat with a canary in her sights. "Perfect." She clears her throat. "Okay, let's go again."

I hold in my sigh and walk back to my mark. I wouldn't have been able to kiss Skye or even hold her hand at the pub anyway, as per our agreement, but I was looking forward to some time away from the rest of the cast.

We shoot the scene ten times, and it takes pretty much the rest of the morning. I'm about to bolt out to find Skye when Minnie booms over the megaphone. "Fifteen-minute break."

I look at the time, and it's already a little after noon. A fifteen-minute break isn't even long enough to get out of costume, which isn't so bad. I've come to quite like the feel of the kilt. I drag myself to the dining room for some coffee. They've taken over the whole thing for a craft service table. Lots of fresh fruit and vegetables, as well as a massive array of just about every cookie known to man, all artfully arranged on the dining room table. I grab a paper cup and fill it from the large carafe of coffee. Is it even worth going to find Skye to have to leave so soon after?

I decide it is. Of course, it is. It always is. I walk purposefully out the door just as Ty is striding into the room. We collide, and my cup smashes into my chest, hot coffee soaking into my light-gray linen shirt. The pain is sharp, and even worse, there goes my time with Skye.

"Shit." I'm so frustrated with having to share the same space with this idiot. How was I ever friends with him?

Ty brushes off his shirt, which has maybe three small spots of coffee on it. "Whoa. You have to look where you're going. Get your head out of the clouds." He walks toward the table and mutters, "Or out of that redhead's skirt, rather."

I whip around on him, rage boiling in my veins. "What did you say?"

"I said you seemed a little unfocused, mate."

Mate? What was he even doing, talking like he's English? I know for a fact he's from Boston. I've met his mom. "I am not your mate."

Ty sighs and runs a hand through his stupidly coiffed hair. "Miles, it was years ago. In the big scheme of things, does it even matter? Just let it go." Ty turns to the table and grabs a cookie.

Let it go? *Let it go?* The room goes red. I swing my arm back and am imagining the satisfying smack it will make when it connects with his face, when my arm gets stuck. Elsie has a hold of it behind me.

"Come on, Miles. Let's get you a new shirt. I'm sure Patty will want to try to get out that stain, too."

Ty doesn't even look in our direction. He has no clue how close he just came to getting knocked out.

Elsie leads me to the costume room, which was a sitting room before we took it over. Each footstep away from Ty calms me down, and I realize how close I almost just came to really crossing the line.

We pass Skye in the hall. I reach my fingers toward hers for just a moment and mouth, *Karaoke tonight?*

She smiles and nods.

Once we step into the sitting room, Elsie looks me dead in the eye and says, "All this shit you have with Ty, you have to ease up. Or if you can't—put it in a box and take it back out when the film is over. Hate him all you want after filming." She throws up her hands. "Hell, knock his block off, get arrested. I'm sure it will be great press for the premiere."

She's right. I thought I had let it go, as Ty so eloquently put it, years ago, but clearly not. I can't focus on it right now. "Okay."

* * *

THE DAY FLEW BY, shooting taking up most of it. After the sun went down, the cast and crew all met out by the vans to head to Thistle House. Skye said she'd ride her bike and meet me there, so it didn't look weird with us coming together. But when I look around at the faces loading into the vans, even Callum is here.

He slaps me on the back. "Miles. Are you going to sing?"

I smile. "Not sure anyone really wants to hear that."

He laughs. "Ah, it's all good fun. We're all crap singers—well, except Skye, and she hasn't sung at one of these in years. Voice of an angel, that one."

I'm really hoping she sings tonight. Maybe she will. I've asked her a few times in the past week, and she said that she might. Callum gets into the van and takes a seat right next to Thora. I get in, and Ava pats the seat next to her.

The ride is quick, and the energy in the van is palpable. Thistle House is decked out for the holiday. Jack-o'-lanterns line the front, ghoulish faces flickering from the candlelight within. We all head inside, bounding in like excited puppies. The place is wall to wall packed—everyone's crowded in with pints in hand, some with masks on. Paper skeletons hang from the ceiling. Each table has a small carved pumpkin on it; some of the faces are silly, while others are downright frightening. Karaoke is already in full swing. They moved the tables to set up a small stage. Someone is on it, belting out and somewhat butchering "You're So Vain" by Carly Simon.

I spot Skye standing by the bar, talking to her friend Kate. She looks amazing. Tight black jeans and a fitted red and black striped sweater. Her hair is curled around her face in large, shiny waves. One stray curl is creeping toward her eye, and I long to brush it behind her ear, for my fingers to linger along her neck. Skye catches me looking, and I can see the twinkle in her blue eyes from across the room. She turns to the bartender, then waves for me to come over. I weave my way through the crowd. The bartender hands her another pint of dark, dark beer, which she hands right to me.

"Happy Halloween," Kate says.

"Yeah, I'm surprised to see all the jack-o'-lanterns. I didn't know you all celebrated it here in Scotland."

They both laugh at this. Skye says, "Are ye kidding me? We practically invented it. Well, the Irish did. They carved turnips to ward off Stingy Jack."

"Stingy Jack?"

"Aye," Kate says. "He tricks people into buying him beers and things. Sold his soul to the devil for one last drink, but tricked him so the devil couldn't collect."

Skye is nodding enthusiastically. "So, when Jack died, he couldn't get into heaven, and the devil wouldn't let him into hell. He roams the earth with his little carved turnip, trying to catch people out."

"I never knew."

Skye musses up my hair a bit. "Read a book sometime."

I laugh. I want to pick her up and toss her over my shoulder, but instead I say, "I'll read you."

She sticks her tongue out at me.

Kate raises her beer. "To Stingy Jack."

We all clink our glasses.

Margie goes up onto the makeshift stage to introduce the next singer. "We have a special treat tonight, lovelies. Please welcome to the stage Skye Ainslie and Kate Donnovan."

I look at Skye, my heart filled like a party balloon. "What are you two going to sing?"

Kate just shakes her head, pulls sunglasses out of her pocket, and puts them on.

Skye whispers in my ear, so close her lips touch my skin, sending goosebumps down my arms. "You'll see."

She pulls a matching pair of sunglasses out of her back pocket, winking at me before her eyes are covered in the mirrored surfaces. They go on stage, their backs turned dramatically to the crowd, their legs in a wide stance. I elbow my way through to the front, not about to miss a single moment of this performance.

Kate starts by counting, and after the three, Skye lets out a guttural, "Uh."

The music kicks in, and I know exactly what song they are singing. I laugh in delight. It's OutKast's "Hey Ya!"

It was the theme song to my teen football movie, so I know the lyrics like the back of my hand. And apparently, so does Skye. Kate struts around behind her, clapping at all the right moments as Skye belts out the song, emphasizing each "uh" with a little hip shake.

By the time she gets to the chorus, everyone is singing along, "Hey ya!" over and over. Thora and Callum are doing something between a jig and twerking, both their faces rosy with laughter. Skye and Kate are performing synchronized dance moves that they must've practiced a thousand times.

Skye belts out the lyrics, and everyone cheers. The crowd is moving like a living, breathing beast. Skye sings out the call and response like a pro. When it's the fellas' turn, I yell along with everyone else.

And here comes the breakdown. Skye and Kate get down in the

crowd and dance lower and lower, inch by inch, while everyone is shaking their Polaroid pictures all over the space in front of the stage. It's joy personified.

I dance my way closer to Skye, and now we are moving in sync, too. Her eyes are on mine. Kate claps along with the crowd, everyone shouting the lyrics at the top of their lungs.

When the song is over, the crowd cheers. Margie yells from the back, "Give us an encore, Skye!"

She shakes her head, her cheeks flushed from dancing, her eyes alive. I want to grab her and kiss her right here.

The crowd won't be deterred. They all chant, "Skye! Skye! Skye!"

I join in. The look she gives me sends shivers from my head to my toes.

Kate is next to me, chanting it as well. Skye moves away and whispers with Callum.

After a beat, she catches my eye. I give her a wink and continue the chant, relishing the feeling of her name on my lips. "Skye! Skye!"

SKYE

*I*t's been an age since I sang. The room is chanting my name, but all I hear is Miles.

"Skye! Skye!"

I know what song they all want to hear. I used to sing it all the time, every month for almost a year, and before that, I used to sing it with my mom. Shaking my head, I head back to the stage to call someone else up to sing, when Dad stops me. His smile is so wide, it fills the room.

"Don't listen to them." He laughs. "I know you won't. You never were one to go with the crowd."

I return his smile and try to hand him the microphone. "I'm sure they'd love something from you."

He shakes his head. "Oh, I'm not saying you shouldn't sing your song. I'm just saying, don't do it for them."

I open my mouth to let out a million reasons why I can't, but my dad puts a gentle hand on my arm. "It used to bring you so much joy. Do you remember when you were wee and I asked you what your favorite thing to do was?"

The memory is there in an instant, like it happened yesterday instead of so many years ago. I was sitting on my dad's knee. He smelled of grass and mint. He asked if I could do anything, anything at all, what would I do. I whispered in his ear like it was a precious secret. *"Sing."*

"You don't have to sing it for any other reason than it's a song you love, surrounded by friends."

I *do* love the song. I haven't even let myself sing it in the shower. Looking around at the warm, familiar faces filling the room, I see Kate standing with Miles. She gives a little wave and a gesture to the stage. Someone in the crowd hands me a whiskey, which I sip before making my way up to the front once more.

The guitar strums, and the crowd settles immediately, their dancing turning into more of a sway. I sing from my soul. "Earthfall." One of the most beautiful, heartfelt songs ever written and it was written by my mother.

I used to sing it with my mom because I loved this song, and because she loved me, she would indulge me. Our voices would mingle together, making one. Then I sang from the depths of my broken heart, for my mother, for my lost love, for my mess of a life. Tonight, I sing it from a new place. I sing for the new story I'm writing and the excitement I feel with each new word on the page.

I sing it for the way Miles looks when the firelight caresses his strong jaw. I sing for the friends I have in this room, filling my heart. I sing it for the shivers Miles sends down my spine when he puts his lips on mine. I sing it for the way he is looking at me right now. I sing for being able to remember my mother on this night with a smile, instead of a gut-wrenching sob.

Lost in my memories, in the song, in Miles's gaze—no one else exists. The end of "Earthfall" almost surprises me. My friends and neighbors cheer so loud you would think I was singing to a packed auditorium instead of a tiny pub in a wee town.

I need air. I weave and bob my way through the sea of people. I catch Miles's eye and tilt my head ever so slightly to the door. He nods, his stare burning a path through the crowd. I keep making my way outside when a man at the corner table catches my eye. Margie passes in front of me. She patters on about how lovely the song was.

I thank her and look again at the table in the corner, but it's empty now. Shaking my head, I go outside, past the people out for a fag, and around the corner. For a second, I thought I saw Finn—*my* Finn. Well, he's not mine. Anyway, it's impossible. Must've been seeing things. Too warm. All the adrenaline.

The chilly night air fills my lungs and cools my cheeks as I lean against the cold stone wall—a welcome sensation after the oven-like pub. Miles comes around the corner, his smile wide.

"That was amazing."

My cheeks grow hot at the compliment, or possibly from the heat of his gaze. It's like standing too close to a fire. He reaches out and tucks a lock of my unruly hair behind my ears, then runs his hand behind my neck. I lick my lips in anticipation. He leans in, and our lips meet, soft at first and then more urgent. He presses me into the stone wall. Our bodies connect. I can feel his excitement as our kiss deepens. His hands move from my neck down the sides of my body, just skimming the places I want him to stop. Teasing. A moan of excitement and frustration escapes me.

A twig snaps, and Miles flies away from me like I'm an over-boiling pan on the stovetop. We both look left and right, but no one is there—just a couple of fellas heading down the road, cigars in hand.

"I thought it might be one of the crew."

I nod. We shouldn't be making out in the open like this. He's explained his precarious situation with the film. Then it occurs to me... "The room."

Miles's eyes light up. "The room? Really?"

I nod.

"What are we waiting for? Let's go!"

"Shh. We still have to be quiet about it."

I lead him around the side to the back of the pub. There is a thick wooden door. Right next to it is a flowerpot with a bunch of unruly rosemary sprouting out of it. I kneel, digging around until I find the

135

key. The back door stays unlocked for all the guests. The key is to the actual room. We open the door and creep up the stairs. At the top, I grab Miles's hand. The hall is dark, lit only by three sconces along the wall. The room Margie keeps open is at the end of the long hallway. We move quickly so that we won't be spotted by any other guests.

With shaking hands, I unlock the door. We're finally going to be alone, in a proper room. I push open the door, my heart hammering in my chest. Once we're both inside, I flick on the lamp with the switch and lock the door.

When I turn around, Miles is standing right there. He puts his hands on my waist and leans down, kissing me softly. His lips are addictive. I need more and more to feel satisfied, and tonight, only kisses won't do. I grab his waistband and pull him closer, the firm muscles of his chest pressing against my breasts. It's still not enough. I push him toward the bed and sit him gently on the edge. I move away so he has a better view, as I take my sweater off. Goosebumps rise on my flesh at the chill of the room and his intense gaze. I shimmy out of my trousers next. Probably not as graceful as I hoped, but they're very tight jeans. He smiles as I throw them across the room.

I come closer. He runs his hands along my waist and over the swell of my hip, gripping it tightly and sending a pulse of want straight through me.

He moves his hands lightly up my ribs, along the silky fabric of my bra, tracing the lines covering my breast. Sticking a pinky finger under the satin, he just barely grazes my nipple, that tightens at his touch. Every nerve ending in my body stands at attention waiting, wanting him to move the fabric, but his hand keeps traveling.

He traces the line between my panties and my lower stomach, his pinky just grazing underneath the silky fabric there. My heart is racing. My breath comes out fast as his pinky skims where I want him to linger.

"Skye," he says, his voice thick, "you are so beautiful."

My chest swells at his voice, his touch. This is so unlike me to be standing in the full light of the lamp in nothing but my underwear. But it feels right with him. I unhook my bra and let it fall to the floor. His eyes turn nearly black. "Then kiss me."

He pulls me on the bed. I straddle him, feeling his ample bulge underneath the thin fabric of my panties. I wiggle a little, getting settled, and the grunt that escapes him makes my core clench.

He brings his lips to mine. It's soft and slow. My hips move in the same rhythm, lightly rubbing on Miles's growing bulge. As the kiss deepens, so do my movements. My breasts press against the soft fabric of his shirt, but I want his skin on mine.

I pull back, grabbing the hem. Miles raises his arms, letting me pull the shirt over his head.

Holy Shite. I run my fingertips over his defined chest, the ridges of his abs, all the way down to the waistband of his jeans. "You still have too many clothes on."

He tugs on the edge of my underwear. "So do you."

I smile and stand pushing down the last bit of my clothes while Miles watches me with a heavy gaze. "Your turn."

He stands and unzips his jeans, and I swear the sound does something to me. My mouth is watering, my cheeks flushed. He lets his pants drop and then his boxers. I drop to my knees, running my hands up his calves, the muscles firm under my palm, to his thighs, then finally to his hard cock.

He sucks in a breath as I stroke, lightly at first, then with a bit more force. I bring my lips to the tip.

"Skye you don't have to."

"I don't do anything I don't want to do."

He runs a hand through my hair, smirking. "What about feeding the chickens?"

"This is a far more handsome cock."

I'm done talking. I put my mouth around him, and he moans. It's a lovely sound. I move my mouth over him, feeling him swell on my tongue. I move my hand as well, until his thighs are shaking.

He pulls at my arms to stand. I do and he leads me back to the bed, laying me down. "My turn. Spread your legs."

I obey.

He brings his fingers to my slit, his eyes widening. "You're so wet. Is this all for me?"

"Yes."

He moves his fingers in a swirl, watching my face intently. "Can I put my mouth on you?"

"You can have me any way you want."

He kisses my neck, moving his way down, stopping at my breast and taking my nipple in his mouth, all the while still swirling. He sucks lightly, then just as he bites, he slides a finger inside me and I cry out with how good it feels.

He moves to my next breast, licking and sucking all the while thrusting his hand deeper and deeper.

As his mouth moves down my stomach, the tide inside me swells. He brings his lips to my slit, swirling and sucking. My hips move, needing more pressure.

"Did you bring a condom?"

He's across the room in an instant, messing with his discarded jeans in a shot and back, the foil package already open, the condom rolling on. "Are you sure?"

"Miles, I want you inside me. Now."

"Yes, mam."

He takes my leg and puts it on his shoulder. I take him, the weight of his cock heavy in my hand, and guide him to my center. He eases in an inch at a time, and I lay back, relaxing my muscles, letting him fill me.

I bring my hands to my breasts, and Miles grunts out. "Fuck yes."

I squeeze them together as his thrusts get harder and faster. The pressure inside me is building. "More oh, Miles."

He thrusts all the way in, his hand tight on my thigh, his other hand moves to my slit and swirls. Stars explode in my vision. My body fills with warmth and tingles. My heart races as wave after wave of pleasure crashes over me.

Miles swells under me, his arms shaking as he calls out my name.

* * *

WE ARE LYING on the bed, both completely spent. Our clothes strewn all over the wee room. As rooms go, it is nicer than I remember. There's an en suite bathroom with a stand-up shower. The window overlooks the streets of Foyers. Most importantly, it has a large bed that came in extremely handy.

Miles is lightly tracing the contours of my stomach and hips. In past relationships, I've always been self-conscious about my stomach. I don't know if it's maturity or Miles, but I don't feel that way with him. A tiny voice in the back of my head pipes up. *"Maybe it's because this is not a real relationship. None of this is real."*

I turn on my side in an attempt to muffle the voice.

Miles smiles and props himself up on his elbow. "Hi."

"Hi yourself," I say in my best old Hollywood starlet voice.

He smiles. He looks so completely and utterly relaxed. I haven't noticed how much tension he holds in his face, except now in its absence.

I run my hand on his jaw to feel its contours, the roughness of his stubble prickling my hand, and remember how hard his face looked as Elsie led him in the hall earlier today. Without thinking, I ask, "What happened in the dining room today?"

He sighs and throws his body back on the pillow.

I quickly backpedal. "Sorry. You don't have to tell me."

"It's fine. I just feel dumb. I almost hit Ty. I would've if Elsie hadn't been there, but thankfully she was."

"What happened?"

"Nothing. I mean, he said some shitty things, but really, it's what happened before."

"Before?" I say.

Miles props himself back on his elbow, facing me and tracing my hip again as he launches into it. "I worked on a film in Barbados. It was a small cast and crew, like this one. I got Ty a role in the film. At the time, he was my best friend. All the main players were all in our early twenties—Ty, and the main actress Lana, and me. We all got really close."

"Lana? As in Lana Freeman?" Lana Freeman—model turned actress, and as it happens, she turned into an excellent one. She won the Golden Globe last year for a limited series where she played Maria Sharapova. The likeness was uncanny—same high cheekbones, same flowing blonde hair, same intensity in the gaze, same uber-toned physique. I resist the urge to cover my body with the sheet.

Miles nods. "Yeah. She and I started seeing each other. She's the one I told you about."

I nod. I remember him telling me by the loch.

"I was reading this great script for a period drama that was going to start production soon. It was about Shakespeare, but the man, not the legend. It was funny and poignant. Some of the more insightful lines were delivered by the best friend. They were interested in me for the role."

I sit up. "*A Dhia*! You were going to be Antonio in *A Walking Shadow*?"

That movie was massive when it came out. It was delightful. They completely swept the Oscars that year and the Golden Globes. I'm trying to remember who ended up playing Antonio in that movie, when suddenly I can picture him clear as day, walking on stage to accept his Oscar.

Ty Marshall.

"I don't understand," I say, shaking my head.

Miles shrugs. "Lana and I had just started seeing each other, and I was so sure she was the one. I pictured our whole life together—big house in Malibu, kids, the whole thing. I turned them down."

"You turned down the role?"

Miles lies back on the pillow again, rubbing his hands over his face. "I sure did."

"Oof. That's rough."

He laughs, but there's no real humor in it. "Oh, but wait, there's more."

"Oh no." I run my hand along his side, and he gives me a genuine smile.

"We kept shooting, and I was really head over heels for Lana. I had a ring shipped there from Tiffany's."

I gasp. "You were going to propose? How long was the shoot?"

He laughs, a real one this time. "It was too soon to propose. I knew that. It was more about showing her how I felt. I went to her bungalow and found she wasn't alone. She and Ty were together. It was… quite a show. After that, I kept to myself, kept my head down, and just got through my lines. I tried to get back into *A Walking Shadow*. My agent contacted the people about the role. They had already filled it."

"With Ty."

He nods. "The movie thing *really* gets me. I mean, all of it was awful, but…I thought we were close, Ty and I. There was a whole day in Barbados where I thought I lost the script. I was frantic. It was confidential. I shouldn't have left it lying around my bungalow in the first place. I confided in Ty, and he kept telling me not to worry, it would turn up. The next day it did, but not before he probably made copies."

I run my hand over Miles's arm. "Maybe they had sent the script to both of you?"

"I thought that too. We both have a similar look. We're up for a lot of the same roles. In the film in Barbados, we were playing brothers. Hell, in this picture we're playing brothers." Miles shakes his head. "My agent got the scoop, though. Ty sent in an audition video to the director. He wasn't even on their radar before. It's a great video. It's in the extra features on the Blu-ray. Have you seen it?"

I shake my head.

"Beautiful white sand beaches behind him. Crystal blue water. The voice that laughs at the end and says, *amazing* is Lana."

I gasp, my eyes going wide. "No."

Miles laughs. "Oh yeah. It's the betrayal that gets me, you know? And the *what if*? What would my career look like right now if I had taken that role? If I hadn't been so blinded by my puppy-dog crush?"

His eyes are far away, and his jaw is clenched.

I caress his cheek softly. He nuzzles his head into my hand, then turns his face to kiss my palm. He grabs my hand and kisses his way up my arm, laying me all the way down on the bed, and climbs on top of me. He doesn't stop his traveling kisses until he's between my thighs. We lose ourselves. All thoughts of Lana, Ty, betrayal, and everything else fades away, eclipsed by the light of us.

MILES

*W*e lie next to each other, her leg draped over mine, my hand moving over the soft skin of her back. Voices from the street have gotten louder in the last twenty minutes as more and more people spill out of the bar, but I'm not ready to let the world in yet.

Skye must hear them too because she says, "I hate to say this, but we have to be back at the pub when the whole crew leaves. You came in the van."

My fingers wander up her spine. "I could text Elsie that I got another ride?"

"Not from me," she says quickly. "Billy. You could tell her Billy drove you back. He's always giving strays rides."

"We have the weekend off. I could even say I went on a little research trip to gain some perspective on the role. My character is a real loner."

She sits up, her hair cascading over her shoulder and catching the light. "The whole weekend?"

I sit up too. "Could you? I know you have obligations."

A slow smile spreads across her face. "I could text Dad. Say I have a writing class in Edinburgh, or something. He should be able to do my chores for a couple of days. I haven't taken a break in a long time. Do you think it'll look too suspicious, us both being gone on the same weekend?"

It will. But at this point I'm not sure that I care. "Maybe a little, but they can't prove we were together. I'll make it worth it."

I snuggle into her neck, kissing the spot behind her ear that I know drives her wild. We both fall back onto the bed.

She laughs. "Okay. We can't stay here, though. There are too many people I know all over this town."

"With the weekend off, the crew might be around more, too," I say. "So where do we go?"

She gets up and grabs her phone. "Let's text all our people we need to. We can stay here tonight and figure out where to go in the morning."

* * *

WE SLEEP IN, a luxury for us both. When we finally peel our bodies away from each other, we make a plan to go to the Isle of Skye. It seems only fitting. We are in the Land Rover, the morning mist clinging to the green hills, fiery orange trees, and the loch. It makes everything look eerie. I can see why Skye writes mysteries, being surrounded by this murky landscape. "Blackbird" plays softly over the stereo. The only thing that would make this perfect would be a steaming cup of coffee. We are on our way to Inverness now to pick up some, along with food and other essentials. Stopping at the Thistle House would've been too suspicious looking, obviously.

Skye is singing along quietly. Her red hair is in a messy bun, with one strand escaping and trailing down her long neck. "Are you named after the island?"

"I was apparently conceived there on my mother's first trip to Scotland," she says, making a puckered face of disgust, and a booming laugh escapes me, the sound echoing off the roof. Skye joins in. "TMI, right?"

I nod. "Definitely. That's nice though, that your parents were... um...passionate. How did they meet?"

Skye keeps her eyes focused on the road, a small smile playing at her lips. "In Hollywood. My dad moved there for a while wanting to be an actor. Mom was performing at some little dive bar. He sat in the front and cheered so loud it shook the floorboards, according to my mom. He bought her a drink and the rest is history."

The corners of her mouth turn down. She seems so lost in thought, I decide not to ask any follow-up questions.

We make a quick stop at the shopping center in Inverness. I want to make it into more of a *Pretty Woman* shopping spree, but Skye insists we just grab some essentials. She doesn't argue with getting some books for the trip, though. We have to pick them up from the stand in the market because the cool bookstore with the wood-burning stove hasn't opened yet for the day. I grab the latest Ruth Ware. She chooses the new Jasmine Guillory book. For a mystery writer, she sure reads a lot of romance.

We drop off our bags and head to a coffee shop. I adjust my purple hat more snugly on my head.

"It's just over here." She holds my hand and pulls me along.

I intertwine my fingers with hers, which makes her smile.

"What's with the hat?"

I smile. "It's so I won't be recognized."

She laughs. "You think that purple tourist hat hides the fact that you are Miles Casey, movie star extraordinaire?"

I shrug. "You'd be surprised."

She leads me to a large stone building on the corner, painted cobalt blue. A matching blue sign hanging overhead reads *Velocite (for the love of bikes)*. Little yellow planters line the door, and a chalkboard propped against the building says they're open. My mouth is already watering at the smell of coffee.

As we walk in, a man with a slick black pompadour behind the counter sings out, "Hello."

The inside is just as charming as the outside, with a long, light wooden bar in the front and matching tables scattered around, half of them filled. A bicycle hangs from the ceiling. I'm still staring at it, trying to figure out how they hung it exactly, as we approach the counter.

"I'll have an Americano with a splash of frothed milk and a halloumi bagel, to go, please. Miles, what would you like?"

I look at the takeaway menu and am debating between the pizza bagel or the squash and pesto bagel, when I realize the man who vaguely resembles Elvis hasn't stopped staring at me. Even though I know it's coming, I plow ahead. "I'll have the squash and pesto bagel and a latte. Thanks."

"You're Miles Casey."

I smile and nod, ignoring Skye whispering beside me, "Clearly the hat didn't work this time."

"I love you." Skye smirks, and Elvis backpeddles. "Your films, I mean." He seems to have found himself again and mercifully starts making our drinks as he talks. "Oh, who am I kidding. *No one*." He sings again. "I love you. I've seen every movie you've ever made. You are magnificent."

Skye's smile is now reaching from ear to ear. Elvis puts the bagels into a bag and goes back to fiddling with the espresso machine.

"Thank you."

Elvis hands our bagels and drinks over the counter, then frantically looks around. "Wait, will you sign..." He pulls his phone out of his apron pocket. "Will you sign my phone?"

I laugh. This is a first. "You want me to sign your phone?"

He shakes his head. "Or a selfie. We could take a selfie—or an 'usie,' as it were."

I nod. "Sure." He hands the phone to Skye and comes around the counter. We stand side by side, just about the same height, in front of the pastry case.

"Say cheers." Skye presses the phone screen a couple more times. Elvis throws his arm around my shoulder and hugs me closer to him.

Some of the other patrons have their phones out now, too. It's time to go.

I hold out my hand to Elvis. "So nice to meet you."

Elvis is fanning himself with one hand. Skye hands his phone back.

We take our breakfast. Once we are in the car with both doors shut, Skye starts laughing.

"I'm surprised he didn't turn around and kiss you."

I laugh, but that has happened before. "What can I say? I have enthusiastic fans." Then I remember the dance that she and Kate choreographed. "Fans who make up dances to the theme songs of my movies and watch them over and over with their best friend."

She turns on the car and immediately turns up the stereo. "All right, all right. We've heard about enough of that. Bloody Kate."

I laugh, but it hits me how close we came to being busted. What if he had taken a picture of Skye and me? What if someone else had and we hadn't noticed? I duck down a little more in my seat. "We should probably be more careful, though."

Skye nods, her eyes on the road.

* * *

THE DRIVE IS GORGEOUS. Lush green hills, massive clouds, and pale-blue sky just peeking out from behind it. We take a turn, and off in the distance, I spot a herd of deer. The buck stands at attention, lifting its head to us as we pass, his massive antlers reaching up to the heavens.

"Look!" I point them out to Skye.

She glances over and nods. "Red deer. Gorgeous, aren't they?"

"They are. Honestly, I've been all over the world, but I've never been somewhere quite so captivating as here. But maybe it's the company."

Skye barks out a surprised laugh. "Wooo, that's quite a line."

She pulls the car over. I check to make sure there are no other cars nearby, no one that could spot us and sell their story to *YHF*. But there's nothing and no one as far as the eye can see. I hop out and take my phone out, snapping some pictures. Skye comes and stands next to me. I turn my phone on her and snap a few pics. Her red hair stands out against the green hills and the gray clouds. She flips me off, and I keep taking photos until she tries to grab my phone. I pull her to me instead, wrapping my arms around her.

I smile. "Have you traveled much?"

Skye shakes her head. "I went to New York."

"I was born in Brooklyn. It still feels like home, even though I've lived in LA for a lot longer than I ever lived there." I shake my head. That doesn't even feel right to say. "What took you to New York?"

Skye keeps her eyes on the deer, her face nestled on my chest. "A boy. Finn. We'd known each other since we were kids, started dating when I was fifteen and he was sixteen. Everyone thought we were made for each other. People talked about us like we were already married. Finn was—well, for all I know, he still is a musician. He wanted to go to New York and start a proper band. We went once we were old enough to be on our own, but it was very clear to me that I needed to go home. Then my dad called. My mom was sick. I came home, we broke up, and Mom died. All in all, it took about three months for my life to be completely unrecognizable from what it was before."

I stroke her hair. "Oh, Skye, that's so fast." I don't want to intrude or poke at her pain, but I want to know everything I can about her, so I ask quietly, "How did she die?"

She presses her head a little harder into my chest as the wind picks up around us. "She had cancer. Lots of tiny tumors in her brain. By the time they found them, there was nothing they could do." Skye pulls away but keeps talking. "And you know, I knew something was off. The whole year before she passed, she was not like herself. She was forgetful, and before that, my mother never forgot a thing. And she was sad. Her doctor said she was depressed and put her on antidepressants. My mom always had her small moments of sadness." I can feel her shake, her head, her hair tickling under my chin. "This was different. It was like a switch. She had no joy. Before, she was always singing when she did anything. Even when she fed those stupid chickens. But then she was just so silent."

A tear falls down Skye's face. I wipe it away. She puts her arms around my neck.

She sniffs back tears and smiles at me. "It's been almost six years. You'd think I'd have a better handle on this."

She looks so beautiful, her eyes glistening. It's like rubber bands are wrapped around my heart to see her so sad, and knowing there is nothing I can do. I shake my head. "I don't think it works like that."

"That's when I started writing. I'd always fiddled with it here and there before. Poems and the like. But I wrote my first novel the year after she passed. It gave me something to do with my hands, with my thoughts: a reason to get out of bed every day and a tangible goal. You know. My first novel was fifty-two thousand words of absolute rubbish written two hundred words at a time, but it saved me."

A car backfires in the distance. We watch the deer bolt across the hill impossibly fast. I lean down and nuzzle her hair. She turns and brings her lips to mine, salty from her tears. I wish my kisses could take her pain away, but I know they can't.

She walks me backward, still kissing me, until we are leaning against the car. Her hands move down my chest, and tiny electric pulses follow them. She moves to kissing my neck, but this feels like an awfully fast shift from sharing confidences.

She moves to kissing right where my jaw and neck meet. I tuck my hands into her coat, placing my hands on her hips. She moves her lips to my ear and whispers, "The back is quite spacious."

I laugh. "Skye Ainslie, are you suggesting we make out on the side of the road?"

She smiles, and I feel it all the way down to my toes. "I'm suggesting we do quite a bit more than that."

It's sweet, but it also feels like a distraction tactic. A way to get us back on the physical side of things and less on the intimate sharing of our lives. I guess we are having a purely physical relationship, right?

But I shake my head. "It's too risky. What if someone drove by? If you didn't like the other picture of you all over the internet, this one would be much worse."

Her eyes smolder, and my heart races in my chest. This is coming out all wrong. And I quickly clarify, "Not that your actual picture would look bad. It would look incredible."

She smiles, and my heart slows. "Fair point. Let's get to where we're going, then."

* * *

THE STEREO IS PLAYING one of Skye's mixes. I turn it up, and we both sing along at top volume to Rolling Stone's "Wild Horses."

On the way to the Airbnb, I get a text from Jake. I try to hide my smirk as I look at the picture he sent, but I do a terrible job of it.

"What are you smiling at on your phone?"

I shake my head, trying to physically wipe the smile away. "Nothing."

"Oh, come on."

"No, really, it's—"

"I will turn this car around."

I laugh. "Remember when you were asking me about fan mail?"

Skye's cheeks turn bright pink. "Was I?"

"Well, I saved a couple, and Jake found them for me. Well, actually Jake's sister."

Skye lets out a heavy breath. "Oh no."

I nod. "Oh yes!"

"No. No. No."

"Let me read you my favorite."

"You really don't need to."

"*Dear Miles,*

My name is Skye, and I live in Scotland. Have you ever been here? It's beautiful. You should definitely come. I love your movies, and I feel like even though we've never met, we have a real connection. Like something they write songs about, like that Beatles song "Across the Universe." It feels like that, except if we met, I feel like it would change my world. Both our worlds. Anyway, if you're ever in Scotland, look me up. Skye."

Skye has gone completely still. I reach over and squeeze her leg. "You weren't wrong."

"It's so embarrassing."

"It's sweet."

She shakes her head. "Do you remember what you sent back?"

A lump forms in my throat, making it hard to swallow. When she sent this, I was at the height of all the *Undercover Quarterback* fame. It had definitely gone to my head.

"I think I sent a headshot."

"Uh-huh. Do you remember what you signed?"

I close my eyes, wishing I had been more clever, or more humble, or more real. "Coo-Coo-Ca-Choo Babe."

"I still have it."

"No! Shit. I was stupid. In my defense, I was only nineteen."

She nods but doesn't take her eyes off the road.

I place a hand on her thigh. "Well, it meant something to me."

"Can we never, ever talk about it ever again?"

"Ever?"

"Miles."

"Okay." I zip my lips and put away my phone.

After another two hours, a quick stop for lunch, another stop for groceries, and some of the most beautiful scenery I have ever seen, we arrive at our tiny cabin. It is in a large field overlooking a massive loch, with virtually no other houses nearby. The cabin itself is modern, with sleek lines, navy siding, massive windows, and a bright-yellow door. It's a jarring contrast to the landscape that looks like hobbits may come tramping over the hill at any moment.

Inside is just as modern. High ceilings, a loft where the bed is, a kitchen that looks straight out of a Crate and Barrel catalogue, a wood-burning stove, and a wall of pure glass overlooking the loch.

I start putting away the groceries.

"I'm going to change into something a little more comfortable," Skye says with a sultry voice that brings flashes of last night back to me.

"Need any help?" I ask with a wink.

She gives me a slow smile but shakes her head before trotting upstairs.

I open a bottle of wine, bringing it over to the coffee table, along with two glasses and a loaf of crispy olive bread. As I light the wood stove, the sun sets out the window, golden streaks reflecting on the dark water.

There's a funky old five-disc changer in the corner of the room. I fiddle with the nobs until it starts to play a Lily Allen album.

"What loch is this?" I ask.

Skye calls down from the loft. "Loch Bracadale."

"Maybe we'll spot a Nessie."

She walks into the room in a black silk nightgown with lace trim tickling her pale calves, her turquoise cardigan falling off one shoulder, and her hair in soft waves around her face.

"Wow."

She smiles and grabs one of the glasses of wine, tucking herself into the couch. "Nessie only lives in Loch Ness. Hence the name."

I grab my glass and join her on the couch. "Right, but there must be other sightings in other lochs."

She lays her legs on my lap, and I run my hand on her silky shins.

"Aye, there are. I've never heard of one here. This loch feeds out into the open ocean, so if we were to see any monster, it would probably be a selkie."

"A selkie?"

She sips her wine, and I continue to run my hand over the soft skin of her leg. "Have you never seen…oh, what was that movie?" She taps a finger on the side of her glass. *Secret of Roan Inish.*

I shake my head, smiling. "Must have missed that one."

"Well, a man fell in love with a creature from the sea. They were married for years and had children. She was a shapeshifter—a seal—but she could live as a woman if she liked. The woman loved her children with all her heart, but she still missed the sea. Her husband knew this, so he hid her seal skin. Most of the time, she was a loving wife and mother. But some days she would wail and beg him to let her return to her watery home."

One day, her son found her seal skin and returned it to her. She slipped it on and disappeared into the water."

"Did she ever come back?" I ask, looking out at the dark water for any odd ripples.

Skye shakes her head. "Sometimes, I felt like my mother was a selkie. Like her singer persona was the real her—her seal skin—and she was suffocating as a housewife."

"But if that were true, she could've returned to the sea, so to speak, at any time."

Skye shrugs.

"And you told me she was happy for the most part. What makes you think she was sad about giving up her music?"

"She seemed happy. Sometimes late at night, though, I would walk by the library, and she would be sitting alone, listening to her old records, just staring into the fire."

"Did you ever talk to her about it?"

Skye shrugs. "I tried. Sort of. I wrote a blog post about it a long time ago when I had a blog. God, I must've been sixteen." She cringes. "I had so many opinions. I think Mom may have read it, even."

The song changes to "Somewhere Only We Know" and Skye changes the subject just as swiftly. She bolts off the couch and turns it up. "I love this song."

I join her, part of me wishing we could've kept talking, sharing. But she looks so adorable standing there in her nightgown. I let it go and hold out my hand. "May I have this dance?"

She curtsies, holding out her nightgown with both hands, and then slips her fair hand in mine. I trained in ballroom dancing for a film, so I know what I'm doing, somewhat. I lead us in a sweeping fairytale–style waltz, the sky out the window darkening into a deep blue, stars just starting to prickle the horizon. And I know, without a doubt, I will replay this moment in my mind until the reel fades.

I lean down and kiss her. The music forgotten, our bodies still. She deepens the kiss, reaching up on tiptoe, bringing her hands to my neck. I move mine to her hips, the silky fabric slick under my touch. I reach her ass and squeeze, lifting her up. She wraps her legs around my waist, and I walk us toward the stairs.

"Too far," she breathes out. Instead, I walk her right in front of the woodstove and lay her down on the soft carpet. The glow from the fire catches on all her curves. The sharp angle of her cheek, the swoop of her collarbone, the ample swell of her breast.

She props herself up on her elbows. "Miles, everything okay?"

I smile, laying down beside her, running my hand along her gown all the way to the hem, then slowly pulling it up. "It's perfect. You're perfect."

SKYE

*M*iles runs his hand up my thigh and leaves goosebumps in its wake. The rug is soft under me, but not quite soft enough. I stand and Miles looks hurt.

"You good?"

I smile, taking his hand and leading him to one of the living room chairs. "Grand."

I shrug off my sweater one shoulder at a time. I can't help but smile at the look on Miles's face as he watches me like I'm the most beautiful woman in the world. When I'm with him, I feel like I am.

My sweater drops to the floor then I remove one strap of my nightgown. Turning around I remove the other and let the fabric drop to a pool by my feet. The cool air of the room hits me, making my nipples hard. I turn around and move my hands up my body, fingertips rubbing over my breasts. Miles grips the sides of the chair for dear life.

I move my hands down and touch my slit as Miles sucks in a breath. My fingers swirl, the sensation heightened by Miles's gaze. How many times have I thought of him while I've done this and now, like a dream, he's here. I move one finger all the way inside my legs trembling with want.

Miles unzips his pants, adjusting his growing bulge.

I pull out and place another finger slowly inside. I moan, "Let me see it."

Miles stands. He quickly tosses aside his shirt, pushes his jeans down, then his boxers, exposing his huge erection.

"Stroke it." I bite my lip, my fingers still moving.

He obeys, sitting back in the chair, his large hand moving up and down his even larger cock.

Warmth is spreading to my cheeks. I pull my fingers out and walk one slow step at time toward him. He grabs my hand and takes my fingers in his mouth, sucking and emitting a pleasant hum.

"Where're the condoms?" I ask.

He doesn't take my fingers out of his mouth, just points at his pants on the floor.

I remove my fingers, placing each hand on his thighs. I spread them apart as I lower slowly to my knees, my face inches from his crotch as I rifle through the pants. Pulling the condom out of the pocket, I rip open the foil and roll it on slow and firm.

Miles's breath comes out heavier at my touch.

I stand and turn around as Miles reaches for my ass, squeezing a handful.

Slowly, I lower onto him, every nerve ending in my body tingling as I let him in deeper.

Miles's hands reach around, squeezing my breasts as I move up and down, going deeper each time until my thighs are trembling and he's filled me completely.

He moves his hands to my hips adjusting the angle, and oh lord he finds a spot that I've never felt before. I cry out, "Yes. Right there."

Miles thrust over and over using his large hands to bring my hips down. I hold the sides of the chair, needing something to ground me.

"Go with it baby," Miles grits out, moving a hand back to my breast. "Come for me."

I let go of the chair and cover his hand with mine. He intertwines our fingers as my whole body tenses, my core squeezing around him so hard we cry out together.

* * *

WE ARE LYING on a big blanket by the fire, sipping wine and looking out at the stars, my body still pleasantly humming. I can say without a doubt that this is the most passionate affair I have ever had. But I have to be more careful.

Something about the way Miles looks at me, the way he leans in, opens me up like a book, and my whole life comes spilling out. All this talk, the way he held me, nestling his nose in my hair, as we looked at the red deer on the side of the road, feels very un-fling-like. I can feel the string between us knot together as warm and strong as one of Kate's scarves.

Nope. We have to keep this strictly physical, surface-level.

Coo-Coo-Ca-Choo, babe.

Miles points to the moon. "Oh, look. It's a banana moon."

"A banana moon?" I laugh. The moon is a perfect pointy crescent. "That, sir, is called a Cheshire Cat moon."

"Ah, of course. The writer whips out the literary references."

I sit up, letting my sweater fall off my shoulder. "And of course the man makes the phallic reference."

Miles smiles and tiptoes his finger on my thigh. "Oooh, I like where your head is at."

I let his fingers roam, but point again to the moon. "Look at it. Can't you just imagine the furry kitty body around it, and then it disappears, and his smile is all that's left?"

Miles nods. "Curiouser and curiouser."

I nuzzle into his neck, kissing the edge of his jaw.

"Who knew quoting *Alice in Wonderland* got you so hot?"

I kiss my way down his body as he keeps talking.

"I love when she asks the rabbit, *How long is forever?*"

"Yes! I've heard that quote. What's the answer again?"

"Sometimes just one second."

"It's not in any of the books," I say between kisses, working my way back up to his mouth.

"Are you sure?"

"Positive. Still very impressive."

We kiss, and it's like falling down the rabbit hole.

He stands and takes my hand, leading me to the bedroom this time.

* * *

IT's our last day on the Isle of Skye. We have to leave this afternoon, so technically, we don't even get the full day. We spent all of Saturday in our cabin, our own little "Somewhere Only We Know" or our SOWK as Miles started calling it. He does it with a fake Boston accent, so it sounds like someone from *Good Will Hunting* saying "sock". It makes me laugh every time.

We've only left for a small walk to explore the stretch of the loch near us. Miles looked the whole time for monsters or selkies. I still can't believe I told him that about my mother. Not that it isn't true—I have often wondered if my mother longed for her singing days the way a selkie longs for the sea, for her life before. I'm just surprised I told Miles. I hadn't expected to share so much more than a warm bed with him. But we've talked nonstop—well, except when our mouths were otherwise occupied. I have to get that in check. *Stop sharing every thought in my head with him.*

This morning, we're dragging ourselves out of bed before the sun, off to the fairy pools. Miles picked the music this morning, so "Annie Laurie" is playing softly over the stereo. He's sipping coffee from his travel mug and staring out the window. The moonlight is highlighting his cheek like a soft kiss. I pry my gaze away, putting it back on the road. Truth be told, I could look at him for hours.

I park the car, and we get out. The sky is just starting to turn a pearly gray. Miles takes my hand in his, and we walk down the path.

"The pools aren't very far."

A slow, unconcerned smile spreads across Miles's handsome face. "I'm up for anything."

We walk on, watching the sky put on a light show just for us. Pinks and oranges outline the glowing clouds, the colors getting deeper the farther we walk. This weekend has been perfect. A stone lodges in my throat as the thought echoes in my head like someone yelling in a cave—we have to go back today.

Somehow, we have to figure out how to sneak into the castle and make it look like we weren't even together. Rushing water buzzes in my ears, making my thoughts even louder. We'll have to pretend we didn't have this amazing time together. They'll shoot their movie, I'll write my words, and then Miles will leave.

It hits me like a swift slap to the face. Miles is still going to leave at the end of this. I was so wrong all those years ago. Our meeting won't change anything about either of our worlds.

The fairy pools come into view, the water reflecting the brilliant colors of the sunrise.

"Wow," Miles says as he squeezes my hand.

My skin is hot from his touch. I drop it. I need to feel something other than my overwhelming feelings for him and this rising panic that none of this is real.

Shrugging off my coat, I kick off my shoes and quickly shimmy out of the rest of my clothes.

Miles's eyes smolder as he watches me. "What are you doing? It'll be freezing."

"Aye." At this moment, I welcome the chill.

Without another thought, I jump into the crystal-clear pool, the icy liquid stealing my breath, or is it the fairies? I move my arms and kick my legs to get my blood moving.

Miles crouches by the edge and puts a tentative hand in the water. He shakes his head. "No way."

I smile and give him a little splash, which he dodges expertly. The water sends ice coursing through my veins, but it is soothing. I float on my back, my face to the glowing clouds, water filling my ears, and everything else fades away. My swirling thoughts have slowed. It was always supposed to be an affair. A harmless little fling.

After a couple more minutes in the icy water, my bones start to feel the cold. I swim to the edge. Miles offers me a hand. He takes off his jumper and wraps it around my shivering body. "Your lips are blue. We should get you back to the fire."

He rubs the sides of my arms. We didn't bring a towel. Honestly, I wasn't planning on wild swimming in November. I pull his cardigan closer, get my pants and shoes back on, and we head back to the car at a quick pace.

Once back at somewhere only we know, Miles plops me in front of the fire and runs me a bath in the clawfoot tub. Goosebumps still cover my flesh as the loch shimmers outside.

"Skye, your bath awaits."

I rise but stop dead in my tracks as something gliding in the loch catches my eye. Barely breathing, I watch as the shadowy figure whirls through the water.

"Skye?"

I glance toward Miles as he comes out of the back.

"Are you okay?"

When I turn back to the loch, it is still as a church on a Tuesday.

*　*　*

I CAN SMELL the bath before I see it. The navy blue clawfoot tub is filled with lavender-scented bubbles. Bubbles higher than the sides. Miles comes over to me and gently pulls my jumper—well, technically his—over my head. He kneels down, skimming my body with his lips on the way to unbutton my jeans.

Once I am completely naked, he gives me a hand into the tub. The water is deliciously warm and feels soft from the bubbles. My whole body relaxes.

Miles gives me his most handsome smile. "I'll give you some privacy."

I reach out, grab his hand, and shake my head. "That's the last thing I want."

His smile grows wider.

I pat the water on the other side of the tub, making little splashes as I do. "Plenty of room."

"You don't have to ask me twice," Miles says as he shimmies out of his clothes. He hops into the tub with a massive splash that we'll without a doubt have to clean up later, but right now that doesn't matter. Nothing matters except our slick skin next to each other in this blissful tub and Miles's lips on my neck.

* * *

SNEAKING BACK into the castle isn't as hard as I thought it would be. Miles had the idea for me to drop him off in Foyers, and he'd find his own way back. It wouldn't look like we were together at all. Still water, no ripples.

After I smuggle our things into my room, I head to my writing room, but stop dead in my tracks at the door. My dad is there, staring out the window. He usually never spends time in this room, even before I took it over. "Dad."

"Ah, pet. You're back. How was the writing class?"

I glance at my laptop on my desk, where it's been all weekend. "Good."

"Thought it was a little funny you went to a writing class without your computer."

So, he clocked it too.

"Yeah. It was all about tapping into your creativity with a paper and pen." Yep, that sounds legit. "No laptops allowed."

Dad narrows his eyes but nods once. He comes over and gives me a kiss on the head. "Be careful, pet."

"With pens?" I laugh, trying to act like I don't know what he's talking about.

"With…" He taps his chest with two fingers.

After he leaves, I close the door and fling myself at my laptop. Words rush out of me. This is not a gentle trickle, but a tidal wave. My grammar is atrocious, but punctuation can't keep up with this deluge. I type until my fingers cramp, until the light dims to evening, my stomach growls, my back creaks, and still the words will not let up. They just keep coming, until finally I'm breathless.

Spent and starving, I head to the kitchen to make myself something to eat. On my way down the stairs, I run into Elsie, in black leggings, a massive green jumper, and her pink hair sticking up at odd angles. Adorable as ever.

"Skye, I was just coming up to see you."

Undeniable joy spreads across my face. It's honestly so nice to have made a new friend, and one that writes. "I'm headed to the kitchen to make a piece. Do you want one?"

"A piece of what?" Elise's brows pull together in confusion.

I laugh. "I forgot I'm surrounded." I do my American accent, which honestly sounds a lot like Kermit the Frog. "A sandwich."

"A sandwich? Brilliant. A piece. I'm going to remember that. I'd love one."

We both head to the kitchen. I make two sandwiches, and we settle in with them at the table. Elsie chews her bite and then carefully sets her sandwich down. "So, I was reading your pages again. They're really wonderful. The voice is just charming. I hope you don't mind, but I sent them to my literary agent friend in New York."

I freeze with a bite in my mouth. Chewing it would take too long, so I grab a napkin and spit into it. "What?"

"I just sent her the first chapter. I let her know it was really rough."

My heart sputters in my chest. "I…um…"

Elsie leans forward and grabs my hand. "She loved it! She wants to read more whenever you're ready."

My eyes are as wide as my smile. I must look like all eyes and teeth. I stand up, knocking my chair over. "Really?"

Elsie stands too. The joy in my chest is bubbling to my brain. I grab both her hands and jump. We squeal like teenagers. This is phenomenal. I might not even need that manuscript contest in February. I might be signed with an agent before then.

* * *

MICKEY AND SORCHA are at it again, my fingers lightly tapping at the keys as Mickey's fingers lightly explore my heroine's body. I take a sip of coffee and stare out the window at those familiar hills. How much sex is too much sex in a sexy book?

The sun refuses to come out today. Dark clouds have settled, looking like a large quilt, but from the frost on the window, probably not snuggly and warm like one. I check the time and sigh. It's a good thing fictional characters can't get blue balls, because this will have to be my stopping point this morning. The demon chickens wait for no mortal man, fictional or otherwise.

It is absolutely Baltic out, most likely going to snow later, so I finish my chores at breakneck speed. Then bundle up the best I can in thermal tights, jeans, thermal top, jumper, coat, hat, gloves, and a scarf. I feel like a child bundled up and ready to be rolled out the door to primary school. I wheel my bike out of the shed and set off into the cold day, pedaling fast to beat the snow.

I keep my eyes peeled, hoping to see Miles out for his morning jog. I haven't seen him hardly at all this week, and last week was even worse. They've been so busy shooting, and I've been busy writing, trying to get a draft done to send to Elsie's agent friend.

I still can't believe she wants to read my work based on the first chapter. I try to temper my expectations. After all, she might not like the rest. It's so hard, though. Being hopeful and excited is one of the best parts about this whole process. It'll hurt just as much if she passes if I was elated or if I was sensible anyway, right? So, I settle my rose-colored glasses firmly on my face and let myself enjoy it.

Pedaling faster, I let hope radiate out of me and churn it into pure energy. The agent will love it, and then there will be a bidding war, and I will sign a book deal with a big, big publisher.

Before I know it, I'm parking my bike outside Thistle House. I open the door, and a rush of warmth greets me. Kate's in her usual spot. I don't even take off my coat as I make a beeline for the fire. I rub my hands together, taking off my gloves, then turn to warm up my backside, which is practically numb from the cold ride over. As I turn, I see Kate is not alone as I had originally assumed, but sitting with none other than Finn fucking McDougall.

MILES

*T*he loch is dark this morning—darker than the clouds, even. It makes it seem like the color is not a reflection, so much as the water itself has turned murky from something beneath. I squat, running my fingers lightly over the surface, a shiver traveling through my entire body.

Off in the distance, a small black figure appears, gliding through the water and sending ripples all the way to the shore. The figure doesn't stop. It keeps coming, getting larger and larger as it does. I walk into the frigid water, my kilt soaking it in like a sponge, and without hesitation, I dive. Fully submerged, the icy liquid steals my breath. It feels like when I was sacked in that silly quarterback movie —the wind knocked right out of me. I'm gasping when I come to the surface. The beast is right in front of me, its inky eyes darker than the water. I can see myself in its reflection. I reach out a hand to touch its scaly gray skin, when I hear, "Cut!"

I swim back to the shore. Minnie is waiting for me with a heated towel. I slip out of my drenched kilt. Feeling like it weighs a hundred pounds, the soaked wool drops to the ground with a plop.

"That was a great take." Minnie lowers her voice. "I thought, anyway."

She trades the wet towel for a heavy blanket. I just nod, too cold to manage even a thanks.

She leads me to my chair that has a heat lamp pointed directly at it. Another PA comes and hands me a warm cup of tea. I'd prefer coffee, but I'm too cold to ask if there is any. I wrap my hands and curl my body as much as I can around the tiny paper cup like I'm huddled next to a fire. The industrial-strength wetsuit I have on must've kept some of the cold out, but it's hard to believe.

The crew is resetting the animatronic beast for another take. Natalie likes to use practical effects as much as possible. She's often been referred to as the younger, hotter female Michel Gondry, but this is her first foray with effects of this scale. They've constructed a massive Loch Ness Monster out of silicone, airbrushing, and a drone submarine device. It's pretty cool and I'm grateful I don't have to pretend something is there. Swimming in the actual waters of the loch, instead of a tank in a studio in front of a green screen, will definitely add some authenticity, maybe even a little magic to the scene. But man, I am freezing my balls off.

There is so much hustle and bustle around, I startle when I hear, "Hey, there."

I turn to see Ava in chocolate brown joggers and a massive fuzzy coat that I'm immediately jealous of, even though this blanket is nice. I give her a half wave and regret removing my arm from my heated cocoon.

Ava pulls a director's chair next to mine. "Mind if I borrow your lamp?"

"Please."

"How's the shoot so far?"

"Good, I think. We've only done one take so far."

"Ah. My scene's up next. How's the water?"

I shake my head, but I don't want her to be too nervous about the shoot. "Cold, but you'll be okay. These wetsuits really do work."

She nods, then fidgets with a loose string on her chair. It feels like she wants to say something. I'm sure she will if she really wants to.

I'm not going to pry it out of her. I stare at the loch and idly wonder how wise it is to put a fake monster somewhere a real monster may live.

"I just wanted to make sure you're still okay with my idea… I wasn't sure since you've been spending so much time with Skye."

I don't have any clue what "idea" she is talking about. But my priority is shooting down whatever impression she has about Skye and me. I shake my head. "I've hardly seen her, really."

This time, I hear the footsteps as Ty approaches. If I could physically tear myself away from this heat lamp, I would find somewhere—anywhere—else to be. But I can't. I sip my tea and try to lose myself in the warmth and spice of the ginger, with a surprising hint of lemon.

Ty pulls up a chair and sets it next to Ava. "Bet you're missing the waters of Barbados right about now."

I shake my head. "Funnily enough, I don't ever miss that shoot."

Ty chuckles. "Right."

Minnie comes over with another steaming cup and hands it to Ava.

"Sweetheart, do you think I could get some coffee and maybe a biscuit if there's one lying around?" Ty asks as he leans back in his chair.

The hair on the back of my neck bristles. Sweetheart? Really. What year is this? And a biscuit. He means a cookie. I want to grab him by the ears and yell, *You're from Southie!*

Minnie nods and gives Ty an odd smile. It's not like any smile she's ever given me before. Ty tosses her a wink as she walks away—well, more like saunters. Is there something going on between Minnie and Ty? No. Minnie's too nice for him. I should say something. Only, it's really none of my business, and they're both grown adults.

What is Ty even doing here today? That thought is the one that comes out. "Ty, why are you here? You don't have a scene today."

"Just being a supportive cast member, mate."

I stand. "Mate? Biscuit? You're not fucking British."

167

"Miles!" Natalie yells at me from the water's edge. She motions me over.

I pull my blanket closer and head to her side.

"Ready for round two?"

I nod.

"Your first take was great. I loved the physicality. But I need more from your expression. This beast has your greatest love's attention. You hate it with every fiber of your being. But when you look into its eyes, you soften and can see the appeal. You can see what she sees. Does that all make sense?"

My brain still feels numb from the swim, that or I'm just denser than I thought. I really don't get it. I knit my brows together in an attempt to massage my brain into working. "No."

Natalie nods but doesn't seem frustrated. She's an extremely patient director. "I want you to look at the monster like you look at Ty. Then, when you look deep into the creature's eyes, I want you to look at it like you look at Skye. Make sense?"

"I don't... It's not..." I fumble. Have we been that obvious? Everyone is talking about us like we've been making out in the hallways. Well, we did that one time, but no one was around.

Natalie waves a hand as if shooing away an invisible fly. "Does it make sense now?"

It does. I nod.

I only need two more takes before we get the shot, and I am wrapped for the day. I change into warm clothes, still bothered by all the talk today about Skye and me.

Does everyone know that we are...? What are we doing? I mean, I know the ins and outs of it, so to speak, but is what we have more than just physical? Back at SOWK, it sure felt like it. I smile at the memory. Every time I put on my admittedly terrible accent, she cracked up like I was literally tickling her.

Once I'm dressed, I stay for a bit to support Ava. The water is freezing, but from her stoic performance, you wouldn't be able to tell. She really is a good actress.

Natalie comes and stands by my side. "These shots are going to be amazing."

I nod as I watch Ava emerge, water rushing off her wetsuit-covered legs.

"I didn't tell you because I didn't want it to affect your performance, but there is a camera in the eye of the monster."

My jaw is on the ground. I stared deep into the blackness of that animatronic beast, and I never would've guessed. "You're kidding."

Natalie rubs her hands together like a cartoon villain, but really, she's probably doing it for warmth. "I can't wait to see them. Hey, don't forget to pack some things tonight. We head out on location in the morning."

That's right. I had forgotten. "Yep, all packed." I'm not. "For how long again?"

"A week, give or take." Natalie runs back over to the shore in her knee-high hunter boots.

After a few takes, Minnie offers to give me a ride back, and I gratefully accept. But once we're in the van, I ask her to take me to Thistle House instead.

"I'm starving, and they have great food there."

Minnie smiles, the dimples in her cheeks appearing. "Sure, no sweat. I don't think I can stay, though. How will you get back?"

I check the time. It's still early, and I'm hoping I might catch Skye there. I know she goes there almost every morning after her chores. What I'm really hoping is we can sneak off to that room upstairs that Skye has the secret key to. But honestly, I'm not sure how I'll get back. The clouds look heavy, like at any moment it may rain—or, with how cold it is, snow. I can figure it out, though. Even five minutes alone with Skye would be well worth the risk. "I can make my way back."

Minnie nods, and I wonder again if something is going on with her and Ty. Should I say something? Warn her that he destroys everything and everyone in his path like a debonair Godzilla? Rizzilla.

"Minnie, I know this is none of my business, but…" I take a deep breath. I just need to trust my instincts, and they are screaming at me to ask her. "Are you and Ty dating?"

"What?" Minnie's neck turns an angry red.

I laugh. "Okay. You don't have to tell me. I just want you to be careful, that's all. He has a tendency to…" How can I say this without sounding like a petty dick? "He doesn't always consider everyone's feelings."

Minnie shakes her head. "Miles, I appreciate you trying to protect me and all, but I'm a grown-up. We have real feelings for each other. He loves me, and more than that, he respects me."

He loves her? That seems too fast to be anything but one of his slick lines. "Did he say that? That he loves you?"

We pull up to Thistle House, and sparklers pop in my heart as I see Skye's familiar yellow bike leaning against the wall.

"Not that it's any of your business, but yeah. Yes, he did."

I swallow hard, not wanting to sound cruel by telling her that it is a massive lie. Minnie must notice, because she sighs. "Ty told me you would do this. He said you've been bad-mouthing him to the whole crew. He says you're just jealous. So, thanks for the advice, but I can take care of myself."

My sparklers turn into a raging fire. He told Minnie I've been bad-mouthing him? Have I? No. She's the only one I've even really talked about him with, besides Elsie, and she knows the whole story already.

"Sorry, Minnie. I was just trying to look out for you." I thank her for the ride and get out of the car. I'm too pissed to go inside, so I stuff my hands into my peacoat pockets and stroll the empty streets of Foyers.

SKYE

"*A*re you mad?" Finn laughs.

I'd like to say I feel nothing for him at all. That seeing him sitting there smiling, laughing, his square jaw covered in stubble, his sandy blond hair, a little longer than I remember, falling into his dark-blue eyes, does absolutely nothing to me. But the truth is, my heart stirs. My stupid heart fucking stirs like it's about to make a nice warm batch of biscuits.

He's wearing the leather coat he had on the last time I saw him. The coat he wore all the time when we were together, and apparently still wears like nothing has changed, the shoulders starting to crack; the only clue any time has passed.

But as soon as the tiny trickle of tenderness seeps in, it's quickly replaced by shame and anger. I shouldn't still have any warmth for him. It's been a long time. It's true I was in love with him for years, but since we broke up, it has been radio silence. He didn't even call when my mother died.

And what about Miles? But it isn't serious with Miles, right? Casual. Physical. A fling. Sooner than I can fathom, he'll be back on a plane to America. Bile fills my mouth at this thought. I swallow it back uncomfortably.

Now Finn is sitting here in my town, like nothing happened, like no time has passed, accusing me of being mad. Well, I am now.

"What are you doing here, Finn?"

Kate laughs, but quickly turns it into a cough and covers her mouth. "Pardon. Still getting over this nasty cold."

"That's some welcome." Finn stands and pulls me into a hug.

My body goes stiff. Any remaining feelings my brain may have had for this man, my body does not share. He even smells different than before. It's minty with a hint of clove. Not a good combination. I pull away.

"You haven't said what ye are doing in town after all these years, Finn," Kate says, still clacking away at her knitting.

"Visiting my ma. Christmas is right around the corner, isn't it? Thought I'd stay for the holidays at the very least."

I do some mental math. It is only the twenty-ninth of November, so Finn is going to be in town for probably a month, maybe more. I shouldn't be that surprised, but in all this time, he hasn't been back. His parents always visit him since his sister is also in America, somewhere in Vermont, last I heard.

Finn scoots one of the other armchairs close to his and pats the cushion, sending small dust particles flying. "Sit. Tell me all about your life. Let me buy you a pint."

I look at my watch. "It's barely ten in the morning."

"Ahh, since when has that bothered us?"

Margie joins us, giving me a weary look.

"Can I have some coffee, Margie?"

"I'll have some too, with a wee bit of the Irish," Finn says with a wink.

Margie asks Kate. "Anything for you, dear?"

Kate is winding her project around her needles. "No, I have to head out. That yarn won't sell itself."

"Aye, but it could, right? If you got one of those fancy self-check-outs. They're all over America," Finn is saying as Kate gives me a kiss on the cheek.

"I can't believe you're leaving," I whisper.

"I have to work. Call me later."

Margie brings over our drinks.

"Thanks, love," Finn says.

"It's good to see you're well, Finn," Margie says before heading back to the bar, icier than I've heard from her in a long time.

We sip our drinks and stare into the fire. Margie, bless her, put actual coffee in mine this time. I'm in no mood for making chit chat with this man who's seen me naked, a man I thought I was going to marry.

"What's new?"

I shrug. "Same old, same old."

"How's your da?"

"Fine." Since when did he ever care about my dad? They never got along, not in any of the years we were together.

"I saw your Instagram. Hanging out with big movie stars, huh?"

And now it makes sense. This is why he's here—the movie.

He keeps chattering on. "Miles Casey. Wow. How'd you two meet?"

I sigh. "He's part of the movie shooting at the castle. You must've heard about it."

He flashes me a sheepish smile. "Yeah. Ma told me all about it. Is Natalie Rodriguez really directing? Did you meet her? I heard Ava Garreth is here, too." Finn whistles. "Wow."

I nod and set my coffee down on the table, feeling foolish. For a moment, just a nanosecond really, I thought Finn might actually want to catch up with me. Apologize, make amends. But he just wants to hear about all these fancy schmancy people. I'm about to leave when Miles walks in the door.

* * *

THE LAST THING I want to do is sit here with my ex-boyfriend and my...well, whatever Miles is to me. He's wearing a wool peacoat and a thick scarf, but even with those, he looks absolutely frozen. But when his eyes land on me, his whole face warms, a wide smile slowly spreading across his handsome mug. He walks over. A shadow crosses his features when he sees I'm not alone, but it's gone as fast as a feather on a windy day.

"Miles!" Margie yells out. "I'll get ye some coffee."

"And some breakfast if you don't mind."

Margie waves at him. "No trouble at all."

Finn stands and extends a hand. "I'm Finn McDougall. It's nice to meet you."

The shadow is back. Miles glances my way, so quick I don't know what my face was doing. Miles takes his hand. "Nice to meet you. I'm..."

"Miles Casey," Finn supplies, as if the man had forgotten his own name.

I sink further into my chair. Could the cushions just swallow me up?

"Pull up a chair," Finn says, motioning to Kate's vacated chair.

Miles sits and smiles, but it's not the beaming grin from when he first spotted me.

"How are you this morning, Skye?"

I nod. Uncomfortable. Wishing we were back on the island. "Okay."

We all make idle chit-chat. Talking about the weather, of all things. I swear, is there a more boring topic of conversation than the weather? Miles tucks into his breakfast that Margie brings over, and we listen to the soft music over the speakers. The Beatles' *Abbey Road* this morning.

Then the music shifts, and my stomach drops like I'm on an untrustworthy elevator. Finn's voice carries over the speakers, accompanied by an acoustic guitar.

He's smiling into his coffee, tapping his foot along to the song. I'm surprised by this new, softer direction his music has taken. Before, he was all electric, very influenced by bands like the Sex Pistols and the Buzzcocks. This sounds more like Elliott Smith. What I'm not surprised about is this shameless bit of self-promotion.

"What do you think?" Finn asks me.

I shrug. "It's different from your usual style." I actually really like it, but I don't want to tell him that.

Finn smiles. "Just recorded it right before I left." He turns to Miles. "You like music?"

Miles nods his cheeks full of a large bite of Scotch egg.

"I've been playing nearly my whole life. Still haven't signed with a label. Weighing my options, you know."

Miles swallows his bite. "Ah, yeah. I've heard it's a hard business to break into."

Finn shrugs. "Maybe. Maybe not. What about acting? How'd you get into that?"

Miles shakes his head. "Damned if I know. Just kind of fell in my lap, really, when I was a kid. My brother started acting, and one day they just put me in the movie too."

"Were you at a shoot this morning?" Finn asks, sitting forward in his chair.

Miles nods. "At the loch—well, technically *in* the loch. We were shooting just a little ways up from that spot that you took me, Skye, with the willow tree."

Finn sits back in his chair like Miles slapped him in the face. He looks at me, and the hurt in his eyes is so intense you would think we were still a couple. "You took him to our spot?"

Now who's mad? *Our* spot? I let out a quick breath. "I've been going to that spot since I was a kid. I found it. It's my spot, and I'll take whomever I please there."

Finn shakes his head, and I realize I don't have to sit here and endure this little chat. I shrug on my coat.

Finn reaches a hand out. "Ah, come on. Don't be like that. I didn't mean anything."

"I have an appointment." I give Miles a smile. "I'll see you later."

Finn throws his head back. "I can see your temper is as fiery as ever."

I take my mug to the counter and stride out the door without a look back. I had been hoping to see Miles this morning. We haven't been properly alone in nearly two weeks. But I didn't want to see him like this. Flustered once again by Finn.

I get on my bike and push down the pedals like they personally wronged me. Like they told me that they didn't like my book, or like they tried to claim my secret spot as their own. I ride straight home.

Once upstairs, I soak in the tub, hoping my feelings will drain away with the bathwater, but my bitterness remains well after the water has gone.

I stomp to my laptop. I can use this frustration. Mickey and Sorcha need some tension, and here it is in a neatly packed, sandy-haired, leather coat–wearing package. Enter the ex-boyfriend, Flynn.

My fingers jab at the keys as the plot twist starts to form. Flynn wants Sorcha back. He's realized that he can't live without her. Well, too bad, Flynny boy, because Sorcha's heart belongs to Mickey now.

I freeze, my fingers hovering over the keys. Is that true? In the book, absolutely, but in life, does my heart belong to Miles? Before I have time to fling myself with wild abandon down that rabbit hole, there is a small knock at the door.

Miles is standing in the alcove with a purple flower. I recognize it immediately as one of the violas from Thistle House.

"Pilfering foliage now, are you?"

Miles smiles, and my knees are jelly. "Well, you know—"

I don't let him finish. I'm across the room as fast as my wobbly knees will take me. I shut the door behind him and put my mouth to his. He runs his hands through my hair, and I let out a moan that I don't even recognize.

"Is it safe? Does the door lock?" Miles asks in a husky voice that sends shivers down my spine.

"No" is all I can manage before my mouth is on his again.

He keeps kissing me and walks me backwards to the couch, but we aren't paying attention and run into the piano. We both laugh.

"No, it isn't safe? Or no, it doesn't lock?"

"Either...or both." I bury my head in his neck, kissing the tender spot under his jaw. He maneuvers me around the piano and closer to the couch. "We could be quick."

Miles throws me on the couch and joins me. "Nothing about what I want to do to you involves being quick, but I'll do my best."

* * *

AFTER WE ARE both blissfully satisfied and back in our clothes, we lie on the couch, Miles the big spoon and me the little one tucked into his body tight so we'll both fit. His fingers traipse on my thigh.

"I was hoping to sneak away to that secret room at Thistle House. That's really why I went there, to find you."

"Ah. Sorry I left so suddenly."

"You don't need to apologize. Was that *the* Finn?"

I nod. "It was indeed."

"Does he come back to visit a lot?"

"No." I don't expand on it. What more is there to say? In all these years, he hasn't been back, and now that he is, it's not to see me, or even his ma, as he said it is, but much more likely because he heard a bunch of famous Hollywood people are hanging about.

"I'm glad I found you," Miles says, maybe sensing that I don't want to talk anymore about Finn. "The shoot is going to another location for about a week, maybe more."

My back prickles, and suddenly the couch feels too small for us both. I get up to put another log on the fire, the wood rough under my fingertips. "Oh. Where are you going?"

"Just around Glen Coe and the other side of the loch." Miles sits up, and his face lights up like a kid at Christmas time. "You could come."

I smile because his enthusiasm is adorable, but I shake my head and sit on the rug near the fire. "No, I can't. How exactly would we keep"—I point to me and then to him—"this secret if I'm tagging along with you on shoots?"

"I could hire you."

"Um, no."

Miles laughs. "Not like that. As my dialect coach. They have an extra room booked because Jake was supposed to be here."

"Wouldn't that look suspicious?"

Miles shrugs. "Probably. But who cares?"

Miles joins me on the rug and takes my hand in his. His hands are so large, his fingers long. He intertwines them with mine. "I don't want to not see you for a whole week."

My stomach clenches like I'm preparing to be hit square in the stomach. Because I am. How much longer does the shoot have altogether? I think Miles told me once they were supposed to wrap before Christmas. It's almost December. And we can't even go a week without seeing each other? How's it going to feel when he skips back off to America, back to his LA life with clear blue swimming pools, fancy cocktail parties, and beautiful women literally everywhere he goes?

I take my hand back. "I can't. I have a life here, you know. I can't drop everything just to go watch you work. I need to finish my book, and I have responsibilities." I stand up and go over to my desk to open my laptop.

"I didn't mean..." Miles sighs. "I just thought it might be fun. I know you have a life."

He puts a hand on my shoulder, and I move so that it falls off.

"I'm going to miss you. We leave in the morning. I'll try to find you before then."

I make a noncommittal mmm-hmm.

"Skye, I lo—"

My heart catches in my throat. Is he going to say that he loves me? I will him not to continue. I'll never be able to keep my nerve if he says the L word.

"I'll miss you." He kisses my shoulder and leaves without another word.

This will be good for us. It'll be like a stepping stone to when he actually leaves. Like sipping a light beer after a month-long whiskey bender.

MILES

*S*kye won't look at me when I leave her to her writing. I didn't mean to offend her by suggesting she come with me on the shoot. And I *really* didn't mean to almost say "I love you."

What was I thinking? The words were tumbling out on their own, but I stopped myself. After our agreement on what our relationship is, it wouldn't have been wise. But when has anyone ever accused me of being that? Never.

It was selfish to ask her to come with me on the shoot. I just don't want to be without her for a whole week or possibly more. It's ridiculous, I suppose. At the end of this month, we will have to part ways, and if a week feels like an eternity, what will our final goodbye feel like?

Maybe it doesn't have to be final. We could do long-distance. Or Skye might want to come to LA. Although with how she reacted to a week away from her life, that doesn't seem likely.

My phone buzzes in my hand. It's Jake.

"Jake. How's your leg?"

"It's healing. But I'm so bored. I got the video games you sent, though. They are currently saving my sanity. How's jolly old Scotland?"

"I'm pretty sure they don't call it that."

"How would I know? How's it going anyway?"

I sigh.

"What's going on? That's not a good sigh. That's a *spiraling into dark thoughts*, sigh."

Jake knows me a little too well. "It's nothing, really. I think the picture is going well." I shut the door to my room and plop down on my bed. "It's just some other stuff."

"It's that redhead from the *YHF* photo, isn't it?"

I sit bolt upright. "How'd you know?"

"Lucky guess."

If Jake can guess that from thousands of miles away, how bad a job have I been doing at hiding our relationship from everyone else?

It couldn't hurt to tell Jake, though. He is, after all, very far away and always discreet. Plus, I'm bursting. I have to talk to someone about Skye. She's all I ever want to talk about, and not being able to is eating me from the inside out.

"Okay, yes, it's Skye. The redhead from the photo. We're…" What are we doing? "We're having a fling."

"A…what?"

I pace around my tiny room. "That's what we agreed upon, but that's the problem, really. I think about her all the time. When I'm on my morning run, when I'm on the set, when I close my eyes to sleep at night, she's all I see."

I can practically hear Jake shaking his head on the other line. "That doesn't sound like a fling."

I put Jake on speakerphone and start packing. "No. It doesn't feel like one either. I'll be honest… It feels a lot like love."

"Love, really?"

I nod and then remember this isn't FaceTime. "Yes. I've honestly never felt this way before. I mean, I thought I loved Lana, but she never felt the same way for me. We had a physical relationship, but to her, it didn't go beyond that. It was just me in my respective corner, pining for her. I've had some strong feelings for other women, too, but this is different. It's all-consuming."

"Have you told her how you feel?"

"No. How can I? We were so clear about what this was. Plus, I just invited her to go with me on location at the next place, and she turned me down. She seemed pissed I'd asked. How would long-distance work if she can't leave the castle for even a week? I can't move to Scotland." I pause with a sweater in my hand, hovering above my bag.

Could I move to Scotland? I could fly to any location that was shooting, which 80% of the time is in LA. But no. My mom is in LA. How could I leave her there? Then again, my brother is there too, and my sister, with her three kids and perfect husband, so my mom wouldn't be lonely. She doesn't really need me there. Moving is not an impossible thought.

"Miles? Are you still there?"

"Yes."

"You can't move to Scotland. Has she even asked you to?"

I sit down on the bed, the soft comforter squishing a little extra under the heaviness of my heart. "No."

"Right. You've said you were both very clear that this was supposed to be casual. So you need to keep it light, right? Give it some space. Go on your shoot. Get some distance. Next week, when you come back, it'll all look different."

Jake is probably right.

"Now, have you been doing the workouts I sent you?"

I've been working out, that's for sure, but not with Jake's set routines as much as I should. "A little."

"Let's do some planks right now. Just a couple two-minute holds. No sweat."

* * *

JAKE WAS WRONG. There's a lot of sweat. In fact, by the time I hang up, I'm covered in sweat. I head to the bathroom for a quick rinse off before bed. When I open the door, light is streaming out from under Skye's door. I want to knock, to give her a goodnight kiss, but Jake's words ring in my head. *Give it some space.*

I turn toward the bathroom instead. Maybe while I'm away, she'll realize she can't live without me. And when I get back, we'll figure out how we can make this work for real. I soak in the tub, letting the warm water soothe my sore muscles. And another thought trickles in...

Or maybe we'll both see it really was just a fling.

After the bath, I try to run through the scenes in my head as I drift off to sleep, but I just see Skye's blue eyes staring at me under hooded lashes. Then I try to mentally pick out what I'm going to eat in the morning, but instead, I see Skye's hair falling in her face as she sits on my lap. It goes on like that until finally I drift off picturing Skye with her legs on my lap, her silky calf in my hands at SOWK.

THE MORNING IS FRANTIC. Calling it "morning" is generous. We're leaving while it's still dark so we can shoot at sunrise. I grab a travel mug of coffee, keeping my eyes peeled the whole time for Skye. But she is nowhere to be seen. For once, I might be up before her. I throw my bag in the van and take a seat near the back. I'm in no mood for conversation.

"There you are," Ava says as she climbs in and takes the seat right next to mine. She has a bright-red beanie on and a matching cropped puffer jacket.

"Want to run lines on the way?"

No. I want to stare out the window and pine, to mope, to act like a sullen teenager who has to leave his girlfriend to go on a stupid family vacation. But I'm not a teenager. I'm a full-grown man. Besides, Ava looks so shiny-faced and earnest. I know this film means a lot to her. It could be her first Oscar. It meant a lot to me, too. *Means.*

"Sure," I say.

Blessedly, Ty is in the other van, and so must be Minnie. Why does their relationship bother me so much? I don't want her to get hurt, and Ty bulldozes through everything and everyone in his life. I thought we were really good friends before he stole my part and my girl, all right under my nose, and I had no idea it was happening. None at all. I don't want her to feel like I felt: betrayed and stupid.

"Miles, it's your line," Ava says.

"Ah, sorry."

We pass the rest of the car ride running through our lines, passing the odd farmhouse here and there, dark shapes against murky fields. There's a good long stretch of road where we follow the water, looking like liquid silver in the dim light. The sky is a pearly gray with wisps of pink caressing snowcapped mountains when we pull up to our site. There is a crystal-clear lake perfectly reflecting the hills behind it. The frosted grass crunches underneath my feet. My breath comes out in white clouds so thick it seems like I could say, *Who are you*, and it would be spelled out just like the caterpillar in *Alice in Wonderland*.

I'm not looking forward to the bare thighs my costume requires this morning.

The crew works fast to erect two tents; one for costumes and one for snacks, both with heat lamps connected to a small generator. I head off toward the costume tent, resigned to my fate. The kilt is made of such thick wool; it's not as bad as I feared, and the cold I do feel helps me get into my character a bit more.

This morning is Thora's last scene. When the film is all finished, she'll only be in the first fifteen minutes of the movie, but we haven't been shooting chronologically, and there are some flashbacks featuring her. They saved her character's death for her final scene, though, which seems fitting.

We are both standing on the sidelines, she's wearing a massive coat to keep the chill out, while they set up the lights.

I nudge her with my shoulder. "You ready for the big scene?"

She nods, her face unreadable. "I am."

"What are you going to do after you've wrapped? Are you going to head right back to the States?"

"No. I'm going to stick around for a while. I really love Scotland. I'm thinking about staying."

"Really?" I'm not sure why this surprises me so much. "In Foyers, or are you going to travel?"

Thora smiles, and it lights up her whole face. You can see the younger woman she used to be, not that she isn't still beautiful. I'm not an ageist by any means. Just that it lightens her. "Actually, I've fallen in love with more than just Scotland."

"Come on," Natalie yells. "It's showtime. Let's set up."

As we head to our marks, my head is reeling. Is Thora in love with Callum? I had noticed they were together a lot, but love? It seems like an awfully short amount of time. Then again, who am I to talk? There's something about those Ainslies. Some kind of magic in their eyes. But move to Scotland? Is she going to live in the castle? Does Skye know?

I'm distracted during the shoot, and it's a few takes before I'm fully submerged in the scene. I feel bad about it. It's so cold, Thora's lips are a little blue, despite the expertly applied lipstick.

Once Natalie yells cut, everyone on the shoot is on their feet, clapping. It is a massive standing ovation for Thora. I join in. She is a true talent. She smiles, her cheeks pink, and gives everyone an exaggerated bow.

I offer her my arm as we both head to the costume tent to warm up. "Sorry about the extra takes. My mind was in the clouds."

She shrugs. "It happens. You're a wonderful actor. I'm sure we got a good one."

The thought of her packing up and moving her whole life to Scotland is still bothering me. "Will you keep acting? If you move here, I mean?"

Thora tilts her head to one side and then the other, as if rolling the question around in her head. "It is my greatest passion. But maybe it's time I explore some new passions in my life. I might try to write my memoir. Or I've thought about trying my hand at cooking, maybe making my own version of what Florence Pugh did on TikTok, *Golden Girls* style, obviously. Have you seen her little cooking bits?"

I shake my head. "TikTok only shows me videos of the North Sea at the moment. It's all raging tides, whirlpools, and pirate dirges."

"Well, the little cooking bits are delightful. I was thinking I could do a longer-form version of learning to cook at the ripe old age of, well, no need for exact numbers, but you get the point. If the right role came along, though, I would snatch it up in a heartbeat."

I nod, amazed by her bravery to try something new. I started acting as a kid. It's all I know, but is it my greatest passion? And if it's not, then what am I doing clinging on to it like it's a life raft in the North Sea?

SKYE

*I*t's been nine days. Miles has been gone for nine days. We've texted a little, but not much. The reception where they are is spotty. And honestly, I haven't been quick to respond. If I let the texts sit unanswered, maybe I won't miss him so much. I can fool myself into being okay with this. Like tapering off contact will make it easier.

He offered for me to visit again. But I can't. They are staying in a small group of cottages all next to each other. How would we sneak around when everyone else is so close? Anyway, I need to finish this book.

In fact, I'm at my laptop right now, killing time until I need to leave for my writing critique group, but the words aren't coming. I got here an hour early to try to get some writing done, since this morning I wrote a whopping one-hundred and thirty-seven words. And also because I didn't want to stay at dinner any longer.

Thora came back a week ago, and tonight she and my father made dinner together.

"Isn't the roast great?" Dad asked, kicking my foot under the table.

Truth be told, it was dry. Very dry.

I smiled. "It's great."

Dad and Thora kept exchanging these looks the whole meal. They had little in-jokes too that didn't make a lick of sense to me, but made Thora giggle. I excused myself after what to me seemed an acceptable amount of time. It's not that I'm against my father dating, if that's what they're doing. But where could it go? Thora lives in LA. Dad lives here. A familiar problem, for sure, but not mine this time.

I thought I'd get more done with the production crew leaving—a quiet castle, no interruptions. But that is definitely not the case. It's like the muse accepted Miles's invitation, packed up, and left with him. The hussy.

I could visit him. What would be the harm?

It's a dry night, so I opt to ride to Thistle House for our meeting. The night swallows me in its cool embrace, the wind in my face refreshing. I didn't give myself enough time, so I'm ten minutes late.

"There she is!" Bella says and claps her hands together as I walk through the door, shrugging off my coat.

Gabby's face is a little pinched, but it always is. It's probably not from my tardiness. Hopefully.

"Sorry I'm late."

Kate hands me a whiskey she had waiting for me with a smile. "What were you getting up to?"

I blush, even though I absolutely wasn't fooling around since Miles isn't even in town.

Gabby smiles. "Ah, yes, probably just furiously typing away."

I laugh. "Not hardly."

"Oh, don't be so modest," Bella says. "You've nearly written a whole novel in…when did you start it again?"

"The beginning of September." When Miles first came here. It feels like a lifetime ago.

I take a seat, settling into the cushions. We talk about Bella's work first. Her killer needs a better motivation to be believable. Right now, the motive is protecting a long-held family recipe for mincemeat pie, and Gabby, Kate, and I agree, we're not sure that's murder worthy.

We talk about Gabby's manuscript. It's flawless, as per usual. She's going to send it out in the new year, since most of publishing takes the holidays off.

Then we come to my pages. They've read all I've written so far. I'm about sixty percent through my manuscript.

Gabby clears her throat. "I'm curious how much of this is... well... autobiographical?"

Kate bites her lip, not saying a word. She's the only one who knows about Miles and me.

I freeze, quite literally, with my whiskey glass halfway to my mouth. "What makes you ask, out of curiosity?"

"I follow your IG account, and back in September, you were tagged in *YHF*'s post. You were walking with Miles Casey. And I noticed in the pages, there are a few times early on, where Mickey is spelled M-L-E-S."

Bella covers her mouth, her eyes wide.

Shit. Find and replace does not replace typos.

"I was just curious. Is Mickey really Miles Casey, and are you Sorcha?"

Gabby is an excellent mystery writer and clearly an excellent detective as well.

I sigh. "Is it really that obvious?"

Bella is shaking her head, but Gabby says, "Yes."

Kate pipes up, "I swear I didn't say anything!"

"I didn't know," Bella insists as she pours more wine into her glass. "But I'm also not on social media. Good Lord, Skye! Are you really dating Miles Casey?"

The whole thing comes spilling out. I tell them all about our romance, sparing the spicy details. Why, I'm not sure, since they've already read about most of them, all exaggerated, I assure them.

Truly, most of them are shockingly accurate...

Gabby is sitting with her drink to her lips, her expression very thoughtful.

Bella is absolutely thrilled.

I pick up my whiskey and take a sip, focusing on the cool glass under my palm and the caramel notes on my tongue, trying not to guess what they might be thinking. I've known these women long enough to know sometimes they all need a minute to process before speaking.

Staring at my glass, the fire dancing behind it as I wait, I end up just staring at my own reflection. It startles me how much I look like my mother in the shiny surface.

Kate clears her throat, pulling me back to the present. "Has Miles read it?"

My stomach churns. I set my wine down, the taste of it heavy on my tongue. Has Miles read it? No. Absolutely not. Hopefully, he never will. But if Bella and Gabby could figure out it was Miles, and Elsie could tell, will it be obvious to everyone? No. They all just know me—well, Elsie doesn't really. Shit.

"Skye?" Gabby says.

"No. He hasn't read it. What if I changed his name to Ben?"

Bella is nodding, but Gabby is shaking her head. "You paint such a vivid picture of him. You describe his face, his body. He's an actor. He was in a teeny bopper football movie. You would need to change more than his name."

My heart sinks into my slippers. Am I going to have to scrap this whole manuscript? I've put so many of my other books to bed. Set them aside after revising going in circles, or a stiff rejection. On to the next shiny new project. But this book is so close to my heart. I can feel the heft of the words on the page. They are like a calming weighted blanket to me. I can't lock this one away. I can't.

Bella sits up, sloshing her wine a little on the floor as she does. "Just ask for his permission. I'm sure he will agree. It'll be grand."

Kate is nodding. "You said he invited you on location, right?"

I nod.

"A drop-dead sexy man has invited you *on location*? What are you still doing chatting with us? You can take some pages and talk to him about it when you aren't otherwise engaged." Bella winks in an exaggerated manner.

The timer dings from Gabby's phone. Always the timekeeper. Gabby and Bella take off first, leaving Kate and me to finish our whiskeys.

"What is stopping you? Why not join Miles on set?"

"What if he changed his mind?"

"He didn't."

I roll my glass in my hands, not able to meet her eyes. "What if he breaks my heart?"

Kate gently touches my chin, our eyes meeting. "At least it will be getting some good use."

I glance over at the bar where Tommy is sitting, staring at us—well, Kate more accurately. "You're one to talk."

She sighs. "I'll go talk to Tommy if you go talk to Miles."

I smile. What am I waiting for? "It's a deal."

Hopping on my bike, I decide I don't even have to show him the pages if it doesn't feel right. Either way, I would get to see him, kiss him, and snuggle in his arms.

That's it, I'm going.

Once home, I open my laptop back up and print out what I have of the manuscript so far, then head to my room to pack. I'm so focused on my task that I nearly run right into my dad.

"Whoa!"

"Sorry, Dad. I'm going on a little trip. Would you mind feeding the chickens?"

I don't wait for his answer; I just continue to my room to pack. I need to go now if I want to get there at any kind of decent hour.

Dad follows me. "Can you go tomorrow? I can feed the chickens, that's no problem. It's just...I'd like to talk to you."

Dad's face is red, and he looks flustered. My dad is never flustered.

I stop walking. "Is everything all right? Are you okay?"

NC BARTON

He laughs. "I'm grand. Oh, pet, look at your face." He smooths the wrinkle between my brows. "I'm great."

"Can we talk now?"

"I'd really like to talk to you over a proper dinner."

"Of course."

He smiles and gives my shoulder a pat. I can leave for Glen Coe after dinner tomorrow. What's one more night?

* * *

THE WRITING in the morning comes like a defective faucet in dribbles and spurts, but I end up with two hundred words, and after the last few days, I take it as a win.

I pack in the afternoon, making sure my manuscript pages are tucked away in the inside pocket of my messenger bag, and toy with the idea of texting Miles to let him know I'm coming. But a surprise would be better. I picture his face as he opens the door to his little cabin, shirtless obviously, because this is my fantasy, and he can wear whatever I imagine. He beams and picks me up, swinging me around the room until we land on the bed—both of us suddenly with no clothes.

The day takes ages to pass by. I fiddle around with the piano, trying to work out the song that seems to always be stuck in my head now. "Somewhere Only We Know." Our song. I make a playlist on my phone for the drive later that I title "To Miles."

When dinner finally does come, I'm surprised to see the table is elegantly set, but Thora is nowhere to be seen. I thought they both wanted to talk to me, and I'm a little ashamed of how thrilled I am that it's just my father and me.

Dad's made a beef stew. The smell of sage and the freshly made loaf of bread has my mouth watering. I sit. After a few minutes, Dad joins me, coming in with a bottle of red wine.

He pours us each a glass and raises his. "A toast."

I raise mine as well. "Cheers."

He mashes his lips together like he's getting the feel for a new coat of gloss. It's his tell. He always does it when he's nervous. "To new beginnings."

New beginnings? What's so grand about new beginnings anyway? When Finn got his new start in America, it was the end of us. When Mom took on her new role as a full-time mom and housewife, it meant the end of her singing career. What will this "new beginning" be the end of?

I clink my glass and change the toast, saying, "Slàinte *mhath*."

Nothing wrong with a little tradition, a little familiarity.

We both drink and tuck into our stew in a comfortable silence. Or what would normally be comfortable, but with the mystery conversation looming over us, it feels like a too-snug pair of pants—not unbearable, but you tell yourself to eat a little less supper tomorrow.

Dad sets down his spoon, takes a long sip of his wine, and then sets that carefully down too. He smashes his lips together. I hold in a sigh. Here it is. Whatever he's been gearing up to. "Skye. Something quite unexpected has happened."

I fiddle with the stem of my wineglass.

"I'll just come out with it. I've fallen in love. With Thora."

I nearly knock over my wine. I knew they had been flirting, but *love*?

"And we've talked about it, and if it's alright with you, well, we'd like it if Thora could move in."

I stand up. "You want to move in together? You've only known her for a couple of months!"

He stands too. "When you know, you know. We're both in our sixties. Why wait?"

My heart is filled with panic, and I don't completely understand why. My mother's been gone for years. I want my father to be happy, so why do I feel this fluttery feeling like I'm about to lose something? Thora seems lovely, but will she stay, or will she set sail after a few months for Hollywood and leave my father brokenhearted and more alone than before she came? "What about her acting?"

"She might travel if a really good film comes up, but she wants to explore other things for now."

"Other things?" But for how long? What if she decides she's had enough of drafty castle life and takes my father with her? What if they want me to be the caretaker indefinitely? I can't. I love this place, but I can't be tied to this castle alone for the rest of my life.

I shake my head. I don't know what to say. "Dad, this is just a lot to take in."

My father's eyes are deeply concerned. "I know, pet."

I cross my arms tightly over my chest, trying to hold myself together the best I can. The look on my father's face threatens to break me. I swallow back my tears like a good stiff shot. Ah, what I wouldn't give for one of those right about now. "It's just…is she really going to be happy here, giving up her acting? Or will it be like Mom with her singing, always wishing she chose the other path?"

Dad steps back, his face wounded but resolute. "I'm not asking Thora to give anything up, just like I didn't ask your mother."

"I know you didn't ask. But she did. And now Thora is. And what if this time she goes back to her old life? I don't want to see you get hurt."

Dad sighs. "It's a risk we all take for love. About your mother, though—"

I blink back tears. "I need a minute."

Heading upstairs, I shut my door with careful, measured movements, my head swimming. This is unbelievable. My father is in love. How can he be so brave about it, after the heartache of losing Mom? Marching right into fire to pursue it. And Thora is willing to leave her career. I pace the room. What have I ever been willing to risk? After about twenty minutes, I'm still pacing and no closer to any answers. There is a small knock at the door.

"Pet. I know you don't want to talk to me, and that's fine. But I have something for you."

I don't respond.

Dad keeps going anyway. "It's from your mother."

I open the door and cross my arms. He's holding a bright-red journal.

"What you said about her giving up her singing career. It wasn't like that. Well, I should let her explain. This is your mother's diary from when she was pregnant with you. I probably should've given it to you a long time ago, but your mother always meant to give it to you when you were pregnant with your own wee bairn. So, I was waiting… but I think you should read it. If you want. The page I've bookmarked, I thought might clear some things up for you. I had no idea you thought that."

I snatch the journal and hug it to me, crossing my arms tightly again. It feels as if I loosen my grip, my heart will literally fall out.

"Read it if you want. This is your home too, so if you're not comfortable with Thora moving in, I can let her know. Just take some time to think about it, okay?"

"It's not that, Dad. I just…"

He places a gentle hand on my arm. "It's a big decision. Let's all take a beat to think about it."

I nod. "I'm still going to go on that trip, just for a couple days."

"Aye. Take as much time and space as you need. I'll feed the damn chickens." He gives my shoulder a small squeeze as he heads down the hall.

I open the journal. My mother's familiar looping script is scrawled across the page, and I can't fight it anymore. A sob rips through my torso. I close the book quickly, not wanting any tears to land on the pages.

I hold the journal close to me as I gather my things. Then I place it carefully in my shoulder bag, put on my coat, and head out to the Land Rover.

* * *

THE RAIN LASHES at the window, my wipers struggling to keep up. My "To Miles" playlist strums softly over the speakers, but I hardly even register a song. My thoughts are tucked firmly in that journal as snugly as the red ribbon bookmark my dad placed on the page he wants me to read. As if I need a bookmark. I'll read the whole thing, over and over, until the words are tattooed on my eyes. I'll be able to close my eyelids softly and reread them at my leisure.

Part of me wants to pull over right now and read it cover to cover. But I'm torn. The other part thinks I should save some, not spend it all at once. I keep going back and forth. Spend it, save it. Spend it, save it. I've landed on spending it. Gobble up all of it at once like a starving man finally sitting down for a fish dinner.

Shimmering eyes and massive antlers pull me back to the present with a jolt. A red deer is standing in the middle of the road. I swerve, and an enormous pop echoes through the night, sending the deer sprinting away. The Land Rover skids off the slick asphalt, the steering impossible to handle, as I head straight for a ditch.

MILES

C/M e: I miss your eyes...

Trying to speak from the heart without sounding too cheesy, I type some more words. I reread my text to Skye before hitting send. I don't have any service to speak of out here, so there's no hurry anyway. It probably won't go through till we're wrapped for the day and back at the cabins.

We're out in the middle of nowhere, a huge snowcapped mountain with a waterfall rushing down it in the distance. There's a charming path of boulders dotted through a stream and then a pebble path beyond through long golden grass leading all the way to the falls. It's so beautiful; it looks like it's been painted.

I read the text again. Is it too sappy? I'm not a writer, but I thought she might appreciate it if I were a little poetic. A sonnet in text form. I don't know, though. I keep sending these long, drawn-out texts, pouring my heart out, and she sends one or two words back hours and hours later. Or sometimes even a GIF. I don't expect her to sit around miserable and missing me, but a little pining might be nice.

"Ooh. Who are you texting?"

Elsie sits in the director's chair next to me. I pocket my phone and smile. "No one."

"Sure. Tell her I say hello." Elsie smiles. "You ready?"

"As I'll ever be."

My big fight scene with Ty is today. The fight coordinator has run through all the moves with both of us several times.

Ty has a monologue they're going to shoot beforehand. They're setting that up now.

Elsie smiles at me. "Are you excited that you get to knock Ty out? I wrote that in especially for you. You're welcome, by the way."

I laugh. Honestly, I haven't thought about it much. I've been too busy missing Skye and trying to figure out what my passion is. Is it still acting? If someone had asked me a couple of months ago, I wouldn't have hesitated to say yes. But now, I'm not so sure.

Ty walks out of the costume tent. "I'm here! Let the fun begin."

The light guys laugh. A couple beats after Ty comes out, Minnie follows, buttoning up her shirt with a quick hand. I look away. It is not my business. Grown adults.

Ty and Natalie are talking low, their heads almost touching. A car drives up as close as the vehicles can get to where we are. Out steps a woman with a button nose, long blonde hair, and even longer legs. She is wearing black leggings and a Prada puffer jacket. She walks over confidently to where we all are.

For a moment, Ty's eyes look scared, but he recovers quickly. "Charlotte!"

She waves.

Ty runs, picks her up, swings her around, and then dips her before planting a sloppy kiss on her mouth.

My eyes find Minnie. She's frozen, holding two coffees, her lips in a tight set line. She starts to move as Ty and Charlotte keep kissing, PDA be damned. Minnie thrusts the coffee at Elsie.

"Oh, Minnie," Elsie whispers.

Minnie shakes her head, tears forming in the corner of her eyes. She turns and heads back to the craft services tent.

Ty leads Charlotte over to the empty director's chair right next to me.

"Hey, Elsie. Miles. I'd like you to meet my girlfriend—"

Charlotte waves her long fingers, heavy with a massive diamond ring, in our direction. "Fiancée."

Ty grins, but it's tight. Not his usual easy-going, *I'm just a laid-back guy* smile. "Right, fiancée, Charlotte. Char, this is Miles and our indispensable screenwriter, Elsie."

Fiancée? Ty has been leading Minnie on this whole time when he is engaged? The pain of this hits me hard and swift, like a splinter that slides right under a thumbnail. Too hard for it to reasonably be only about Minnie. Even I can see that.

I clench my jaw to keep from saying anything I don't mean to.

"It is so nice to meet you both," Charlotte says with a light southern twang. She takes the empty seat right next to me, and without thinking, I shift my body slightly away. Ty plants a light kiss on her cheek and heads back to his mark.

Charlotte stretches out, resting both elbows on the armrests and making it impossible for me to take any more space unless I physically move my chair away.

"Miles Casey." She shakes her head. "I'm a huge fan. I loved you in *The Last Candle*."

Of course, she loved *The Last Candle*. It was an indie film I made in my late teens, and it made the small awards circuit. There was a buzz of Oscar talk, but no nominations. I say, "Thanks."

"I mean it. That performance moved me so much. It literally changed me as a person. It's why I got into acting."

"Oh, are you an actor?"

"I'm a model. I just got into acting a couple of months ago. Elsie, you should write me a great role like the female lead in *Swipe* or like Ava's in this movie or something and put me on the map."

Elsie giggles uncomfortably, still holding the two coffees Minnie handed her before she ran off. Elsie thrusts one at me. Charlotte perks up. "Ooh, coffee. I'd love one. It's freezing out here."

Minnie walks by with a steaming cup, beelining it to Natalie. One of these coffees had probably been for her in the first place. She's not even looking in our direction, her eyes solely focused ahead, her mouth set in a grim line, her cheeks splotchy like she's been crying. On her way back from handing off the cup, Charlotte grabs her arm. "Excuse me… Do you think you could get me one of those coffees?"

Minnie nods, looking down at the ground the whole time.

"And a blanket if it's not too much trouble?" Charlotte looks toward us. "Y'all got blankets out here for while you're waiting or watching, I guess?"

Elsie shakes her head like she's watching a car crash. It seems I'm not the only one who knew about Minnie and Ty. "I…uh…I'm not sure."

Minnie says in a small voice, barely above a whisper, "I'll see what I can find."

"Oh, honey," Charlotte says, patting Minnie's arm. "You gotta learn to speak up if you ever want to be heard. Women gotta speak twice as loud. You know what I'm saying? Otherwise, people'll just walk all over you."

Minnie makes eye contact with Charlotte now, and if looks could set someone on fire, that one would for sure. She nods and leaves.

"Sweet kid." Charlotte smiles. She seems pleased with herself for having imparted some wisdom to this young girl in the industry. I'm sure she means well. That's when it dawns on me that Minnie is not the only one betrayed here.

* * *

Ty's monologue is on the sixth take when I head to get for more coffee. I'm about to enter when I hear a soft sniffle coming from behind the tent. I follow the noise and find Minnie, her arms wrapped tightly around herself, tears rolling down her face.

She quickly wipes them away when she sees me. "You were right about him."

"Minnie." I hold out my arms to hug her, but she shakes her head. "I didn't want to be right. I'm so sorry. Is there anything I can do?"

"No." She stands a little straighter. "I'm fine, really. I'm going to get that horrible woman a blanket, even if I have to knit it myself."

I put a hand on her shoulder. "I'll find her something. Why don't you go take a break? Maybe you could head back to the cabins for the day? I can let Natalie know you weren't feeling well."

"Really? You think it would be okay?"

I nod and find another member of the crew, ask him to drive Minnie back to the cabins, and he agrees. While I'm at it, I also ask him to grab a blanket, even though I shouldn't care if Charlotte freezes. Although she didn't do anything wrong. This whole mess is Ty's fault. He hasn't changed at all—still using people, destroying everything in his path.

Ty's monologue calls for thirteen takes. Natalie clearly isn't the superstitious type. I've known some directors who would do one more take just to not end on thirteen. But not her. I hate to admit it, but that last take was really something special. He might get a supporting actor nod out of this whole thing.

The afternoon is a mix of gray and gold, the clouds dark, the opening in between shining brighter as if to make up for it. We don't have much daylight left today. Around here, the sun sets before four p.m. these days. And I thought the days were short during winter in Brooklyn.

The PA is back with a blanket for Charlotte. "Oh, thanks, hon. You know, I never did get a coffee."

After all this time, why hasn't she just gone and gotten her own damn coffee? No one else is being waited on hand and foot. How can Ty choose this self-absorbed princess over Minnie?

I find my mark for the fight scene, still seething about how careless Ty is with people. Natalie's words from the beginning of the production echo in my head: *Make it work for you.*

Ty gets to his mark after a quick costume adjustment. He gives me a wink—an honest-to-God wink. "Ready for this, old man?"

Old man? He's only like a year younger than me. Rage is bubbling its way up to my brain. "As ready as I'll ever be."

The fight is supposed to start with me punching Ty in the face—fake, of course. Then he punches me in the stomach. We grapple, wrestle on the ground, and roll into the water. There is a moment where my character debates holding his brother under, but he can't do it. He lets up, and then Ty is sucked out into the water by a massive dark mass, waves of water in their wake. I go after him and pull him back to shore.

This will be the last scene of the day since we'll be freezing, and exhausted afterward. I suggest we film it in two sections: the wet part and the dry part, but Natalie wants it all as one take. From the very first call of *action*, it all goes wrong. I punch the air near Ty's face, but it's too far away to look realistic. We reset after a costume change into dry clothes. Ty gets closer for the next take. I pull my arm back and bring it forward, focusing on channeling my anger at Ty into my expression. My foot slips a little, bringing me even closer, and my fist connects with Ty's cheek in a sickening and, if I'm being totally honest, satisfying smack.

Ty immediately falls to the ground, clutching his face, and any satisfaction I momentarily felt dissipates in the reality of the situation.

Oh shit.

I hit Ty in the face.

I leap toward him. "Are you okay?"

Ty backs away, scooching on the ground like I might hit him again. "Get the fuck away from me."

The medics swarm around Ty like ants to a fallen crumb.

"You did that on purpose."

Natalie is over by us now. "Are you okay?"

Charlotte joins the group. She kneels next to Ty, practically shoving one of the medics out of the way. "Oh, baby. Your face."

Ty ignores her, stands, and speaks directly to Natalie. "First he throws coffee at me…" I try to protest, but Ty is too loud. "Now he hit me on purpose. He's had a grudge against me this whole time. I can't work with him."

Natalie takes a quick breath. "Ty, it looked like an honest accident."

"It was an accident, I swear." My limbs feel heavy. I know it was an accident, but even I can admit it doesn't seem like it.

"He needs to be replaced." Ty points his finger at me. "And he's been sleeping with the host's daughter. I've seen them sneaking around."

My stomach drops to my toes like I'm in a free fall. Everything slows down. Everyone looks at me, even the medics. Natalie's eyes are like a wounded animal, then, in an instant, go ice hard.

I shake my head, but is there really any use in denying it? It's not like I've broken any contract. But I did break a promise, and it's written all over Natalie's face what that means.

Ty holds the ice from the medics to his cheek. "Either he goes, or I go."

* * *

WE WRAP for the day and all head back. I feel awful, so instead of heading straight for my cabin, I walk to the little pub nearby. After buying the best bottle of Scotch they have, I bring it to Ty's cabin and knock, but there is no answer. Searching my pockets, I find a pen and a scrap of paper.

Didn't mean to hit you. It was an accident, I swear. Hope this helps.

Leaving the note and the whiskey on the porch, I head back to the pub. I drown my sorrows in a whiskey, and then another, and another. It's not like this is the only time anyone has ever accidentally gotten hurt on set. On *The Princess Bride* set, Mandy Patinkin bruised a rib holding in his laughter during the Miracle Max scene. It's not like he threatened to quit if Billy Crystal wasn't fired. Harrison Ford hit Ryan Gosling on *Blade Runner*, and they all laughed about it on *The Graham Norton Show*. Me hitting Ty a simple accident, wasn't it?

My text to Skye says delivered, but it doesn't show that it was read. She's probably busy writing or biking—well, maybe not in the dark. She could be meeting with her writing group. No, that would've been yesterday. Honestly, it doesn't matter what she's doing. In a couple weeks, maybe sooner now, I'll never know what she's doing. She'll be here, and I'll be back in LA.

I order one more whiskey and swish this thought around like the amber liquid in the glass.

Skye was completely upfront about just wanting something casual —a fling. I can't pout, because that's exactly what we ended up with. Of course she doesn't want to be with me; I've been like a love-sick puppy, dropping everything to spend more time with her and not focusing enough on the film or my career. What little of one I have left.

I stumble back to my cabin, a candle burning in the window. That wasn't very safe of me to leave that burning. Did I leave it like that all day?

When I open the door to my little studio bungalow, I notice right away there is a lump in the bed, the blankets moving rhythmically up and down with each of their heavy breaths.

SKYE

loody hell. Once the car stops (snugly in a ditch, but stopped), I get out to see what happened. When I swerved in the road, I must've run over something. My front left tire is as flat as a pancake and no longer straight like the other wheels, but at an odd angle. I take a deep breath and mean to let it out in one calming gust, but what comes out instead as I stare at my demolished tire in the dark night and feel the first fat rain drop of many to be sure, is a primal rage-filled scream.

As I get back in the car, the rain really starts to come down, the sound echoing on the metal of the roof. At least it's not snow…yet. Even if I changed the tire, with it bent that odd way, I couldn't drive it anywhere. My phone has absolutely no service and two missed texts. The first is from Dad.

Dad: Drive safe, pet.

Ha! Too late for that advice, Dad. The second is from Miles.

Miles: I miss your eyes. The first time I saw them, I thought they looked like the sky on a sunny day on a tropical island, and now I know they are the sun itself. I miss their warmth upon me.

Tears spring to the corner of my eyes as I read and reread it. And he says he's not the writer. I miss him too. More than I'd like to admit. I miss his hands on me. I miss his laugh. I miss his eyes when they light up with an idea. This will be what our relationship is like if we keep seeing each other after he goes back to America—just a bunch of words on the screen and an ever-present longing.

Headlights are coming down the road, startling me out of my thoughts. I hop out of the Land Rover, throw my bag on my shoulder, and wave, jumping up and down like a mad thing. The car, a white sedan with a prominent dent on the side, mercifully slows to a stop. I've seen this car and that dent before.

The window rolls down, and Finn leans over. "What are you doing out here jumping like a nutter?"

Because I am a nutter, I think, but just shake my head, water droplets flying out of my hair.

"Get in."

I do. What choice do I have?

"Thanks."

He nods, his blond hair falling over his eye. "What are you doing out here?"

I tell him about the deer and the flat tire. He gets out, braving the downpour, his phone out with the little flashlight on. After a few minutes, he gets back in the car with a shiver. "Yeah, it's properly fucked."

I nod.

"You're lucky I came by. You might have been stuck out here all night. Where are you going?"

Should I just ask him to take me back home? But he was headed the opposite way, and I'm probably only about half an hour from the address Miles sent me when he was trying to convince me to come. Maybe an hour.

I fish out the page I printed out from the holiday park's website and hand it to Finn. "I'm headed here, but you can take me home if that's the way you're headed."

"Nah, this isn't too far out of my way."

Relief washes over me so completely that it feels like dunking my head under in a warm bath. "Thanks."

He pulls back out on the road, the windshield wipers struggling to keep up.

"Where are you going this fine evening?"

Finn laughs, the booming sound filling the small car, his mom's car. It reminds me of when we were kids and used to ride around in this heap for hours playing an old Sonic Youth cassette tape and looking for adventure or trouble, whichever we could find. I was in the car when he put that dent in it, trying to park a little too close to a pole. "Fine evening indeed. Can't say I've missed the weather here, that's for sure. In Brooklyn, when it rains, it's a whoosh all at once, a couple of minutes, and then it's over. Sunny skies again. Not like this constant dirge."

I bristle at this. It's one thing for me to complain or joke about the weather. I love it here. When Finn does it, it feels like a slight. "Well, we can't all be Brooklyn."

Finn smiles like I was joking. "I'm going to an old buddy's gig at Grog and Gruel. You could come with if you want? He's putting me up after the show. I actually stayed with him for a couple of weeks when I first arrived. Wasn't quite ready to face everybody. You, anyway."

There is an awkward silence. I don't know what to say to that, and his cheeks are pink as a fresh rose.

He keeps talking. "I'm sure there would be room for you to stay the night, too. It's Nate Haggarty. Remember him?"

I smile. "Ah, Nate. I haven't seen him in an age."

"Want to come?"

I shake my head.

"Who are you off to see, then?"

I falter, "Um...I..."

Finn laughs again. "It's alright. It's none of my business anyway."

I nod, and we're quiet for a moment. The silence is heavy with unsaid things. For the life of me, I can't think of one small-talk type of topic. The only thing that comes to mind is *Why did you ghost me when I needed you the most?* But I can't say that. The answer wouldn't even matter.

It's like Finn can read my thoughts. He fiddles with the heat, putting it on full blast, and then says, "I'm sorry."

He's so quiet, I can hardly hear him over the whoosh from the vents. "Sorry?"

Finn nods. "I should've called when I heard your mom died. I should've been there for you."

It's so unexpected, I don't know what to say. I know I'm supposed to say *that's okay*, or *don't worry*, but I can't. It wasn't okay. "Why didn't you?"

Finn runs a hand through his hair. "It was hard the first few years in New York. I was broke as fuck. The band wasn't going well. I was afraid that if I talked to you, I'd come running back home, and I wasn't ready to give up my dream."

Finn turns down the dirt road, thick with trees on either side.

"I wasn't asking you to give up your dream or to come home, even."

"Aye. I see that now. And my dreams have...not changed, exactly, but shifted. I'm moving back."

My mouth falls open. "Moving back, for good?"

Finn nods. "That's the plan. And I was really hoping you would forgive me and that you might want to hang out a bit?"

The holiday park comes into view with two neat rows of cabins on either side of the road, lit by their dim porch lights, some with glowing windows.

Finn stops the car and looks at me with his blue eyes glistening in the dim light. He takes my hand. "Please forgive me, Skye."

I take my hand back and clutch my bag to my chest. "I have to go."

Finn blows out a small breath. "You sure you're going to be alright here?"

I nod.

"If you need a ride back, just call. I promise I'll answer. I'll always answer from now on."

I don't know what to say, but part of me wants to yell *too little too late*, and the other part wants to call right now just to try it out. Just to have Finn be there for me. A rewrite of history. But you can't rewrite history. I get out of the car without another word.

"Take care," Finn says after me.

* * *

FINN SWINGS HIS CAR AROUND, coming very close to hitting one of the cabin's little porches, still a terrible driver. It seems some things never change. I'm reeling from his apology. Never in a million years did I expect him to come back, let alone hear the words *I'm sorry* from him. Accountability was never Finn's strong suit. Even when he made that dent in his mom's car, he told her he came back from the shop and it was like that. But I guess we all grow up. What exactly did he mean by *hang out*? Does he want to *date*?

Not that it matters what he wants. It's absolutely not what I want anymore. I'm here to see Miles. I check our text thread for his cabin number. Cabin eleven. I walk past one, then three, odd numbers on one side and even on the other. It's late, so I climb the porch stairs to eleven at almost tiptoe, but then notice all the lights are on inside. I can just make out Miles's shadow in the window. He's pacing back and forth and probably running lines. Even though he says he's been more distracted on this film, he works so hard, and he's equally as hard on himself about it. I think it's one of the things we share—our persistence in the process, me with my writing and him with his acting.

I pause for a moment, watching him, when another shadow passes in front of the window, a distinctly female shadow. My hand flies to my mouth to muffle my cry of outrage. I creep a little closer on the porch, feeling like I'm moving through molasses. Time slows as I peek through the small opening in the curtain.

Miles is in his jeans—the tight black ones that make me crazy—and no shirt, shaking his head. The female figure comes into view and grabs his hands. It's Ava, in red satin shorts and a nearly see-through white tank top that hardly comes down past her taut belly. She grabs his hand and leans her face up to his. There is a scratch on his chin. From shaving? Or from her?

My stomach seizes as if from a physical blow. But no matter how hard I clench, it'll never be as flat as Ava's. I want to cry, but not here.

How long have they been seeing each other? Have they been together the whole time we have? Late-night shoots... Were they really late nights caressing Ava? And their runs together every morning. Were they stopping in hidden places? Was she giving him a diddy ride amongst the trees? I know Miles and I said it was just a fling, but I just never thought he was sleeping around. We never discussed monogamy. I just assumed.

I turn to leave, my bag swinging and hitting the house on the way with a thud. The door opens behind me, the creaking hinges as loud as a scream in the quiet night. I keep going.

"Skye. Wait."

I stop but don't turn around. I can't look into his eyes now. I'll break like that record carelessly yanked off the shelf by another American.

"Skye, it's not what it looks like."

I wave my hand. "It's fine." *It's not fine.* "I should've texted." *It was supposed to be a sexy surprise.* "I didn't know you'd be busy." *I didn't know you were sleeping with your co-worker.* "It's not a big deal." *There has never been a bigger deal in the history of deals.*

"Not a big deal?" I turn now, and Miles's perfect lips are in a frown, his brow creased.

"Yeah. We never said this was exclusive. The only promise we made to each other was to keep it light. You're free to see whoever you like, however you like." My words come out so calm and measured, I'm thoroughly impressed with myself. Miles isn't the only actor on this porch.

Miles crosses his arms over his bare chest. It's freezing out here. He must be cold, but his eyes are focused on me. "Have you been… I mean… Are you seeing someone else?"

I want to say no, that there is absolutely no room in my heart for anyone else, but how pathetic is that when he's clearly sold the cow and is still sippin' the milk. I could tell him I have been seeing some-one, level the playing field. He'll feel better. I'll save face. But I can't bring myself to lie to him outright. So, I just shrug, like that stupid *I don't know* emoji.

Miles nods. "Is that why you hardly respond to my texts? Is that why you never want to FaceTime?"

My stomach finally unclenches and is immediately filled with fire. "Your texts? I've responded to every single text you've sent."

He shakes his head. "Not the last one."

"I was on the road, coming to see you."

He lets out a long breath. "When you do respond, it feels like you're doing it out of obligation. Not like you really want to talk to me. Did you even miss me at all?"

My face is numb with shock, or possibly the absolutely Baltic air. My hands lose their grip on my bag, and it slips off my shoulder, all of its contents spilling onto the deck, some skidding off the side and into the bushes. Is Miles really going to stand here, half-naked on his porch, with an equally half-naked woman in his cabin, and accuse me of not being interested in him?

Light snowflakes start to fall. One flutters in the wind and lands on Miles's bare shoulder. In an alternate reality, I would kiss the spot it landed, melt it with my mouth. If I hadn't gotten a flat or if I'd left yesterday like I wanted to, maybe Ava wouldn't have been here, and I would've never known he was sleeping with both of us. My *Sliding Doors* moment. Maybe after this, I'll get a jaunty haircut and meet a witty man on the tube. No tube around here, though, so fat chance, and my hair would never lie flat like Gwyneth's.

"It's Finn, isn't it? You're seeing him. It was clear that day in the pub that he's still in love with you. I just didn't realize you felt the same."

What? How did my walking in on Miles and Ava, turn into him accusing me of being in love with Finn? My mouth is dry. I feel dizzy.

I bend to scoop my things back into my bag. My lip balm rolls out of reach and falls between the cracks. It's my favorite, but I couldn't care less. Miles is sleeping with the most beautiful woman I have ever met in real life. Who gives a fuck about chapped lips? I put a firm hand on my mother's journal and fit it snuggly inside the bag—some things do still matter—throwing the whole thing over my body and turn toward the stairs. "I have to go."

"Skye it's not what it looked like. Nothing happened between me and Ava."

I face him, swallowing back tears. His face is sincere, but even if nothing happened it's a huge wake-up call that this, us, is not going to work. I try to smile. "Miles it's fine. Really. You two would be good together."

I run down the porch stairs, down the road, and into the black night, wishing it could swallow me whole. Part of me—all of me, really—wants Miles to run after me. The door shuts, the hinges creak, and I'm still running alone.

There's a small pub on the road into the holiday park, and I drag my heavy bones inside and take the only empty seat at the bar. I order a whiskey and a pint.

The bartender places my drinks down, bringing me back to the present. What am I going to do now? No car. No place to stay. No Miles.

I pull out my phone and send a text. At least the pub has Wi-Fi. The first whiskey goes down fast and smooth, so I order another. The vision of Ava's long bare legs in Miles's cabin gets fuzzier with each sip. If Miles says nothing happened, I really do believe him. I think. But either way this will never work.

Finn walks into the bar and smiles once his eyes find mine.

As I'm paying my tab, Elsie comes up behind me. "Skye! You're here! Let's get a pint."

Elsie's face falls as I turn around. I must look as bad as I feel.

"What's wrong?"

I just shake my head. "Ask Miles."

Finn takes my hand in his. "Ready to go?"

I nod and give Elsie a small wave on my way out the door.

MILES

*M*y brain is still fuzzy from too much whiskey. Skye doesn't care. She wants me to date other people, but that's the last thing I want. Ava is sitting on the bed and has even put another log on the fire.

"Ava, you have to go."

"Fine." She sighs and shimmies into a pair of sweats over her sleep shorts. "Miles, I don't understand. We discussed this. Several times. Why are you acting like you didn't know I was going to be here tonight? You know our love scene is tomorrow."

I shake my head. Talked about what? "Ava, I honestly don't know what you're talking about. When did we discuss this?"

"The first night I came. It's part of my process to be close with my co-stars off-screen before any big love scene. It's not sexual. It's just a sleepover, a pajama party if you will. It will make the scene less awkward tomorrow if we spend some intimate time together. You could've told me you had a guest coming."

I shake my head. Shit. "I didn't know she was."

Ava throws on her sweater and slips into her boots. "Can we hug it out before I go? We still have to be very much in love first thing in the morning."

I nod and wrap her in my arms. It feels wrong. I should've run after Skye, but what's the point? She's back with Finn. Skye never took me or my feelings seriously. I was only ever a distraction from her real life.

Ava is rubbing my back slowly with the tips of her nails, bringing me back to the present.

My stomach lurches, and I pull away. "You can't stay. I'm sorry. I'm in love with Skye."

Ava frowns. "I understand. From what I heard from the porch, though, she doesn't feel the same."

My whole body heaves with the heaviness of the fact. She doesn't love me back. How many times can one man endure unrequited love? So far, the count is two. Even so, I can't deny my feelings. "That's probably true. Sadly, it doesn't change how I feel about her."

Ava smiles and gives me a pat on the shoulder. "Really putting the hopeless in hopeless romantic, huh?"

I laugh.

"Not that I'm one to talk. I'm miserably in love with a man who writes letters. No texts, no calls… Actual letters." She shakes her head. "I'll see you in the morning, Miles."

I SHOULD TRY TO SLEEP. Call time is seven tomorrow morning, which means I need to be up at five to fit in my workout. But how can I sleep? I pick up my phone and open the text thread with Skye. Should I send her one? Where did she go? I didn't even see her car.

I start to type.

Me: Nothing is going on between Ava and me. She basically wanted to rehearse our love scene.

Delete. Delete. Delete. It doesn't matter what I say. It won't change her feelings for Finn. But did she actually *say* she had feelings for Finn? Or did I just say it? Either way, it won't change the fact that she doesn't have any for me.

I throw on a coat and go outside to the porch. The snow is starting to pile up. The night is muffled, the moon glinting off the white-capped roofs. I look down the road for Skye or her car. A green folder catches my eye, nearly camouflaged in the bush next to the deck. It must've fallen out of Skye's bag. I brush off the snow and open the front cover. *Insert Amazing Title Here: A Novel by Skye Ainslie.*

My pulse picks up like the beat of a drum. This is Skye's mystery novel. I bring it back inside with one last glance down the road. She must've left it. I pick up my phone again.

Me: You dropped your manuscript. Come back and get it, and we can talk.

Delete. Delete. Delete.

It sounds like I'm holding her novel hostage. I can just give it to her when we get to the castle. We should be wrapped here in the next couple of days. Then there are only a few scenes left to shoot, and we're done. Fin. God, I hate that word now.

All of us will head back to America—well, most of the crew is from Edinburgh, but I will head back. Back to my big, lonely house in LA. No, it's not lonely. I have friends over. It's just the way I like it. I have my space. Everything is set up just how I like it. I can swim in the pool, watch a movie in my home theater, and take a shower with massive amounts of water pressure whenever I want.

I try again to sleep but end up staring at the ceiling, wondering what Skye is doing right now. Is she thinking about me? Probably not. I stare at our texts, willing the three little dots to appear, saying she's typing. But it's late. She's probably sleeping by now.

My chest vibrates as three dots appear. I sit up. She's texting me. But then, as quick as they emerged, they vanish. I stare at my phone until her texts are branded on my eyes like I've been staring at the sun. The dots are gone. There is just my sappy, sad sack text about her eyes. She must be sick of people talking about her eyes. I couldn't have been more original and talked about her ankles, or maybe the spot underneath her left breast where she has an adorable little mole.

I put my phone on the bedside table and yank on the chain of the lamp with a clang. Sleep is not going to come today. Best to move on. I make myself a cup of coffee with the Keurig machine in the little kitchenette.

Once it's ready, I grab the manuscript and my coffee and settle myself under the covers. I feel like I should ask Skye's permission to read her novel, but my curiosity can't take it anymore.

I open the cover and begin to read.

Hell of a Meet Cute

Delight fills my chest. That's what I said to Skye when we first met. Am I in this book? I continue reading.

The wind was as crisp as the crunchy leaves beneath Sorcha's tires. She rode her bike home from coffee at the pub as usual that morning, blissfully unaware that day would be the day that changed her life.

As the castle that had been her home all her life came into view, so did he. He was tall, dark, and oh so handsome, but he was dressed ridiculously for a Wednesday morning, in a kilt and tuxedo jacket, his bow tie hanging loosely around his neck, and a backpack slung over one shoulder.

Holy shit. It's me. She's writing about me, about us meeting. But why? I thought this was a mystery. Does she kill me? Am I the victim? Or, oh no, am I the murderer? I keep reading until the words are swimming on the page.

It's not a murder mystery at all.

It's a love story.

Skye has written our love story.

SKYE

The bar is loud, too loud, stereo blasting the Sex Pistols. I want to go home. That's not even true. I want to go back to somewhere only we know and back in time to before Miles and I made the stupid agreement to keep our relationship light.

A fling? Really? What was I thinking? There had been so many times when it seemed like Miles was about to tell me he loved me. What if I had let him instead of changing the subject or kissing him to shut him up?

Finn comes over and puts his arm around me, his whiskey sloshing in his other hand. When he picked me up, we came to Grogg and Gruel for Nate's show. He finished playing half an hour ago, and everyone is still hanging out, drinking steadily—everyone except me. I cut myself off when I nearly sent Miles a drunk text saying…

That was part of the problem. I don't know what to say.

"Need a refill?"

"No." I want to ask when we are going to head out, but I don't want to be rude. Finn rescued me twice tonight. I should be gracious enough not to push him to leave. But at the rate he's going on the whiskey, we won't be able to drive anywhere, unless he lets me drive his car for once.

As if reading my mind, Finn says, "Nate's going to let us stay at his place. He has a nice big couch." Finn pulls me closer to his side. "We can share it. We've snuggled up in tighter spaces."

I don't want to share a small couch with Finn. I don't want Finn at all. We don't have anything in common anymore. His life is filled with shows, drinks, and buddies. Even if we did have similar lives, I don't have feelings for Finn anymore.

As the night drags, Ava holding Miles's hand in those skimpy shorts replays in my mind. It's very clear to me now that I've been fooling myself that I could just keep things light with Miles.

Finally, we head back to Nate's. It's a small one-bedroom apartment above a bakery. It has beautiful hardwood floors, big bay windows, and enough houseplants that I'm pretty sure Nate doesn't travel much for his music.

Nate gets us a sleeping bag and a couple of pillows, then stumbles to bed after telling us to make ourselves at home. I kick off my boots. All I want to do is sleep. My eyelids are heavy, and my heart weighs a metric ton.

Finn sits next to me on the couch, so close that his thigh touches mine. I scoot over, but am met with the armrest. He reaches out and clumsily tucks a strand of my hair behind my ear. It's an old move, one that used to send chills through my skin, but now I don't feel anything.

"Finn," I start, but before I can continue, his mouth is on mine. So many years, I thought this was all I wanted—for Finn to return, for us to get back together, for him to want me. But it's not what I want, definitely not what I need. I am no longer in love with Finn McDougall.

I push him away. "Finn, no."

"I know I hurt you by leaving. But I'm here now, really here. I'm not going anywhere. I won't ever leave you again. I love you, Skye."

I shake my head. "It's fine that you left. I get it. Either way, though, I don't love you anymore, Finn."

* * *

My head is pounding out the tune to Beck's nineties classic, "Loser." I sit up on the couch and bring my ear to my shoulder, each vertebrae popping on the way. Finn is on the floor, his bare leg half out of his sleeping bag, his mouth wide open, snoring peacefully.

Water. I need water. I head to the kitchen and move some dishes out of the sink so I can pour myself a glass. Finn took my rejection well. He said he's not even really sure if he's going to stay or head back to America. He graciously took the floor and let me sleep on the couch alone—all alone—as I should get used to being for the rest of my life, apparently.

Out the window, the snow lining the street is too bright but gorgeous. I wonder what Miles is doing. I wish we could be snuggled under a blanket somewhere, watching the light snowfall with steaming mugs of coffee. My head tingles. I just want to be with Miles all the time. I want to wake up with him, go to bed with him, and watch Netflix with him. But that's all a silly fantasy.

My stomach writhes, and I head to the bathroom. I grab my bag and rummage around for my toothbrush, I notice my manuscript is gone. *Bloody hell.* It must've fallen out when I dropped my bag. Oh well. It's just a copy and not even finished. I'm still not sure how to end it.

I brush my teeth and check the time. It's only eight thirty. I can't possibly wake up Finn for a couple more hours, but all I want to do is go home.

I try curling up on the couch to sleep some more, but I can't stop thinking about Miles. Instead, I get out my phone, and without checking myself, I go to Miles's Instagram page and start to doom scroll. I've never checked out his page before. I was so enamored with *us* that I didn't want to see him with anyone else or be reminded of his other life in LA. The one he would be going back to after us. I expect to find picture after picture of Ava.

But what I actually find is a whole bunch of landscapes of Scotland. There is a picture taken from my secret spot, where we had our first kiss. I click on it. The caption reads: *Please forward my mail here to this exact spot. It's so magical, I don't know if I can ever leave.*

Back to his page, another photo catches my eye, and I suck in a breath as the picture zooms larger on my phone. It's the loch near Somewhere Only We Know. The sky is a hazy purple with little pink wisps. He must've taken it that morning I slept in and he went for a run. I can practically hear the wind whipping through the long grass bent at a stiff angle. The caption reads: *Is this the place that I've been dreaming of? There's no falling about it. I am in love.*

Tears spring to the corner of my eyes, and I know deep in my gut that he's not talking about the landscape. It's me. He's talking about me. Miles is in love with me, or he was before I pushed him away.

Finn moans from the floor. He sits up and puts his head in his hands. "Too much sunlight."

I laugh. "I think you mean too much whiskey."

He lies back down, throwing the sleeping bag over his head.

I CONVINCE Finn to let me drive. The roads are covered in snow, and the trip takes hours, even longer since I keep having to pull over for Finn for various reasons. To pee. To retch. To get some snacks. You name it, he needs to stop for it. I'm anxious to be back at home, to escape into the clickety clack of the keys on my laptop.

Finally, I pull up to the castle, and Finn gets out to take over the driver's seat.

"Thank you for the ride."

Finn nods. "Anytime. I mean it."

The look in his eyes, so sincere and so intense, makes me look away. I head into the castle with Finn's eyes still on me and give a little wave from the door.

Dad strides out from the kitchen. "Pet! You're back. Why did Finn give you a ride? Where's the car?"

I nearly forgot the Land Rover is still on the side of the road. "In a ditch."

"What?"

Thora comes out into the entryway from the kitchen, too, coming to stand behind my dad. I also completely forgot why I had been so upset when I left. My dad is in love. I should be happy for him. I *am* happy for him. It's just…everything is going to change. My dad has found a second love of his life, and I can't even make *one* work.

It's all too much. My soul aches like I've been in a bicycle accident. Tears fall from my eyes.

"Oh, pet." Dad comes and wraps me in a bear hug, smelling like bacon and woodsmoke. It's such a comforting smell, I cry harder, my shoulders shaking. He pats my back like he used to when I was a child. "It's okay. I can tow the car. Billy can fix it up for us. It's not a big deal."

I pull away and try to catch my breath, but like an obstinate chicken, it won't be caught. "It's not the car," I say through gasps. "I was so childish when you told me about you and Thora. I'm sorry."

My sobs take over.

"Pet, is that all? It's forgiven. There's no need to get so upset."

I shake my head. That's definitely not all.

Thora puts a soft hand on my back. "Let's get you something warm to drink."

I let her lead me to the kitchen table. She sets some coffee in front of me. After a few sips, the bitterness and warmth calm me. We all sit in silence for a bit, sipping coffee, my dad's face pinched in worry, Thora's calm as a loch on a windless day.

"Pet, what—"

Thora shakes her head. "She'll talk when she's ready."

My dad nods but starts tapping his foot under the table. Thora puts a hand on his knee. My heart is just starting to return to a normal pace, but I'm not ready to talk yet. I may never be. Dad drums his fingers on the side of the mug.

"Callum, why don't you go take care of the car?"

He nods and stands. "Yes. Is that alright with you? Will you be okay?"

I try to smile, but it's like my face has forgotten how, so I just nod instead.

"We'll be fine." Thora stands and walks Dad out the door.

When she returns, she still doesn't press me. Just sits quietly sipping her coffee and staring out the window at the snow-covered field.

A small bunny hops through the snow, tail bobbing with each leap. It leaves adorable little paw prints when it goes. Miles would get such a kick out of that. I can practically hear his laugh. My arms feel heavy, and a fresh wave of tears roll down my cheeks. "I messed everything up."

Thora shakes her head. "Oh dear. Do you mean with Miles?"

I gasp. "How did you know?"

"Anyone with eyes in their head can see the way you two look at each other."

"Does everyone know?"

She shrugs. "I'm not sure. Does it really matter? I know Natalie told Miles he couldn't date you. She tried to tell me the same about Callum. I let her know she could kindly mind her own business and I would mind mine."

I smile. "I'm sure she loved that."

Thora shrugs. "She was just worried about losing this location. This is a big movie for her."

I nod. "I told Miles I didn't want anything serious. We agreed upon having a casual fling."

"A Highland fling. How cute."

I shake my head. "I thought so. But it seemed like he wanted more. And I kept shrugging it off, keeping it light, and now I told him he should date Ava."

Thora slams down her coffee cup on the table. "Ava?" She shakes her head. "That'll never happen, dear. Ava is in love with a man living in Sweden. They exchange love letters. It's very Jane Austen. Very romantic, but I think it's driving her crazy at the same time. Where did you get this idea?"

I let it all pour out. The whole story from beginning to end. All about seeing Miles and Ava together, how Miles said nothing happened and I really do believe him but I told him he should go for it like I'd completely lost my mind.

Thora nods, leaning in toward me. "You should talk about all of this to Miles. Tell him how you feel."

A chill passes through me. I put both hands around my mug as if I could warm my whole body from what little coffee is left. "He's going back to America soon. And I will be here."

Thora's eyes are soft. "If you want, you two could probably figure out a solution to that, too."

"Like your solution to give up your whole life to be with my father." I cover my mouth and instantly regret my words. "I'm sorry. I shouldn't have said that. It's just... It's exactly what my mother did. The woman always has to change. To mold herself into something that will fit into the man's life better. I love it here." In the back of my mind, I know that's not entirely true. I do love it here, but part of me yearns to set off on my own adventure. Then the real truth comes out. "I don't want to give up who I am to be with someone."

Thora scoots back in her chair. "I'm not giving up my life. I have never contorted myself to fit anyone's expectations. I'm choosing to come here because I've fallen in love with Scotland just as much as your father, and I need a change in my life. I've been putting out a film, sometimes two or three a year, for decades. I want time and space to breathe. I want to learn to bake a loaf of bread or at least fry an egg."

She pauses before continuing. "That being said, all relationships do involve some compromise on each person's part." Her brow furrows for a brief moment. "Compromise isn't the word I'm looking for… Collaboration. That's it. You have to change some things if you want to be a 'we' instead of a 'me.' It doesn't mean losing yourself. It's more about learning about each other and how you fit together."

Her words make sense, but a voice in my head is still screaming at me that I would be the only one to change. Just like my mother did.

MILES

*B*y the time I head out for call time, I've read eighty-seven pages of Skye's manuscript, and I am sure of two things. One—Skye is a beautiful writer. Her words are concise and poetic when they need to be. Her writing is funny and warm, but at times biting and fiery, just like her. Reading about our first kiss, seeing it through her eyes, through her exquisite words, is an experience I will hold close to my heart for the rest of my days. And two—despite everything Skye said about keeping things light between us, if there is an ounce of truth in anything she's written, then she loves me.

That last one, I'm more hopeful than completely certain of. What if there is more fiction and less truth in her writing? She could've just used our relationship as a starting point and added all the feelings in her writing for dramatic effect.

The crew is packing up the vans. Natalie is discussing something with Minnie when I approach.

"Miles," Natalie says. "You can head back to your cabin."

Shit. This is not good. "Am I fired?"

Natalie walks closer to me so she can lower her voice. "Right now," she begins, "I'm not sure what to do. I told you we couldn't risk the location, no relationships with the hosts. How long have we known each other?"

"A long time." I look down at our boots in the snow. What can I say? She asked me not to date Skye, and I did. But I didn't sign anything. And I've shown up to set and done my job.

"Close to twelve years. And you blow me off, betray my trust for a hookup?"

Hookup? That phrase sends a fire to my belly. But isn't that what Skye and I agreed we were doing? My head is swimming. "It wasn't just a hookup, okay? She's important to me."

Natalie looks me in the eye, hurt still written all over her face. "More important than the film?"

The question hangs between us with our cloudy breaths. When I started this film, I had such a commitment to it, to the part, to the success of this odd, heartfelt monster movie. But through the filming, I've lost focus. Is Skye more important to me than the film? And the real question is, if she is, what does that mean?

Natalie sighs. "We're taking the day off. Hopefully this snow melts tomorrow. If not, we'll have to shoot it with a green screen and add in the background later."

"A green screen? What about all your practical effects?"

Natalie barks out a humorless laugh. "Won't it just be hilarious to have a monster all done with real-life materials, and the background is the thing CGed?" She shakes her head. "Some things can't be helped, though. I can't keep all these people here, employed, waiting for the weather to shift."

I nod. I'm relieved to have the day off, but also very aware that she didn't outright say I'm not fired.

I head right back to my cabin, make myself another cup of coffee, and settle back in with Skye's manuscript. The light moves across the room, the shadows shifting, as I read and read. Before I know it, I have to turn the lamp back on, my stomach is growling, and Skye's novel is starting to shake in my hands. I need to eat, but I don't want to stop reading. I could bring it with me to the pub. Get a beer, some food, and keep reading.

I shrug on my coat, tucking the manuscript into the inside pocket, and lace up my boots. I think about grabbing my thistle hat, my disguise, but there are so many film people around, there's no hiding really. The night is clear and cold, my breath coming out in white, cloudy bursts. Stars dot the sky like snowflakes frozen in midair. It's beautiful. Skye would love it.

The pub is a blast of hot air, both welcome and stifling from the peaceful cold of the night, like walking from the freezer straight into a toaster oven. Scottish folk music plays, and the chatter of the people filling the space is jarring. I'm looking for an open seat when Charlotte stands up from a booth in the corner and waves me over.

She's sitting with Elsie, who is furiously scribbling on a notepad, but I don't see Ty anywhere, so I head over. Not like I have much of a choice. There's literally nowhere else to sit.

"Miles. Sit! Sit!"

Elsie lifts her pint to me but doesn't look up from her notes.

Charlotte laughs. "You can keep me company. This one is too busy *working*."

Elsie shrugs and goes back to writing.

"I'll just get a beer. Either of you need anything?"

Elsie raises her hand. "I'll take another."

Charlotte smiles. "I'd love another white wine."

I make my way through the crowded room to the bar, leaning into an open space and order our drinks and a fish dinner. I accidentally bump into the large man on the stool next to me and say, "Sorry."

"Watch it, laddie."

I nod and grab our drinks, precariously carrying all three back to the table.

"Thank you," Charlotte says as she takes the wine.

Elsie downs the rest of her beer and grabs the next one without ever looking at me once.

Charlotte holds up her glass. "To new places and new friends."

I hold up mine and clink it while Elsie ignores us both to keep writing.

With Elsie working right next to me, I want to pull out Skye's novel and keep reading, but Charlotte is set on chit-chat. We talk about the snow, the film, and her and Ty's upcoming wedding.

"We're getting married in June. I want an outdoor wedding with lots of flowers."

"That will be nice."

"It will." She smiles. "I'd invite you, but honestly, Ty would probably be pissed I'm even talking to you right now after you clocked him yesterday."

"It was an accident."

She shrugs. "Sure it was. He wanted to sue. But I talked him out of it. You're welcome."

Sue? Could he even sue? Why would she talk him out of it anyway? "You didn't have to do that."

Charlotte waves a hand at me. "What are friends for?"

Are we friends? Charlotte keeps talking. "I really think you two should sit down and make up. You're so good together on screen. I must've seen *Swipe* a billion times. It's one of the reasons I wanted to start acting." She pushes Elsie's notepad a little. "Are you working on the sequel?"

Elsie shakes her head. "No. It's something new. A love story set in the Pacific Northwest between a screenwriter and a Bigfoot tour guide who doesn't actually believe in him."

I smile, happy Elsie is continuing to explore this new *mystical creatures* theme. "Any parts for me?"

Elise sets down her pen and looks at me properly now. "*You*? I wrote this part for you, and you seem to be more concerned with yourself than the character."

I sit back, feeling like she slapped me. Now Elsie is pissed at me, too? I thought if anyone would understand, it would be her. "I've still been acting my ass off. I'm allowed to have a life."

"Yes. You are allowed to date whomever you please." She lets out a long breath. "But you're not putting a lot of heart into that either."

"What?"

"I saw Skye last night, and she looked like her dog had just died. Know anything about that?"

"You saw Skye?"

Charlotte asks, leaning forward. "Who's Skye?"

Elsie ignores her. "She was here, but not for long. She left with a handsome blond guy."

"She did?"

Elsie nods. "They were holding hands."

Finn. She must've left with Finn. Who else? But why was he out here with her? I assumed she came here to see me, spend time with me. But what if she came here to break up with me face-to-face? No wonder she didn't mind when she found me with Ava; she said it was fine. Skye really doesn't care who I sleep with or not because she is back together with Finn. But that can't be true. I've read the manuscript. There are real feelings there.

The bartender sets down my food, but I'm no longer hungry. I'm nauseous and dizzy, and I just want to go home. All the way home. Why did I ever take this role in the first place?

I push my plate away. "I have to go."

Elsie says, "Miles, wait."

I'm not listening anymore. The voices in the pub are too loud, and the clanking of silverware on plates echoes in my head. In my hurry to get outside, I run into the same man I bumped into at the bar.

"Sorry." I hold up both hands in surrender.

"Do ye have a problem with me, laddie?"

"No. I just wasn't looking where I was going."

"Yeah, why look at us peasants? Ye Hollywood types taking over. I've had enough of it. Square-go!"

I nod. "I'll go. I'll go."

The man, who is a good three inches taller and has at least fifty pounds on me, looks just as angry when I say I'll go. He follows me outside, fists up at his chest, a group of people following behind him.

"Look..." I turn to face him. "I just want to go."

"And go we will." The man arches his arm back and brings it toward me, fist balled tight, in slow motion. I'm still in awe that this is really happening. I haven't been in an honest-to-God fight since first grade, when I wore the same sneakers as the class bully. I duck but end up slipping on the snow and winding up flat on my ass to a roar of laughter from the crowd.

"Ye don't even need me to beat you up. You'll do it all on your own." The burly man waves a hand at me and leaves me lying in the snow. He heads back into the pub, followed by the crowd of people.

I look up at the stars. If I smoked, I'd pull one out right now and light up. What's the use in getting up?

I hear footsteps crunching in the snow. Ty looms over me. "Need a hand?"

I sigh and reluctantly take his outstretched hand. He heaves me up with a bit more force than necessary. Always showing off.

"Thanks for the whiskey."

I nod and take a deep breath. *Be the bigger man.* "I'm really sorry I hit you. I slipped."

Ty nods. "It's okay. It's not like you even really hit that hard. I was just upset. Heat of the moment. You've hated me for no reason for years now, so I just assumed it was on purpose."

He's got to be kidding. "No reason? You call stealing my girl and my part in the same week 'no reason'?"

Ty shakes his head, genuinely confused. "What are you talking about? You mean Barbados?"

I step closer, my anger threatening to melt all the snow surrounding us. "Yes. I mean Barbados."

Ty holds up his hands. "Look, Miles. Lana came onto me. I did you a favor by showing you who she really was. And the movie... Well, the movie I couldn't pass up. I was meant to play that role, and I was right. Plus, didn't you turn the role down?"

There is a beat of silence where I neither deny nor confirm, but we both know he's right.

Ty continues, "You can't steal a part, though. If they had wanted you for it, you would have gotten it. Just like you can't steal a person. If Lana wanted you, she would've chosen you. Don't blame me."

"What about Minnie?"

Ty looks like I punched him again. "That's none of your business."

"You're engaged, and you let her believe you loved her."

"I do love her," Ty yells, his chest puffed up. He lets out an exhale and shrinks back. "It's complicated. You wouldn't understand. You're so closed off, so easygoing, you never really open yourself up to anyone, not in a real way. You keep people at arm's length, just let them in enough to be friendly, but not enough to be meaningful. Like with us. I thought we were really close, but after Barbados, you wouldn't even talk to me."

Is that true? Do I not let people in? No, I do—well, I did. Until he took everything that was important to me. "You stole my life in Barbados. What was I supposed to say to that?"

"You should be thanking me. I just showed you Lana wasn't worth it. What if you had married her and then she cheated on you? It would've been so much worse."

"That's rich coming from a cheater."

Ty turns and heads into the bar, muttering over his shoulder, "Stay out of it."

SKYE

I throw my messenger bag down on the couch and make myself a cup of coffee in my writing room. I light my candle. It's been a while since I've done my pre-writing rituals. The words have come so easily, I've just been sitting down and getting right to it. But today the rituals feel comforting. I open my laptop and pull up my manuscript. I'm so close to the end, it's time for the grand gesture, but I can't see it yet.

I start to type.

Sorcha was like a wild horse. She could not be tamed, could not be broken. As much as her heart yearned to be with Mickey, her head wouldn't let her. So, she pushed him away. She stopped making herself so available to meet at any moment of the day. She stopped returning texts right away and sometimes at all. Until one day Mickey stopped texting. He went back to America, and they never spoke again. Their love became like her Loch Ness Monster sighting from when she was a child. Whenever she thought of it, she got that same rush of feeling, but as much as she scanned the waters for glimpses, she never saw it again.

Delete. Delete. Delete.

No. This is a romance. Not women's fiction. They have to have a happily ever after. I'm just not sure I can write one. Why didn't I just stick to murder? I get up and walk around the room, my messenger bag catching my eye. My mother's journal spilled out and is sitting on the couch like an old friend waiting to chat.

I grab my coffee, and settle under a blanket on the couch. I open the first page, and my breath catches as I read the words.

Dear peanut,

She always called me peanut, and I haven't heard it since she's been gone.

I just came from the doctor. He told me I'm pregnant with you! Can you believe it? I found it hard myself. I thought I just had a stomach bug or something. But it's a baby. It's you, baby. Your father is over the moon, and so am I. I'm not sure how this will affect my tour schedule, but we'll figure it out together. We are a family now.

I lose myself in my mother's letters to me. Some are funny, some sad, one is hilarious—she went to a gig and was so sick, she ran off stage into the crowd, vomited in a trash can behind the bar, and then went on like nothing had happened.

After my drink has grown cold and my legs stiff, I get to the page that my father bookmarked for me.

Peanut,

It's me, Mom. Even though I can feel you squirming around in there, this is still all a little surreal, but these letters are making it real. Normal even. I made a big decision today, and since we are a family, I thought we should discuss it. I'm hanging up my microphone. These past few months, and if I'm being honest, even before I found out I was pregnant, I haven't felt the same about my music career as I used to. I still love to sing, but I don't always love doing it for drunk assholes. Oof. Gotta work on the swearing. I love the music, hate the career part of it. On my last album, my two favorite songs were left off because the studio producing it didn't feel they were the right tone. Now they'll never see the light of day.

And the tour... Before I signed with anyone, I could sing places I knew, to people I loved. But a booked tour is totally different. The road is hard. And before I was pregnant, I drank too much to try to make it easier. To relax, or because I deserved it, or because I was bonding with the other musicians. I don't want to go back to that. I didn't always make the best decisions on those hazy nights.

And then there's you—my not-so-little-anymore squirming bun in the oven. I don't want to drag you along with me from town to town, bar to bar, and I don't want to be away from you. I want to be there with you as you grow up. I want to show you the beach and teach you how to tend a garden. Your father has assured me that if this is what I really want to do, we can swing it financially.

I just hope you don't think I'm a quitter. I'm not. But I'm not so proud to admit that I've changed, and the things I hold dear, my priorities, have changed too. There is nothing more beautiful than embracing the change in your heart. The trees can't cling to their leaves as they turn from green to red.

So, my little peanut, we will sing lullabies together and both get to know this new version of me. And if I can teach you anything by my example, it is to always follow your heart—even when it seems like it's leading you off of your carefully-mapped-out journey, even when it seems like it's leading you off the road altogether into unknown waters. Listen and learn to swim.

Love,

Your adoring mother

I close the journal so my tears won't smudge the precious writing. Mom was not a selkie longing to return to the ocean, to the wild adventure of being a professional diva. I was the adventure, I was her watery home, and leaving all of that behind to raise me was the bold, uncertain choice.

I keep reading until the fire is the only thing lighting the pages, the sun having dipped below the hills. The journal goes all the way up to my first birthday. Each sentence feels as warm as she was. I can almost smell her rose-scented perfume and feel the tickle of her hair on my face as I read. When I finish, I go back to the page my father has marked and read it again.

Have I been following my heart? Or have I buried my head in the sand, tucked myself away in this castle, terrified of more change since my mother passed? I know the answer. I know I have been living each day just like the last, shuffling along. The only real bravery or reach for any kind of future was in the queries I sent out, and even then, one stiff rejection sent me hiding under my covers.

Until Miles showed up.

Everything changed: I felt lighter, more myself. Each day suddenly had a rosy glow of hope cast over it. Hope that I will see him, or kiss him, or make him laugh.

I get up, feeling my body adjust to not being curled on the couch, and look out the window. The night is clear, the moon a perfect sliver —a cheshire cat moon. A bloody banana moon. I wish Miles were here to see it. It hits me, and I feel like Alice falling down the rabbit hole, hitting the bottom with a massive thud. I have been lying to myself as much as Miles. This is not a fling.

I am in love with Miles Casey.

* * *

I TRY TO SLEEP, but sleep won't come. I'm in love with Miles. I am. But now what? Will he forgive me for being distant, for basically shutting him out?

I reach for my phone and see I have a *YHF* news article alert. I click it and watch in horror as a very large man is about to punch Miles. Miles ends up flat on his back in the snow. I can't tell if the guy actually punched him or if he slipped. Without thinking, I go over to my texts and type.

Me: Are you okay? I saw you got in a fight.

I send it and then instantly regret it. No hi, no how are you? Just *I saw you got in a fight.* What was I thinking?

I watch my phone for a few minutes, hoping for a reply from Miles, but nothing comes.

In the morning, I check my phone first thing, but still nothing. I sigh. It's going to take more than a text to get through to Miles after all the things I said. But what?

I tinker with different ideas at my laptop. I need a grand gesture, both for my manuscript and with Miles. Something to show him how much I love him. Show him that I'm done living in fear—I'm ready to believe in love, in us. I could take him back to Somewhere Only We Know, but how? That's not right anyway. I don't want us to sneak around anymore.

Maybe I could sing to him, at the pub—serenade him with "Can't Take My Eyes Off You", like Heath Ledger in *10 Things I Hate About You*. No, that's silly. I don't even know if he likes that movie, although who doesn't? It's delightful.

What does he do at the end of his football movie, *Undercover Quarterback*? Oh, right. He has fans in the stands hold up signs saying "I love you." That might work, except I don't have a stadium or a crowd.

The ideas keep bouncing around in the back of my brain while I open a new document, a fresh story. This one is about a mother and daughter. One is a writer, the other a singer. It's told in a dual timeline, both of them at age twenty-four. There is a love story in both as well, but it's more about the two women finding themselves.

I write like my keys are on fire and my fingertips are the only thing that can smother the flame threatening to consume me. I think about it all day as I patch another hole in the hall ceiling, as I check on the cows, as Thora, my dad, and I put up the Christmas tree. Each ornament that reminds me of my mother sparks a new idea in my manuscript.

The next morning, I make myself some coffee, light my candle, and get back to work. This has a lot of me and my mother in it, but it is a departure. They are their own characters, and the story starts to become its own living, breathing beast as well.

I finish a full synopsis, the first chapter, and half of the second, and take a deep breath. A new story. It's satisfying to know that I don't need Miles to write. But I still want him. I shut my laptop once the light peeks over the hills, no closer to knowing how to finish my novel or tell Miles how I feel.

Putting on my warmest coat and my heavy boots, I head out into the Baltic morning to feed the chickens. Their little coop heater is plugging away, and if I didn't know better, I'd think they almost missed me.

"Hey, buddies." I throw some feed at the ground. "How would you tell someone that you loved them, in a big way? In an *I'm sorry I was ghosting you, I was just trying to protect my heart, but I've decided I'd rather give it to you than keep it, even if that means it might get broken* way?"

A booming laugh sounds from the door. I look up to see Dad, chicken feed in hand. "You're asking an awful lot of very specific questions of a bunch of bird brains."

"Yeah."

"I wasn't sure you were back on chicken duty."

I sprinkle another handful of feed. "I'm back."

He smiles. "You're in love with Miles?"

I nod, no longer surprised that everyone seems to know we have feelings for each other.

"Thora said as much," Dad says.

"I like her."

He smiles. "Me too. Look at us. What a fine pair." He runs a hand over his beard. "You could just tell him. Be honest, speak from the heart."

"He won't even respond to my texts. Well, the one text I sent anyway."

A rumble of engines and crunching of tires comes from the drive. "Sounds like they're back. You can talk to him in person."

My chest fills like a party balloon. I hand the feed to Dad and run gingerly over the snow to the front of the castle. The crew is unloading equipment and lugging it into the castle. Bundled up, Ava jogs lightly toward the house. She stops when she sees me.

"Skye. I have to talk to you."

I hold in a sigh. I don't want to talk to the perfect woman who was practically naked with the man I love. "Uh, I can't right now—"

"I just wanted to let you know that nothing happened with Miles and me. The whole thing was my idea, really. It's part of my process to spend time with my co-stars right before a big love scene. I find it makes the performances on the day less awkward. But it's never sexual. It's a sleepover, really."

I nod. What she's saying makes sense, sort of. "Okay."

"But Miles wasn't into it at all. He was sending me away before you even got there. Really. He's crazy about you."

Her last words ring in my head. *He's crazy about me. Me!*

I throw my arms around Ava, and she lets out a surprised laugh.

"Thank you! Have you seen him?"

Ava shakes her head and jogs inside.

I keep looking for Miles. Ty is holding hands with a glamourous woman I've never seen before. Did they take on a new cast member?

I search through the faces but can't find Miles anywhere. Elsie climbs out of the second van.

"Elsie!"

"Skye!"

"Where's Miles?"

Elsie rolls her eyes. "Who knows?"

I shake my head. It doesn't make sense. Did they just leave him in Glen Coe?

"He didn't come back with you all?"

She shakes her head. "He took Charlotte's rental car to the train station."

My heart sinks. Charlotte. Who the hell is Charlotte? He's leaving? For good? Without even coming back to say goodbye. I head to my Land Rover before I remember it's in the shop.

I run back to Elsie, nearly sliding into her when I try to stop. "What train station?"

"The one in Inverness. The train to London. But Skye—"

I wave behind me. "No time!"

I bolt to my dad's rusted old jeep, the keys dangling from the ignition as always. Elsie jogs after me, and I roll down the window.

"He asked me to give you this."

She hands me my manuscript in a bright green folder. There is a Post-It stuck to the front with a note scribbled on it.

I hope you don't mind. I read your book. I love it. But how does it end?
-Miles

I toss it on the seat next to me.

"Thanks. Wish me luck."

I don't even let the car warm up as I fishtail onto the road headed for Inverness.

MILES

The roads are thick with snow, and the car is silent. I want to plug my phone in for some music, but it's completely shattered. It was in my back pocket when I landed on my ass in the snow. At least I was able to borrow Elsie's laptop before we left to finish up some important business—order a new phone, make a big swing toward winning Skye's heart, write some emails toward pursuing a new passion in life.

It was a productive morning to say the least. We waited out the snow for a whole entire day so I had plenty of time. It's not really a new passion, more a new direction. I still have a passion for movies and stories, and I would like to try my hand at producing. It seems like the next logical step in my career. I'd like to see a film through from idea to completion, and I think I know what I'd like to produce.

I turn to Minnie, who's staring out the window. "Do you want to plug in?" I hold up the cord. "Maybe put on some music."

"No."

The film is not wrapped. We still have a few scenes to shoot in the castle and one at the loch. Minnie, however, is finished and handed in her notice effective immediately.

I park the car at the shopping center first, placing my thistle hat firmly on my head. "I just have to run in and pick up my new phone. Do you want to come, or do you want to wait?"

"Wait."

I turn toward Minnie. Her eyes are rimmed red, her hair up in a messy bun, and her arms are wrapped tightly around her torso. "Minnie, are you okay?"

"I feel so stupid." She shakes her head. "I thought he really loved me."

She bends forward, sobs shaking her shoulders.

I put a gentle hand on her arm. "Minnie, he's a dope. Anyone who doesn't see how amazing you are is a complete dumbass. I'm sure if you were with anyone else, anyone at all, it would be different. But this is just what Ty does."

She sits up straighter and takes a deep, shaky breath. "Not anymore."

I'm not sure what that means, but I know I can't leave her to wallow in the cold car. "Come in and get some coffee."

"Okay."

Leaving Minnie in the food court scrolling her phone, I pick up my new device, and the gentleman working helps me set up all my information. It's downloading or whatever the guy said when we head back to the car. Minnie looks much calmer, latte in hand.

The drive to the train station takes longer than I'd hoped on the snow-slick roads. Once we get there, I help Minnie with her luggage. We make our way through the crowded station. It's charming. Flocked garland and twinkle lights hang from the walls. There is a massive silver Christmas tree, and when we get closer to it on our way to the ticket booth, I see it's all made of CDs. There must be hundreds of them. They reflect the twinkle lights on the wall in rainbows.

We get the ticket situation all squared away. We're lucky there is a train leaving in the next thirty minutes to London, and we head toward our platform, weaving through people. My phone rings in my pocket. I'll have to remember to turn the sounds off.

A woman stops me for a photograph, even with my hat. I smile, and we pose quickly. I glance around the crowded station and hope it doesn't turn into a selfie line.

The phone call went to voicemail. We continue on towards our platform. Minnie takes a seat, and I set her bag down next to her. There is a band set up, with a keyboardist, guitar player, and singer near the waiting area playing "Silent Night". I move away with a finger to one ear, my phone pressed to the other to listen to the voicemail. It's Jake.

"Miles, everything should be in order. The lawyers were able to handle most of it. Papers are all signed. Check is cashed. You're crazy, but they'll meet you this afternoon. I'll text you the address of the pub where you can pick up the keys. Oh, have you seen the news this morning about Ty? Not too surprising, but yikes. Call me later."

I take a seat next to Minnie. She has earbuds in and is scrolling again. I check the time. Still twenty minutes until the train. I pull up the internet browser on my phone and google Ty Marshall. The first thing that pops up is an image of him kissing a red-haired woman, taken as a selfie, the loch shimmering behind them. The red-haired woman looks an awful lot like Minnie. My stomach sinks into my shoes. Not this on top of everything else she's been through.

I click the link, and an article pops up from *You Heard It First*.

Hanky Panky on the Set of the New Ty Marshall Movie

My spine stiffens. It's really more the new Miles Casey movie or, more accurately, the new Natalie Rodriguez movie. I read on.

An anonymous source sent one of our news affiliates a treasure trove of behind-the-scenes pictures from the new Ty Marshall movie currently filming in Scotland, and over half of them, as you can see, feature Ty macking on a young woman working as a PA on the film. Sources say the two acted very much in love, sneaking off together on day trips, often sleeping in the same room (we doubt any sleeping was done), and making lovey-dovey eyes at each other on set. This would all be well and good if Ty weren't already engaged to Charlotte Romine, the supermodel trying to turn actress.

At the time of this article, we have reached out to some of the involved parties for comment, but have not heard back. Stay tuned as this drama unfolds. And if their movie is half as steamy as some of their backstage shenanigans, we'll be first in line for tickets.

Oh shit. I cover my mouth as I read the article again. How will Minnie take this? Not only was she betrayed by Ty, but now their relationship is all over the internet. I show Minnie the screen lit up with a picture of Minnie and Ty cheersing two beers. "Have you seen this? Minnie, they have photos of you and Ty."

Her face breaks into a wide smile as she takes my phone and scrolls to one of the photos. "I thought this one was a particularly flattering shot of me."

My eyes go wide. "Minnie!"

She hands me back my phone. "What?"

"You leaked these photos?"

"I have no idea what you're talking about." Her smile is positively beaming. "Ty can't just keep chewing people up and spitting them out with no consequences."

I sit back and chuckle. "Wow. Okay. Note to self, don't fuck with Minnie Le Blanc."

"Damn straight." Minnie turns to me. "Miles, I should've listened. I'm sorry I said you were jealous."

I wave her away. "You don't need to apologize. I get it. I've been in love before." The words *right now* blare in my head. "I know what it's like."

A few people walk by, staring at Minnie the whole way, and one even takes a photo.

Minnie half laughs. "I didn't expect to be quite so recognized, though."

"Weird, huh?" I take my hat off and hand it over. "You can borrow my disguise if you want. Works half the time." I consider and laugh. "Maybe more like thirty percent."

Minnie laughs, tucking her hair into the ball cap. "I'll give it a shot." She smiles and slips her earbuds back in.

The band has stopped playing, making the voices of the hordes of travelers seem louder. When it starts again, they're playing "Fairytale of New York" and I wish Skye were here so fiercely, it feels like my heart might crack.

An announcement comes over the loudspeaker for the train to London. As we make our way onto the platform. I check over my email. The signed contracts are sitting right there at the top. A mix of uncertainty and excitement washes over me. I sure hope this plan works.

SKYE

*J*run through the station. An announcement comes over the loudspeaker that the train to London is now boarding. Shite. I might be too late. I run faster, wishing I had my bike. I can't believe Miles actually likes doing this, arms pumping, legs burning. "Fairytale of New York" plays from a band set up in the corner. The platform is crowded. Streams of people bundled up for the weather, presents in tow, board the train. I scan for Miles but can't find him.

My eyes keep roaming. It's like trying to find an individual snowflake in a blizzard. But then, through the window, I see it. That ugly purple hat Miles thinks is somehow a disguise. He's seated near a window, the glass tinted, turned the other way so I can't see his face, but the window next to him is mercifully open a crack.

"Miles! Miles!"

I jump up, but I can't quite reach the glass to knock. He doesn't turn toward me. I'm not even sure he can hear me, or maybe he's still upset.

"Miles, I read my mother's journal, and do you know what I realized? I'm terrified of change. So much has happened that's been entirely out of my control, and I thought, well, I felt if nothing ever changes, then everything would be fine. If nothing ever changes, nothing can get worse. Then you came, and everything changed. You really did change my world, but for the better."

People are turning to look. My cheeks grow hotter than they already were from the exercise. A few more of the windows have come down on the train.

The train makes a loud noise just as I say, "Miles, I love you."

Little lights on phones twinkle like stars. I'm sure this will be all over the internet. I think of that picture of us walking into the bookstore. How mortified I was to see my face on *YHF*. But right now I couldn't care less. Film away. Post it all over Instagram, TikTok, and any other social media I'm not hip enough to know about. The whole world can know.

I scream it this time to make sure he hears me. "I love you, Miles Casey."

The train starts to pull away, and I run after it. I swear I've never run this much in my whole life. He starts to turn in the window. I see that bright-purple hat standing from the seat, then fiddle with the window.

"Miles, you can't leave. I mean, of course you can, but I'm asking you to stay. We don't have to stay here. I'm asking you to stay with me. We can decide where we want to live or how to date long distance."

The figure in the purple hat leans out the window, and I see clearly now it's not Miles.

It's Minnie. She points and makes her hands into the shape of a heart. I stop, my shoulders slump, my chest heaves, my breath ragged. All that, and it wasn't even Miles.

A deep voice behind me says, "We?"

I turn to see Miles standing behind me, smiling ear to ear, slightly out of breath himself, with a small crowd around us, some with phones out.

"I was trying to catch you, but you were so focused."

I laugh. "That I was. Did you hear any of it?"

He nods. "All of it."

He picks me up and swings me around, the world a blur of white and Christmas lights. The crowd cheers. He sets me down, pulls me close, and we kiss. It is a proper, knees-to-jelly, leave-the-world-behind kiss. We would have kissed longer, but the wolf whistles from the crowd signal it's time to find a more private location for this conversation. The conductor announces another train arrival, and some of our adoring fans dissipate.

"Miles, don't go."

He shakes his head. "I'm not. Well, I do have somewhere I need to be, but I'm not getting on a train."

"You're not?"

"Nope. Minnie has family in London. She quit, and I was just giving her a ride."

He pulls me closer, and I laugh into his neck. "So, I didn't have to run after a rolling train and pour out my heart in front of a bunch of strangers?"

He shakes his head. "No, but I liked it."

"You *liked* it? Do you see how many bloody people I just yelled like a nutter in front of…"

He kisses my neck behind my ear, and I let my sentence trail off. He takes my hands in his. "I loved it. I love you. You've changed my world, too."

I smile. "Coo-Coo-Ca-Choo, babe."

We kiss, and the train station falls away. Nothing exists but this man and his lips, his smoky-sweet scent, and his broad chest. After an eternity, yet not long enough, our lips part. He smiles his most charming smile. "Let's get out of here."

"Miles, I love you."

* * *

MILES'S HAND feels solid and strong in mine as we make our way into the pub. We returned the rental car and took my dad's Jeep all the way to Fort Augustus, but as much as I pester him, Miles won't tell me what we're doing.

"Is it a good surprise?"

Miles laughs. "Of course it's good. Why would I keep something bad from you?"

I nod. He wouldn't. I know that. The pub is a cute brick house right across from the Caledonian Canal. We enter, and a couple with matching silver hair waves from the corner. Miles waves back and squeezes my hand.

"Miles Casey," the woman says, adjusting her heavy cardigan. "As I live and breathe."

Miles holds out his hand to shake, but the woman pulls him into a hug.

The older man with her laughs. "Let the boy go, Isla."

We all laugh at this. Introductions are made around, and we all order pints. After a good fifteen minutes pass, I start wondering what we are doing here. Who are these people to Miles? I'm just about to ask how they all met, when Isla pulls out a set of keys, the bright-yellow keychain catching the light shimmering through the windows, and passes them across the table.

"Here ye are. I hope you enjoy it as much as we have over the years."

My mind is trying to sort through what's going on, but I can't quite catch up. I look at Miles. His smile is luminous. He hands me the keys. I look down at them in my hand, a glittery sunshine hanging off the chain along with two small house keys. "Miles?"

"I bought you a house."

Isla nods. "Paid a pretty penny for it, too."

The older gentleman finishes his beer and stands. "Come on. Let's give these two some privacy. It's not every day a man buys a woman a house."

We say our goodbyes, and Miles walks them out, thanking them the whole way out the door.

He comes back and sits.

I'm still in shock. "You bought me a house?"

"More specifically, I bought you Somewhere Only We Know."

My heart blooms. It's one of the most beautiful places I've ever stayed. I picture Miles and me making dinner, starting a fire, gazing out at the stars while snuggled up on the couch. But he keeps saying he bought it for *me*, so maybe he doesn't plan on being there a whole lot. My face must look as confused as I feel.

Miles reaches out and smooths the wrinkle in my brow. "There's quite a bit of land that comes with the house. We could probably build an addition, or I was thinking we could build another, smaller house as a writing office for you. There's room for a garden, too. I thought... Well, I was hoping...we could stay there together when I'm in Scotland. I'll still have to go back and forth for work, and you've made it clear that Scotland is your home. I don't want to try to change you. I just want to be with you, whatever that looks like for us. I love you, Skye."

The last words sink into my skin, like submerging myself in a hot bubble bath. I sigh and close my eyes. "Would you mind saying that last part again?"

I hear Miles move in his chair, and then his breath is hot on my ear. "I love you, Skye Ainslie."

I open my eyes and turn my face to Miles and kiss him.

When we part, I say, "I'm more open to the idea of travel than I was before."

"You are?"

I nod and look down at the keys. I hold them up and jangle them. "Let's go now."

Miles nods. "I have one last scene to shoot for the film, not tomorrow but the next day, so we'll have to be at the castle by then."

"Sure, but then if we want, we can go right back?"

Miles nods.

A warm smile melts over my face like butter on toast.

* * *

THE SUN IS SETTING by the time we make it to our new house. I get out of the car, and Miles sweeps me off my feet and carries me over the threshold, with some complicated one-handed juggling to unlock the door.

We hardly even shut the front door before we tear each other's clothes off, the sky awash in pink light out the windows behind us.

Miles runs his hands down my back and whispers in my ear, "I love you."

I can't hear it enough. It's as rich and decadent as a form-fitting ball gown but also feels as cozy and everyday as my softest blue sweater. I try explaining this to Miles as I'm lying on the rug in front of the wood stove, the throw blanket from the couch wrapped around my shoulders. Miles is making a fire, and I'm trying not to take over.

"So, our love is your ratty old cardigan?"

I shake my head. "No, well, sort of—hey, it's not ratty. It's well-worn."

He laughs, putting another log on the fire. "You're the writer, so I'll leave the analogies to you. Oh, I read your book. Did Elsie give it back to you?"

My heart hammers in my chest. I wanted to ask about the book the whole way here. I'm dying to know what he thinks, but I also didn't want to be the one to bring it up. Since he hadn't mentioned it yet, I am almost certain that he hates it. He probably didn't connect with the characters. *Story of my life.* Particularly gutting, seeing as he is basically one of them. "She did. It's just a first draft. I still have a lot of work to do, fleshing it out—"

"I loved it. It's warm and funny but also cutting and emotional. Just like you."

It feels like the summer sun has come out and shone just on me; I can practically feel the warmth. Or maybe Miles got the fire to catch. "You loved it?"

"I did. And I've been thinking." He shuts the door to the wood stove, the fire blazing inside, and comes to sit next to me on the rug. "I'm so impressed with everyone's bravery lately. Thora is starting a brand-new life in Scotland, Minnie quitting, you writing this amazing novel, which is a totally different genre for you, right?"

I nod, touched that he remembered. Touched but not surprised. Miles remembers things about me. He really listens. It's part of what I love about him.

"And I was thinking to myself, have I been brave? The last couple of years, I've taken the safe roles—well, except for this film, really, but even this film, I just had to show up and do my job, right? I want to produce. I want to see a film from inception to reception."

"Ooh, and I thought I was the writer."

He waves me off. "I have my moments. But I was wondering, I was hoping, what if we made your book into a movie?"

I sit up as if jolted with a shock of electricity. "You want to make my manuscript into a movie?"

He nods, a massive smile on his face.

"But it's not even a book yet."

He shrugs. "Well, it needs an ending, but given the slightly autobiographical nature of the story, I kinda figured we were working on that right now." He runs a hand on my thigh under the blanket, and I get another, entirely different shock of electricity.

* * *

THE WATER RIPPLES. It's small at first, so small you can hardly see it—in fact, if you blinked, you wouldn't. The wind blows on my cheeks, and I'm grateful that I wore my woolly hat, scarf, and my warmest coat. The ripple expands and all of a sudden erupts, sending shock waves lapping at the shore. The beast emerges from the depths, water rolling off its scaly back. Miles approaches the edge of the water, his strong calves stunning in his long socks and kilt. He must be absolutely freezing.

The creature approaches the shore. Miles reaches out his hand to the beast's face. He caresses Nessie's cheek as gently as a lover.

"He's gone. They're all gone. I have no family left. No lover. Just you."

The beast nuzzles its head into his hand, then turns around, diving under and leaving Miles alone on the shore. Miles motions with his body like he's going to dive in the water, but stops himself, and Natalie yells, "Cut."

"That's a wrap."

The whole crew cheers. Several of them pop champagne, while three of them get the animatronic Loch Ness Monster out of the water and quickly onto the trailer they use to haul it.

Miles runs to me, picking me up off my feet and swinging me around. The landscape swirls around me. The tree, the loch, and the crew all come in and out of focus as we spin. They've chosen my favorite spot in the world for the final shot of the film, and I couldn't be happier. It's funny to think that just a few months ago, if I'd seen anyone else here that I hadn't brought myself, I probably would've shoved them into the loch. But now, sharing it feels right. It's a magical place, and it turns out that sharing it with others has only enhanced its charm.

A PA hands us both a clear plastic flute filled with bubbly.

Once everyone has a glass, Natalie holds hers in the air. "Thank you all for being a part of this crazy idea."

Elsie pipes up. "Hey, who are you calling crazy?"

Everyone laughs.

Natalie continues. "If you're crazy, we're all right there with you. From the bottom of my heart, thank you for going all in. I couldn't have asked for a better location or better hosts—"

Dad holds up his glass and, in his booming voice, says, "You're welcome."

More laughter.

"But really, I couldn't have dreamed up a better crew or a more invested cast. Thank you. Thank you for your commitment to the story, to the film, to each other."

Miles pulls me a little closer to him. Tears are forming in the corner of my eyes, and as if on cue, it almost seems like another trick of movie magic, a light snow starts to fall.

"The heart and the love that you all embraced during this shoot…" Natalie takes a deep breath and places a hand on her chest. "Well, it's changed me on a molecular level. I started this project thinking I could control every detail, control all of you, just like I do when mapping out my storyboards. It's worked for me in the past, set up rules, run a tight ship." She waves a hand. "Now I can see control is not the path to great art. Collaboration is."

There is a ripple of nods, and a wave of applause erupts at this.

Natalie holds up her glass. "The end is just the beginning. Slàinte *mhath*."

We all echo her words. "Slàinte *mhath*."

Dad says, "Party back at the castle."

The crew whoops.

I lay my head on Miles's shoulder.

He kisses my cheek. "I'm just going to grab my stuff and throw on some sweats before they dismantle the costume tent. Then we can head to the party?"

Miles weaves his way through people, hugging and shaking hands, and I turn to stare out at the loch, perfectly still once more. The snow is so light, it's hardly causing a tremble on the glassy surface. But then there is one—way off in the distance. A large black mass rises to the surface and ducks under just as quickly, like a shadow just went for a quick dip. I go to yell out, but my breath is stuck, like it rose, hit the air, and froze in my throat.

Miles joins me. I can sense it's him by his scent, his presence that displaces the air, changing it in an indescribable way, but I can't tear my eyes off the water.

He puts his hand on the small of my back. "Ready to go?"

I smile, but my eyes are still fixed.

Miles peers into my face. "Everything okay?"

I shake myself and look deep into Miles's rich brown eyes. "Everything is perfect."

SKYE. LATE JUNE, AROUND A YEAR AND A HALF LATER

New York feels completely different this time. It still has the undeniable energy, like the ocean at high tide, but instead of threatening to pull me under, it feels like it's pushing me forward, like I'm riding the wave. The pink skirt of my sundress billows around my knees, roused by my momentum.

I'm off to The Ripped Bodice in Brooklyn, the first stop on my book tour.

My book tour. I love hearing that term.

It's about a month long, with seven stops on the East Coast and then five on the West. It'll wrap up near the end of July, just in time for Dad and Thora's wedding back at the castle. They both keep saying they're going to keep it simple, but knowing the two of them, it'll be grand, with more flowers than a garden store.

I check my phone. Miles is supposed to meet me at the bookstore.

We've been splitting our time between Scotland and LA, but the past month or so, I tucked myself away at our little slice of heaven on the Isle of Skye, working on my latest book. It's not due to my publisher for a good six months, but I was so excited about it that I couldn't wait to pick up where I left off. After finishing my romance,

I sent it to Elsie's agent friend and signed with her a few weeks later. When she sold this book, I really did get a two-book deal.

My first, the romance about Miles and me, just came out last Tuesday, and so far, the response has been exciting. Lots of people have given it five stars on Goodreads, and I'm getting tagged left and right in reels on IG and TikTok. Miles bought the rights to the film, even before it was published, which I think may have sped up the process. He asked if I wanted to write the screenplay, but I wanted to focus on my next book. And I'm still tinkering with the story inspired by my mother.

After my last delicious sip of my iced coffee, I throw it in a nearby trash can and take a deep breath. I can do this. I can read from my book in front of a handful of people. Easy peasy.

The Ripped Bodice is impossible to miss. Both the awning and the building itself under the storefront window are bright pink, almost the exact pink of my dress. The bells chime as I swing the glass door open to a packed house. Far more crowded than I've ever seen a bookstore at four o'clock on a Wednesday afternoon. I almost turn right around and leave before the door can close, noticing as I do *HAPPILY EVER AFTER* and a smattering of *HEA*'s are hand-painted above the door.

One of the owners comes over, the excitement in her cheeks grounding me. "We're so thrilled you're here! Can I get you anything? Water, juice, coffee?"

I nod. "Water would be great, thanks."

"We're just going to be right up there." She points to two velvet rose-colored chairs in the back of the store, sitting in front of a gorgeous display with three large arched window frames, book pages hanging where the glass would go. I make my way through the crowd, looking for Miles. Each face I peer into is friendly but unfamiliar, until I get to one I know.

"Minnie!"

"Skye!" Minnie throws her thin arms around me. "This is amazing! Look at all these people here for you!"

I frown and nod. "It's a little intimidating."

She squeezes my arm. "You're going to be amazing."

"I hope so. What have you been up to?"

"Well, I got a new job at LightStream Productions. We're shooting a movie a couple of blocks over."

"Oh fun!"

"It is, but it's a ton of work. I actually have to head back. I snuck off set just to wish you luck."

"Thank you."

Minnie blows me a kiss before running off on her next adventure.

I make my way through the chairs, and before I know it, it's time to start. I read a few excerpts, ending on one of my favorites.

"*Sorcha curtsies, holding out her threadbare slip with both hands, doing her best impression of Audrey Hepburn in Roman Holiday. Mickey takes her hand and fits her body close to his at first, then adjusts to a perfect waltzing position. They glide through the room, the walls of the little house fading away, like they're in a grand palace. The stars out the window are like candles burning; the rustic wood floor has been transformed into marble tile. Sorcha has never felt more lithe on her feet, never felt sexier, never felt so much in love as she does at this moment. She worries there may not be enough room inside her to contain it all—that it may be too heavy, but then she looks in Mickey's eyes and realizes she doesn't have to carry it alone.*"

The crowd, even larger than when I started reading, definitely a lot larger than my agent and publicist anticipated, claps. Slow at first and then building. My cheeks warm when everyone stands up and continues to applaud. From the back, I hear a low whistle. I look to see Miles banging his hands together like a man possessed. I laugh.

The bookstore owner gets on the microphone. "Wow. I just can't get enough of Sorcha and Mickey." She holds up a printed list with a red circle in the middle. "We have a little surprise for you from your agent and publisher. Ms. Ainslie, as of this morning, is a New York Times Bestselling author!"

My jaw almost hits the black and pink tile floor in front of me.

Did I hear her right? She hands me the paper, and there it is, printed in black and white. My agent mentioned a surprise at the signing, but in all the excitement, it slipped my mind.

Sorcha and Mickey: A Somewhat True, but Mostly Fictional Love Story is number eight on the New York Times bestseller list. My eyes go to where I saw Miles in the crowd earlier, but he's gone. I scan and find him running along the edges in back, trying to find a way to the front.

I leap forward and weave my way through the fans to more cheers. Affectionate hands pat my shoulders, and some of the women hold up their hands for high fives, which I enthusiastically give as I strut through the crowd to Miles.

His eyes are like fireworks. "You did it!"

The smile on my face grows wider, a feat I didn't think possible. I have no words.

The corner of his lips turns into a playful smirk. "The writer is speechless?"

I laugh.

Miles leans in and whispers, "Let's give them something to talk about, then."

He pulls me into his arms, and the applause gets louder. He dips and dramatically kisses me like the end of an old Hollywood movie. All under the fitting painted wall saying *HAPPILY EVER AFTER.*

The Q&A and the signing that follows have a celebratory feel. When it's time to go, Miles takes my hand. As soon as we step outside the store, I pull out my phone. "I have to call my dad. He's going to be so excited. I've been dying to tell him since I heard the news."

Miles is nodding. "Yes, of course." But something about him seems nervous, and he's texting. Probably work stuff.

Dad picks up on the first ring. I hadn't even thought about what time it must be there.

"Pet, is everything all right?"

I nod and realize he can't see that. "More than all right. Dad, I have some very exciting news."

"Ahh, so Miles finally did it?" Dad yells to Thora in the background. I can't make it all out. "I wondered what the holdup was. He asked me for my blessing ages ago."

"Your blessing?" More indistinct chatter in the background, but I don't wait for an answer. "Dad, I'll have to call you back."

Miles is running his hand over his face and shaking his head.

A smirk pulls at my lips. I knew it. I knew Miles Casey was up to something. "Miles, my dad said something about you asking for his blessing? What do you think he means? What could you possibly need his blessing for?"

Miles laughs. "I was trying to text him. I knew he'd think that's what you meant. Can't I have one surprise?"

"What did he think I meant? Do you have something to tell me? Or should I say, ask me?" I hold out my hand, wiggling my fingers.

Miles sighs, then takes my hand. He looks me in the eye. "Skye, I wanted this moment to be epic. It just took me a while to figure out what to do. I thought about doing it at our place, but that seemed too *everyday*. Then I thought maybe while you were here, I could take you to the Empire State Building, but that didn't feel right either."

My heart is soaring. How is this my life? Can this many good things happen in one day?

"I have a picnic all set up at Central Park." Miles looks around. "But the Universe wants it here."

Miles gets down on one knee, pulls a velvet ring box out of his pocket, and then takes my hand in his again.

"Skye. I love you. I love your laugh, I love your wit, I love your crazy hair, I love your long legs, I love your eyes, and the way they look at me. I want to spend the rest of my life with you, and I was hoping you might want that too. Skye, will you marry me?"

He opens the ring box to reveal a perfect marquise-cut diamond ring, which twinkles in the summer sun. My heart is beating so fast, I feel like it's trying to reach out of my chest. I can barely contain my tears, my emotions threatening to overwhelm me. "Aye," I say in a trembling voice.

Cheers erupt from the bookstore behind us. We turn to find many of the women from my reading pressed against the glass door, peeking out the windows, some with phones held up, some clapping, and some with tears of joy trickling down their faces.

Miles stands, picks me up, and swings me around. Then he sets me down and kisses me—my first kiss from my fiancé.

He takes my hand. "Still up for a picnic in the park?"

I smile. "I'm up for anything, as long as it's with you."

ACKNOWLEDGMENTS

Thank you reader, for joining me for this new series, Love on Location. Minnie's story is next, coming in 2026. I'm also busy writing more from Fortune Falls.

I wrote this book (the first draft) a couple of years ago, when my daughter was very young. This book is for her. Thank you, Aggie, for inspiring me to do my best, to embrace change, to be brave. And thank you for making me a mama. It's the most precious adventure and truly the most fun I've had in my entire life.

Thank you to Andy for always being there for me. For also making me a mama. I love you.

Thank you to Alaina for reading and loving this book. For always being so encouraging of my endeavors. And for always being there, whether to bounce ideas off of, watch a rom-com, crochet and/or come to the zoo with us for the billionth time. I love you.

Thank you to my parents for always being there for us all.

Thank you to everyone who has worked on this book and read it over the years. Thank you to Mary and Francie for shifting genres with me.

A huge thank you to Robin Blackburn for reading and loving this book and for buying me a Highland cow (stuffie). It has offered me comfort and encouragement at much-needed times, and it's so SOFT!

Thank you to Jenny Rarden for copyediting. I love working with you.

Thank you to Cierra Paige for the proofreading.

And thank you again, reader, for being here and reading my books. I hope you enjoyed it.

ABOUT THE AUTHOR

I received a BFA in mixed media studio art. With a degree in the arts and no solid plan, I've had the opportunity to hold many different jobs; video store manager, barista, photographer's assistant, toy store clerk, and yoga instructor at a retreat in Puerto Rico are just a few. Hands on research for her books.

Currently, when I'm not writing, you can find me working at a title one elementary school library, crafting with my little girl, or hosting the podcast, *So I Wrote a Book...Now What*, where I interview fellow authors about their revision process.

Want to join my newsletter?

ALSO BY NC BARTON

The Now in Forever: A Small Town Second Chance Romance

The Art of the Meet Cute: A Small Town Found Family Romance

The Road Not Taken: A Friends to Lovers Christmas Roadtrip Romance